PROTECTIVE IMPULSE
CRIMSON POINT PROTECTORS

KAYLEA CROSS

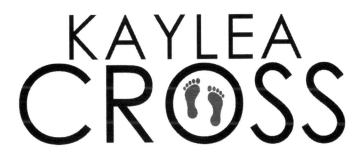

PROTECTIVE IMPULSE

Copyright © 2023 Kaylea Cross

Cover Art: Sweet 'N Spicy Designs
Developmental edits: Kelli Collins
Line Edits: Joan Nichols
Digital Formatting: LK Campbell

This book is a work of fiction. The names, characters, places, and incidents are products of the writer's imagination or have been used fictitiously and are not to be construed as real. Any resemblance to persons, living or dead, actual events, locales or organizations is entirely coincidental.

All rights reserved. With the exception of quotes used in reviews, this book may not be reproduced or used in whole or in part by any means existing without written permission from the author.

ISBN: 9798372579798

PROLOGUE

Port-au-Prince, Haiti
28 years ago

"Come on, hurry," her mother snapped, tugging impatiently on her hand.

Anaya lurched forward, her bare feet squishing in the sticky mud at the bottom of the thigh-deep water they were slogging through on the ruined road. It was still dark out, the rain soaking through her clothes. They had been walking for hours. She was so tired and hungry, didn't even know where they were going.

"I'm tired too, but we can't stop to rest yet. We have to keep going."

She remained quiet, watching around her and clutching her blanket tight with her free arm. Just like their village, everything here was destroyed too. Trucks and cars had been swallowed up by water and mud. Some of the buildings and the people inside them had been swept away.

A terrible storm had raged over the island. Hurricane Gordon, she'd heard *Maman* say. It had unleashed so much rain that the mountain above their village had melted like shaved ice in the sun, sending it tumbling down into the valley where they lived in an avalanche of destruction.

She shivered, soaked through to the skin. Last night had been terrifying. She'd been woken from a deep sleep when her mother dragged her out of bed in the middle of the night and raced outside with her toward the forest while the landslide rumbled like thunder behind them.

Anaya had heard people screaming, houses and trees cracking. It had frightened her. She didn't know how long they had hidden deep in the forest, but when they had finally come out, their village was gone, along with many people Anaya had known.

Now they had no home, and no family to take them in. What would happen to them?

Her stomach rumbled angrily. The last things she'd eaten was a little plate of rice and beans one of the neighbors had shared with them yesterday afternoon because *Maman* couldn't get any fuel for their fire with the storm howling outside their little home.

It was starting to get lighter out now. They had been walking all night, the two of them part of a long line of people carrying their most prized possessions down from the mountains.

The winding, muddy road began to straighten out before them as it stretched uphill. Up ahead she could see signs of people moving around in the faint gray light. A city loomed ahead, emerging out of the hazy shadows. Some buildings and cars were ruined here too, but not as many as back home.

She wanted to go home. Wanted the doll her grandmother had made for her on her last birthday, left in her bed. Was it buried in the mud too?

She and her mother walked for another hour or more, back

downhill to wade through water that came above her knees. Every step was a struggle, exhaustion dragging at her legs and feet along with the water and mud. She wanted to stop. To curl up at the side of the road and sleep under her filthy, wet blanket.

Eventually the water and mud ran out, leaving giant puddles everywhere. Tall buildings rose like dark trees in the distance. When they got closer, Anaya saw that these buildings were undamaged. Cars were still driving on the muddy roads, and people were busy carrying things to and from the market.

The hazy shapes up ahead became clearer. More buildings, far bigger than anything near their village. Then the tall, pointed spire of a church.

Suddenly she couldn't stay quiet any longer. "Where are we going?"

Her mother's face was drawn and sad looking, her lips tight. "Hush. We're almost there."

Where? she wanted to ask but held her tongue. Her mother was upset but seemed to know exactly where to go. Anaya hoped they would have food there.

They passed the church, painted all white with blue lettering above the front door, and started down a narrow, winding street nearby. A low building stood at the end of it.

Something about it made Anaya's stomach tighten in foreboding. She stopped walking, but her mother muttered something under her breath and jerked her forward once more.

Anaya went along reluctantly, unable to shake away the thought that something bad was about to happen. Her heart thudded hard as they stood on the doorstep. Her mother pulled on a rope. A bell rang inside.

Moments later a woman opened the door. She was old, with pale skin, and only her face showed in the middle of a black and white flowing scarf and robe that covered the rest of her. She looked at them both standing there in their wet, filthy clothes, and Anaya could see the woman felt sorry for them. "Come in, both of you."

Anaya was put in a chair near the window with a piece of bread and a glass of milk while her mother went into another room with the old woman and shut the door. She glanced down. Her bare feet and legs were coated in orange mud. Her nightgown was ruined, and her blanket might be too.

After finishing her bread her stomach rumbled for more, but she was suddenly too tired to care. Her eyelids grew heavy, and her head with it. It kept falling forward until she finally slid out of the chair and curled up on the hard stone floor to sleep, clutching her blanket to her.

Maybe this was all a bad dream. Maybe when she woke up everything would be all right again.

The next thing she knew, her mother was shaking her awake. Anaya blinked slowly, struggling to sit up. She was still so tired. Couldn't concentrate on what her mother was saying.

Then the urgency on her mother's face registered, and she shot upright. She stared up into her mother's wide brown eyes, the sheen of tears there frightening her.

"I have to go," her mother said softly.

Go?

"The sisters will take care of you." Her mother smiled but her lips trembled, and she looked so sad, Anaya reached out to grip her arm, stomach pulled into a hard knot.

"I don't want to stay here," she said in a voice that shook. Her birthday was coming up. She was turning six. Her mother had been saving up money for weeks to take her into town to get a new book. "You already take care of me."

Tears flashed down her mother's cheeks. "I can't anymore. These people will give you what you need."

What? "No, *Maman*—"

"I want you to have this." Reaching up, she undid the thin

gold chain from around her neck. The tiny cross pendant winked in the light coming through the window as she fastened it behind Anaya's neck.

Then she cupped Anaya's chin in her hand. "Be a good girl. Promise me you'll be good, and remember that I love you." She dropped her hand and stood, turning away and striding for the door.

Anaya's heart lurched. She shot to her feet, panic roaring through her. "No," she cried, hurrying after her. This couldn't be happening.

Her mother paused. Looked back at her. And the stricken look on her face made Anaya go cold all over. "I'm sorry, my angel. I love you. I will always love you, but things are bad here and you deserve more than I can—" She choked out the last words and stopped, then spun away and rushed for the door.

Anaya raced after her, heart hammering. Terrified and not understanding what was happening. "*Maman*!"

This time her mother didn't stop. Didn't slow down. Just walked out the front door at a brisk pace without a backward glance.

A wave of terror crashed over her. Anaya bolted for the door, determined to go with her. "*Maman*, please!" she cried, her voice shaking as much as her limbs.

Adult arms caged her from behind. "Don't, my child."

She kicked. Struggled. Tried to wrestle out of that imprisoning grasp, her eyes glued to her mother's retreating form. *No! Don't leave me! Please don't leave me!*

Her mother kept going. Had now reached the end of the narrow street they'd walked up earlier, her figure silhouetted against the bright morning light. "Come back!" Anaya cried.

Anaya had to catch her, before it was too late. She gulped in a breath, her chest hurting. Had she done something bad and made *Maman* angry with her? She must have, for her to leave her here. "I'll be good!" she screamed at the retreating figure, sobbing. "*Maman*, please, I'll be good!"

Her mother turned the corner and vanished from sight.

Anaya stopped struggling and stood frozen inside the doorway, staring at that spot. The terrible realization hit her just like the wall of mud that had destroyed their home last night.

Her mother had left her. And deep down, Anaya knew she wasn't coming back.

ONE

Present day
Crimson Point, OR

"There's my little princess!" Anaya crouched down and held her arms out to little Ferhana as the baby toddled out of the hallway and into the kitchen.

Her adopted niece froze when she saw her, clinging to her mom's hand and eyeing Anaya warily.

"It's Auntie Nay-Nay," her sister said brightly. When the baby didn't budge, Nadia chuckled and urged her new daughter forward. "Give her a few minutes. I think she's still trying to wake up."

Anaya sat down on the kitchen floor and folded her legs, waiting. They'd "visited" by video call three times a week since Nadia and Callum had decided to adopt her weeks ago, but Anaya guessed seeing each other in person must be a shock for the eleven-month-old.

Her patience was rewarded soon thereafter, however, because Ferhana cast aside her caution, tugged free of Nadia's grip and toddled toward Anaya with a toothy grin. "Nay!"

"Yes, that's right!" Anaya held out her arms again with a big, animated smile. She caught the toddler and scooped her up, peppering her face and neck with kisses, a bittersweet pang hitting her in spite of her resolve not to think about what might have been. "How's my girl?" Ferhana smelled like baby shampoo and pure innocence. Anaya could just eat her up.

Ferhana giggled, then started squirming until Anaya set her down, and made an unsteady dash for the adjoining living room. "She's getting so big."

Nadia started after her. "I know. She's also getting faster and picks up more words every day. It's amazing how quickly she's adjusted."

The side door opened and Callum walked in. Her Viking-like future brother-in-law's ginger-bearded face broke into a big grin when Ferhana shrieked and raced toward him as fast as her short, unsteady little legs would carry her.

"Hi, sweetie," he said on a laugh and swept her up in his thickly roped arms, placing smacking kisses on the side of her neck.

Ferhana gave another happy shriek and then broke into a helpless giggle that made them all burst out laughing. Anaya was charmed all over again. That belly chuckle had to be one of the best sounds in the whole world.

Watching her sister, Callum and Ferhana together, she felt a wistful pang hit dead in the center of her chest. But the deep love between them filled her with warmth. Ferhana had endured so much in her short life, and thankfully was too young to remember any of it. Now that Nadia and Callum had adopted her, she would have a solid, stable and loving home to grow up in, a world away from war and the oppression of the Taliban that had taken back control of Afghanistan.

Still, Anaya couldn't ignore a twinge of sadness. This is what she'd wanted for herself. What she'd always wanted—an unshakable sense of security and belonging. Of unconditional love and support with a man who loved her as they built a life and family together.

So far, it wasn't meant to be. She hadn't had it as a young child, though being adopted had somewhat eased that old trauma. But if it hadn't been for Nadia and their dad's unwavering love and support in the midst of their unconventional and highly dysfunctional family, Anaya would have crumbled inside long ago.

Callum came toward her holding Ferhana in the crook of one arm and gave her a warm smile. "Drive down from Portland went okay?" he asked, reaching out to wrap his other arm around her.

She adored him. He'd risked everything—including his life—to get Nadia safely out of Afghanistan after she'd been trapped there in the wake of the American withdrawal in July, and then been the one to suggest they adopt Ferhana.

She'd never seen Nadia so happy, and for her guarded sister to put aside her deep reservations about relationships and give her heart to him already told Anaya everything she needed to know about his character. "Thanks to GPS, yes."

He walked over to kiss Nadia, then faced Anaya again. "Oh, Jaia said you called the office earlier, when Ryder and I were both in meetings. What did you want to talk to us about?"

Nadia shot her a frown. "Is everything okay?"

Anaya sighed. She had a lot on her mind, had intended to wait until later to bring this up, but no point avoiding it any longer. Of course phoning Crimson Point Security earlier would raise questions. "Yes, fine. I've just got a couple things coming up this weekend that I'm feeling a little unsure about, so I was actually calling to see if you might be able to come with me to Seattle over the weekend. I tried your cell before but your voicemail was full."

Nadia frowned at her, and Callum's red-gold eyebrows rose. "Why, what's happening?" Callum asked.

With them both staring at her, she felt suddenly embarrassed, and wondered if maybe she'd overreacted to her situation. "It's not like I'm in danger or anything," she added quickly.

"Then what's going on?" he pressed, his demeanor calm as his hazel eyes remained locked on hers. Giving her a glimpse of the elite SOF soldier he'd been until not very long ago.

Oh, hell. Fine. "Can you pour me that wine now?" she asked her sister, who rushed to get her a glass of white. "I'll explain everything while I help you finish getting dinner ready."

Nadia handed her the wine as Callum sat on a stool at the island and fed Ferhana bites of cut fruit and cheese.

Anaya took a sip before whisking together the fresh lemon vinaigrette she'd made for the salad. "I've got these high-level meetings at Boeing Field over the next week."

"Right," Callum answered, watching her steadily.

"I just found out that they're flying in their top legal team from back east to deal with the contracts. I've dealt with them before, and the firm has an incredible rep within the industry, except I've had…issues with one of their younger lawyers in the past."

"In what way?"

"Inappropriate behavior, sexual harassment, and borderline stalking."

Callum's eyebrows snapped together, and her sister whirled to face her. "Not the guy you met in DC last year?" Nadia demanded, spatula poised in her hand like a weapon.

"That's the one. Anthony Riggs. Total sleaze ball." Her skin prickled just thinking about him and his smarmy face. "He's disgusting, and I called him on his behavior last year when he wouldn't take the hint and leave me alone. My boss was able to have him removed from the proceedings for that particular job, but the whole thing was stressful and embarrassing." She'd hated how people had looked at her differently after the incident. As if she was to blame for causing the situation in the first place.

"What happened to him after?" Callum asked.

"He was placed on unpaid administrative leave, then made to see a therapist and take 'sensitivity training,' but I'm sure it was a total waste of everyone's time and money. Anyway, he's since been reinstated and will be at these meetings."

"Of course he will," Nadia muttered in disgust.

"Yep, and there's this big formal dinner Saturday night for some of the top executives from our team and the French delegation coming in. Given the history between he and I, I'd feel more comfortable bringing someone as a plus one to make sure he keeps his distance this time. Preferably a big, intimidating guy who could act as a buffer. Someone who wouldn't be afraid to step in and put Riggs in his place if necessary." She smiled at Callum. "Know anyone like that?"

He winced. "I wish I could go with you, but I've already got meetings this weekend and I can't get out of them. Is it just the dinner you're worried about?"

"No." They stared at her expectantly, even Ferhana, watching her with big brown eyes as she chewed on a piece of cheese. "I'm also meeting my biological father this weekend as well and want someone with me when I do."

Nadia gasped and flicked off the burner, eyes wide. "No. When did this come about?"

"Two days ago. I emailed him last week to say I was coming to Seattle, and he answered saying he'd love to meet me while I'm in town. So we set up a time."

"He's got a criminal record," Callum said, frowning. Nadia

must have told him about Anaya's saga to find her bio dad, and how a distant cousin had at last filled in the gaps after she had done a DNA test with a genealogy database.

"Yes." Armed robbery and aggravated assault. She wasn't clear on the details. "He was released from prison in Haiti five years ago for good behavior after serving his sentence. Somehow he still got a visa and was able to enter the US legally. He started off in Florida, apparently, then moved to Chicago for a few years before coming to Seattle seven months ago. Anyway, given his record and that I don't know him, I don't want to meet him alone."

"Shit no, you can't go alone," Callum said. "Would you be open to hiring someone through the company?"

"Maybe." She'd hoped to go with Callum because she knew and trusted him, but if that wasn't an option, she needed to be open-minded.

He rubbed his jaw, took out his phone. "I think Myers might be available."

As in Donovan Myers? Her pulse tripped at the mention of that name, even though she didn't really know him. She'd talked to him on the phone once while he and Callum had been looking for Nadia in Kabul, then met him briefly at the airport in DC a few days after they'd rescued her. But in those few minutes, he'd made one hell of an impression.

Tall and ruggedly masculine. Broad-shouldered. Dark and brooding with piercing green eyes. One look at him and it was obvious that he could handle himself.

She pictured him beside her at the dinner this weekend. Imagined Riggs wilting like a dying plant when Donovan aimed his intense stare at him across the table.

It was such a great image.

Yeah, but you've also fantasized about plenty of other scenarios involving him over the past few weeks too.

Okay, she had, and she only felt a little bit guilty about it because he was the first guy who'd stirred any interest in her since...

Well. Maybe it was a sign she was finally ready to put what had happened two years ago behind her. She hoped so, because for a long time afterward she'd been convinced she would never recover from it.

"I'll give him a call right now," Callum said, breaking into her thoughts, putting his phone to his ear.

A ringtone went off from the depths of her purse, wrecking her concentration. She grabbed it, tensed slightly when she saw it was her mom, and immediately silenced it. Awkward.

"Who was that?" Nadia asked.

She didn't want to lie to her. "Mom."

"Oh." Nadia's face shuttered, then she turned away and kept prepping their meal.

Anaya hated the tension the mention of their mother caused. Nadia had made the decision to go low contact with her after getting back from Afghanistan, limiting their communication to the occasional text only. Because their mom had somehow managed to twist even *that* situation around to make it all about her, complaining how hurt she was that no one had kept her in the loop during Nadia's rescue, and how upsetting it was that Nadia hadn't introduced her to Callum and Ferhana.

Some things never changed. Their emotionally fragile adoptive mom had never once accepted responsibility for her behavior and would never see that she was the source of most of the family drama.

"You can talk to her in front of me," Nadia said as she stirred the contents of the pan. "I don't mind." Her tone made it clear she didn't want to be included in the call, however. Anaya understood. She respected her sister's decision.

Be a good girl, that constant little voice in the back of Anaya's mind insisted.

"No, it's okay," she said with an easy smile, automatically assuming her role as peacemaker. She'd done it for as long as she could remember, running interference between her mom and the others because she couldn't stand the tension. "I'll call her later." When she was alone, and her mom couldn't try to pressure or guilt her into putting Nadia or Ferhana on the phone.

She moved in beside Nadia, gave her a little hip bump. They shared a smile as they worked together in easy silence while she secretly kept most of her attention on what Callum was saying in the background.

She *really* hoped Donovan said yes.

TWO

Donovan reached for his back pocket when his phone rang. Seeing it was one of his bosses calling, he immediately silenced it. He'd get back to Callum later.

"You can answer your phone while I'm here. I don't mind," Shae said from across his kitchen table.

"It can wait." It was just the two of them on a rare Wednesday night together and he intended to make the most of it. Unless Callum sent an urgent text, he was leaving it until after Shae left.

"No, really. Go ahead."

He turned to raise an eyebrow at her. "How often do we get to hang out together? Especially now that you're in college." Hard to believe his daughter had already graduated high school this past summer. Time went by too damn fast. He felt like he'd blinked and missed everything—but the real kick in the ass was that he had no one to blame for it but himself.

She rolled green eyes that were identical to his, yet in that moment her expression made her look exactly like her late mother. Donovan had had a brief relationship with Jillian before shipping out on a deployment when he was twenty-one, only to learn a few months into his tour that she was pregnant. Neither of them had planned or been ready for it.

"Seriously, you can take calls if you want. It's fine," Shae said.

"It'll keep." He was making a concerted effort to spend quality one-on-one time with her without distractions whenever he got the chance. God knew he had a lot to make up for. He was lucky Shae was giving him the chance to try. "How's the steak?"

"Good. What did you put on it?" She peered at the sauce on her plate.

"Garlic and rosemary. I threw them and some butter in with the steaks as they finished cooking and spooned it over the top to baste them."

Her eyes widened. "Where'd you learn to do that?"

"Cooking channel. Saw it on a show the other night and thought I'd try it." That's how bad he wanted this second chance with her. His free nights were now spent at home alone watching cooking shows. He barely recognized himself.

"And these scalloped potatoes?"

He snorted in feigned insult. "Potatoes dauphinoise, thank you very much. Saw the recipe and thought it'd go well with the steaks and asparagus."

"Ooh, fancy." She laughed softly. "Look at you, getting all domestic."

A wry grin tugged at his mouth. "Let's not get carried away. I only eat this fancy when you come over." He wanted her to know he put in extra effort for her because he loved her. And it still bothered him to think she hadn't always really *known* that deep inside. Of all his regrets, that was the hardest one to live with and impossible to forgive himself for.

She looked down at her plate and forked up a bite of the

cheesy, creamy potatoes, the little smile on her lips telling him she was as pleased by his words as she was his effort.

Now a young woman, she was a mystery to him in a lot of ways. He'd missed out on a lot of the important milestones while she was growing up because of his military, government and then contracting work. Since her mom passed, he'd been doing his damnedest to bridge the gap that had formed during the time they'd lost together.

One of the best things he'd done was moving here to the Oregon Coast recently to be closer to her. The biggest reason he'd taken the job with Crimson Point Security was so that he would be around for her more often, since he no longer had to do any long deployments or travel overseas much anymore.

"So, how are classes going so far?" he asked her, reaching for his bottle of beer.

"Okay. Most of them are more boring than I expected though."

He chuckled. "Yeah, the first year or two is kind of a drag. Still thinking business admin?"

"For right now, yeah. But I'm open to changing my program if something else catches my interest in the meantime."

"Always good to keep your options open." Covertly studying her while she enjoyed her dinner, it stunned him all over again how grown up she was. At eighteen she was more grounded, responsible and mature than he'd been at twenty-five. He was damn proud of her—not that he could take any credit for how she'd turned out. That was all her, Jillian, and Shae's stepdad Walker's doing.

A lengthy silence stretched between them as they ate. The slight stiffening of her body language told him it was starting to make her uncomfortable. They'd made huge strides in repairing their relationship, but sometimes it felt like he hadn't done enough. It was a work in progress, both of them still finding their way.

"You seeing anybody?" he asked finally, spearing up his last bite of asparagus. He'd always hated asparagus, but it turned out that was because he'd only eaten it boiled or canned. Roasting it in the oven for a few minutes with olive oil, salt and pepper at a high temperature was a game changer, because it was still crisp on the inside, not in the least slimy and soggy.

"No. Been too busy to even think about dating." She looked up at him, sudden interest glinting in her eyes. "Why, you seeing anyone?"

"Nope, same. Too busy." And not all that interested in dating right now anyway. He'd learned pretty quick that online dating was like trying to safely navigate through a minefield. There were too many toxic, desperate people out there, and the whole online thing created the perfect environment for fake profiles and manipulation.

On the rare occasions he did go out with someone, he looked for casual and fun. So far, no one he'd met had ticked both those boxes.

There was only one woman he'd met lately who might make him change his mind about dating, but it would be somewhat complicated, and she lived on the opposite side of the country. Probably a good thing, since he was concentrating on his daughter and work right now.

After they finished eating, Shae helped him clear the table. His phone buzzed in his pocket as he carried the leftover potatoes to the counter. He checked it, found a text from Callum.

You home?

He would have ignored it, but if Callum was texting it must be important, and Shae wouldn't be here much longer now anyway. *Yes. What's up?* he answered.

Just on the road. Can I stop by quickly? Need to talk to you about something.

Sure, he replied, and tucked the phone away.

"Callum's gonna drop by. I've got a chocolate cake if you want some," he said while Shae rinsed plates and he loaded the dishwasher. He hated the chaotic way most people loaded them, so he preferred to do it himself.

She shot him a disbelieving look, holding a plate under the flow of water from the tap. "Don't tell me you made that too."

"No, I know my limits. Bought it at Whale's Tale this afternoon. Poppy said it's to die for." The sheriff's wife owned and ran the popular local café and bookstore on the waterfront. Everyone adored her because she was kind with a sunny personality. And everything there was amazing.

Shae passed him the plate. "Are you kidding, she's still working? Last time I saw her a couple weeks ago she already looked about to pop."

"She was there today. But yeah, she has to be close to her due date by now." He took the cake out of its box and was just cutting them both slices when a brisk rap came at his front door.

He set the knife down and answered the door. "Hey," he said to Callum.

"Hi." Callum glanced past him to Shae. "Hey, Shae."

"Something wrong?" Donovan asked him.

"No, but I need a favor."

"Sure, name it."

"It's a job, actually. This weekend in Seattle."

Okay, that was pretty last minute, but this might work out perfectly because he was already planning to meet someone there on Sunday. Maybe he could fit in both. "Who's the client?"

"Anaya Bishop."

Her face instantly popped into his head, along with a

sudden spike in interest. He'd heard from Callum that she was coming into town, and after meeting her in person at the airport, well...she was hard to forget. "Why does she need a bodyguard?"

"She's got high-level meetings with Boeing, and one of the lawyers has harassed her previously. To the point that she had to take formal action."

He bristled at the thought of some asshole preying on her. "Can she give me more details?"

"Yeah. She's in the truck, actually, if you want to talk to her."

She was here? His pulse sped up. "Sure, bring her in."

Callum turned around and waved at his truck. Anaya stepped around the corner of the house moments later. The instant Donovan saw her, something flared to life inside him. Something hot and primal he couldn't control as he tried not to stare.

She paused a few feet behind Callum and flashed him a smile that made him feel like he'd just walked out of the cold shadows into a warm ray of sunshine. Her hair was down. Tight, black spiral curls that bounced around her shoulders. The coral-pink dress she wore hugged the rounded curves of her breasts and the indent of her waist before flaring out over her hips to swirl around her knees, the color making her gorgeous brown skin seem to glow from within.

"Hi, Donovan."

Damn, that voice was exactly as he recalled it from their phone call in Kabul. Silky. Sexy. "Hi." When they'd met at the airport, she'd told him she hoped to see him again when she came here to visit her sister. He hadn't imagined their next meeting would be about a job.

She glanced past him into the house. "Oh, you've got company." She waved a hand in dismissal, gave him an apologetic look and took a step back. "We can talk over the phone later—"

"No, it's okay." She was even more beautiful than he remembered, and he remembered *plenty*. Had thought about her way more than he wanted to admit ever since she'd walked up and flung her arms around him at the airport for helping her sister.

Realizing he was staring, he snapped himself out of the semi-trance she'd put him in and stepped back. "Come on in."

She hesitated, her gaze straying past him once more. "Are you sure?"

"Yeah, it's all good." He turned around and headed back into the kitchen, catching Shae's curious expression where she stood at the sink. "This is Shae." He gestured behind him. "This is Anaya, Nadia's sister."

"Oh. Nice to meet you," Shae said, watching her with open curiosity.

"Hi, Shae," Anaya said with another warm smile he wished had been aimed at him instead.

"Donovan was just cutting us some cake. You guys want some? It's from Whale's Tale."

"I never say no to anything from Whale's Tale," Callum said, pulling out a chair for Anaya at the table.

"You want some?" Donovan asked her, picking up the knife. He wanted to know all the details about what she was looking for in terms of protection this weekend, and about the asshole who'd harassed her.

"Sure, thank you."

He turned away to resume cutting up the cake, the picture she made still vivid in his mind. He carried the plates over and set the first one down in front of her, the little smile he got sending a rush of heat through him.

Against his will, his gaze dropped to her lips, noting how

full they were, and suddenly all he could think about was tasting them instead of the cake. Sliding his fingers into those springy curls, gripping tight while he took slow, thorough possession of her mouth.

She's Nadia's sister, man. Your boss's future sister-in-law. And potentially your next client.

Three very good reasons to snap his brain back into line.

Once everyone had their cake, he sat down in his spot across from Shae. "So, what's the job?" he asked Anaya, seeing no reason to drag this out.

She explained her situation, beginning with the asshole lawyer who'd hassled her before, and ending with meeting her biological father. "I know it's not your usual assignment," she said. "It's not like I need a bodyguard per se, but Callum can't go, and I need someone who can intervene if necessary. I would feel a lot better if you were there with me, just in case."

He'd take that as a compliment. Especially since they barely knew each other. And he'd be lying if he didn't admit that something about her triggered his protective instincts on the deepest level. As well as some baser ones he needed to fucking stop thinking about.

"Unless you're busy already," she added quickly.

"He's not busy," Shae answered. He shot her a look and she shrugged at him. "Well, you're not."

No, but she didn't need to broadcast it to the gorgeous, sexy woman next to her. "I'm not," he told Anaya wryly, having already noted the absence of a ring on her left hand.

"Donovan will keep that creep away from you at the dinner and any other time this weekend," Shae added fiercely. She'd called him by his first name since she was little. Dad was reserved for Walker, and he deserved the title after stepping up and helping raise her from the age of six with Jillian.

Yeah, Donovan certainly would handle Riggs—if he took

the job. "Why didn't you just call me yourself?" he asked Anaya. "You could've gotten my number from Callum."

"Callum and I both thought you'd be more comfortable if I did this through the company. Then you hopefully wouldn't feel obligated to say yes just because I'm Nadia's sister."

She was stunning in that coral summer dress, but it was her eyes that captivated him. Deep and dark, with long, curling black lashes, they were almost hypnotic. Pulling him in. "What do you do, anyway?" he asked her.

"Oh, I'm an aeronautical engineer."

So she was hot, sweet *and* brilliant. "Very cool."

She shrugged. "I'm part of the design team for this new engine, but that's not the whole reason I was asked to be at these meetings. My boss really wanted me here because I speak French."

"Yeah?" Her accent was pure American.

She nodded. "I was born in Haiti. When the Bishops adopted me and brought me to the States, they made sure I retained my mother tongue as I learned English. Anyway, the executives we're meeting with are from France, and a few of them don't speak much English. My boss wants me to help sell them on the new engine, and act as translator when the need arises."

Impressive. He'd wondered about her background. Callum had told him that her and Nadia's parents had adopted kids from all over the world when they'd first been married. But from things Nadia had said, it sounded like a chaotic...unconventional family to grow up in.

"I don't want to pressure you," she went on. "Please feel free to think it over for a while before you make up your mind."

He'd already made up his mind the moment he'd seen her step onto his front walkway. "If you want to officially hire me through the company, that's fine." Given his powerful attraction to her, keeping things strictly professional was best, and it would reinforce that this was business only.

Her face brightened. "So you'll do it?"

He dipped his chin. "Yeah." He didn't want her dealing with this alone, and there was no way he was letting her meet a guy with a criminal record on her own, even if he was her father. People were crazy.

"Oh, that's great. Thank you," she said, visibly relieved.

"Sure," he said, a bit uncomfortable with her gratitude. He was a professional. She needed his services and had hired him to do a job. Pure and simple.

She and Callum stayed long enough to eat their cake and chat for a few minutes with Shae. Donovan grew more curious about her by the minute. He wondered about her childhood in Haiti. Wondered what had happened to her bio parents and how and why she'd been given up for adoption. Wondered what an aeronautical engineer did for fun in her downtime.

He saw them out after, locked up, and when he turned around, Shae was sprawled on the sofa in the adjoining living room, watching him with a grin that was way too shrewd.

"What?" he asked.

"Sounds like you're gonna be busy this weekend."

"Yeah, guess so." He went to the sink to rinse the dessert plates and load them into the dishwasher. Everything was organized the way he liked it, small plates in front of the big ones, all the knives in one part of the utensil rack and the forks in another, all facing the same way.

"Anaya seems nice," Shae said, a little too casually.

"Yeah, she does." Another reason he intended to keep a professional distance between them, contract or not.

"She seemed to want you specifically."

"Because I helped bring her sister home from Afghanistan."

Nothing more. And if she knew the truth about his past, she might have changed her mind.

"She's really pretty, too."

He didn't answer, still stuck on that last thought. It wasn't a comfortable place to be.

"What, you don't think she's pretty?"

He shot her a stern look over his shoulder. Her grin widened. "It's not a weekend getaway, Shae, she's hiring me to look out for her." And pretty was way too bland a description for her. More like stunning.

Shae lost the smile and rolled her eyes. "It's a short job that'll be over by next week at the latest. Then all your hardcore rules about client boundaries won't apply anymore."

He understood where she was heading with this but he wasn't going there, even mentally. Because the idea was way too damn tempting. He was looking at this as him protecting a good person who needed some backup for a couple days. Nothing more.

And maybe, just maybe, it might help tip the karmic scale back a little bit toward his favor.

THREE

Anaya kept her attention on the head of the French delegation as he spoke, while studiously ignoring the man standing across from her. Anthony Riggs hadn't stopped staring at her since the meeting started over an hour ago. Sometimes she could feel anger emanating from him, and other times an undisguised lust that made her stomach turn.

As she'd suspected, the "sensitivity training" and "therapy" had done nothing. The man was a predator and always would be. And she refused to give him the satisfaction of acknowledging him with so much as a single glance unless she was required to address him directly.

"When do you expect to have the first prototype completed?" the French CEO asked her in their native tongue.

"In five months," she answered, mostly enjoying herself. She didn't get to speak French often anymore.

Everything had gone smoothly thus far. The tour of the facilities at Boeing had been flawless, and the French delegation seemed both fascinated and impressed by everything they'd seen so far today. That boded well for getting a deal signed sometime next week after negotiations were complete. An order that size would pump hundreds of millions of dollars back into the company and allow them to finance development of the new project Anaya was excited to start.

The CEO adjusted the brim of his white hard hat that they were all wearing for the tour of the facility and peered more closely at the mock-up prototype on display before them. "How is this different from the designs we've seen previously?"

Anaya translated for her boss, Darren, who then gave her a smile and nodded for her to take the lead on this one. She launched into an explanation of all the modifications her team had made with this model, showing them on the prototype itself, and on the computer program they had ready on a laptop.

She kept it short and tight, putting most of it in layman's terms while throwing in a few technical ones for clarity. When she started in on the physics of the design, the CEO's mouth twitched. He held up a hand. "That all went flying over my head," he joked, and everyone there who understood French laughed at his pun. "But it sounds impressive."

Anaya smiled at him. "Thank you. It really was a pleasure to work on." It had taken her team almost three years to get to this point. Now they were so close to getting a deal she could taste it, but would leave all the negotiations to the business experts. Her wheelhouse was in design and the engineering side, not the boardroom.

They finished the session with a tour of the rest of the fabrication facility. All the equipment was state-of-the-art, a dream come true for any aeronautical nerd, and she was a huge one.

"Will you be joining us all for dinner tonight, Mademoiselle Bishop?" the CEO asked as they walked outside afterward. The noise of aircraft engines on the tarmac filled the air along with a tinge of aviation fuel.

As far as she was concerned, September in the Pacific Northwest was paradise. The days were filled with bright blue sky and warm sunshine, the temps cool and comfortable yet holding the cool nip of approaching fall in the evenings.

"Yes, I will," she answered. She liked him. He was far warmer and more human than most of the businessmen of his level she came into contact with. "I was wondering... Could I perhaps interest you and your team in a field trip before you leave Seattle?"

He gave her an intrigued look. "What did you have in mind?"

"I've been here several times and never visited The Museum of Flight. I've heard it's phenomenal, well worth the visit." She cocked her head. "Would you care to go with me if I arranged it?"

His lined face broke into a wide smile. "I think I would go anywhere you asked, my dear." He shook a finger at her and tossed a grin at Darren. "*Elle est très charmante,*" he said, and chuckled to himself as he strode toward the waiting limousine out front.

"What did you say to him?" Darren whispered as they stood watching the French team enter the vehicle.

"That I'm going to set up a private visit to The Museum of Flight while they're here. I've always wanted to go, and I think Henri would really enjoy it. He seemed interested."

"He certainly did." His lips quirked. "I think I'd better bring you to the negotiation table with us. You might be the key to this whole deal."

She laughed. "The right price is going to be the key to this whole deal."

"True, but you two have a really genuine connection. I want you to be there."

"All right." She'd hoped for more time with Nadia, Callum

and the baby, but this was an opportunity to make a big impression on the higher-ups.

He unknotted his tie and undid the top button on his collar, sighing in relief. "Hate wearing these damn things. You coming for drinks with us now?"

"No, sadly, I have to pass. I have an appointment I need to be at."

"But you're coming to dinner, right?"

She grinned at his anxious tone. "Yes, I'll be there."

"Good." He patted her shoulder. "Great work today. *Really* great."

"Thank you," she murmured, secretly thrilled by the praise, and went back inside. She used the washroom and freshened her lip gloss, then walked out into the lobby and almost ran straight into Riggs.

He'd positioned himself between her and the front doors, preventing her from getting past him without an interaction. She glanced past him through the glass doors. Donovan had texted earlier saying he would pick her up in a black SUV but there was no sign of him yet.

"Are you planning to ignore me through this whole thing?" Riggs said coldly.

Keeping her composure firmly in place, refusing to let him know he rattled her, she faced him head on and lifted her chin. "Can I help you with something?"

He was young and good-looking, successful—and disgustingly full of himself. Utterly confident in his power over women, and secure in the knowledge that his charm and money would mitigate any real and meaningful consequences for his actions. And right now, he was looking at her with thinly veiled resentment.

"I wanted to clear the air between us after the unfortunate

misunderstanding the last time we saw each other," he said tightly.

He hadn't changed at all. Hadn't even attempted to, she'd bet, because guys like him never saw anything wrong with their behavior. They took no responsibility or ownership for their words or actions, it was always the woman's fault for being too sensitive or touchy.

"I understood you perfectly last time," she told him. He'd wanted this confrontation, been waiting for it, and she wasn't letting him walk away unscathed.

Shock flickered in his eyes briefly, then his mouth tightened. "Look, you didn't need to try and blow up my career over what happened. I thought you were attracted to me—"

She gave a humorless laugh, stopping him cold. "I'm not, never was, and never did or said anything to suggest otherwise. You were in the wrong, not me, and sexual harassment has consequences. And my ride's here now, so if you'll excuse me."

She swept past him, her strides heavier than normal in her anger. God, he was such a piece of shit, and she hated that she would be forced to see him again.

The black SUV pulled up just as she stepped outside, and seeing Donovan behind the wheel brought a rush of relief along with an odd blend of safety and desire she didn't want to examine too closely. He leaned over to open her door for her, and the moment his green eyes connected with hers, a rush of awareness swept through her.

Anthony Riggs could only *wish* in his wildest imaginings that she would react this way to him.

"Hi," she said as she climbed into the seat, pulse picking up. She could smell the leather of his jacket and something else spicy and masculine that made heat curl low in her belly.

"Hi." His dark hair was cut short in the back and a little longer in front, and his muscular torso filled out the jacket to perfection. At his house the other night, she'd caught herself staring at his roped arms revealed by the sleeves of his T-shirt. "How did it go?"

"Really well, until just now." Her gaze trailed back to the automatic doors at the front of the building.

He stopped the vehicle, his gaze snapping to the front of the building as if he was thinking about marching through the doors. "The lawyer?"

"Yep, but I firmly put him in his place and if he doesn't take the hint this time and leave me alone, I'm not going to wait until the end of the meetings to do something about it. Honestly, I'm surprised he had the balls to confront me just now. I'm sure he was told to stay away from me. I'll talk to my boss about it later tonight."

"Good." The corner of his mouth kicked up in a sexy grin as he swung the vehicle around in a circle to head back for the main gate. "So, where to now? Off to meet your dad?"

"Jean Luc," she corrected. "Frank Bishop's my dad."

"Right, my bad. Do you have a location yet?"

"He sent me an address earlier." She got out her phone and read it to him.

He frowned as they neared the front gates. "That's a really sketchy area of town. Way worse now than the last time you were out here."

"Well, then I'm even more glad I've got you with me," she said, determined to make the best of this potentially awkward situation. She was nervous enough already.

"I think you should consider doing this somewhere else."

"I only have an hour or so before I need to get ready for the dinner. I'd prefer to meet him where he asked this time." In case there was a next time.

Donovan didn't look happy about it, but he didn't argue. "Okay."

They didn't speak while he got them on the freeway and headed north toward downtown Seattle, its cluster of tall buildings and the Space Needle visible in the distance. He didn't use a GPS or the vehicle's navigation system, but he knew exactly where they were going because he exited the freeway and navigated the one-way streets of the downtown core with ease.

Little flutters of anxiety in the pit of her stomach intensified into a constant buzz as they neared the waterfront. She was nervous as hell, wondering how this was going to go. Last night's call with her mom hadn't helped either. She had made it clear right from the start of this that she disapproved of what Anaya was doing. That she was just asking for trouble and should leave the past in the past.

But Anaya couldn't pass up this chance to meet him. And she knew her mother's reaction was less about worrying for Anaya's safety than it was her mother's jealousy and insecurity. Her mom was far more concerned that she might have more competition for Anaya's attention and affection.

Although she had accepted long ago that it was just how her mother was and shrugged it off as best she could, this one had stung more than usual.

Outside the vehicle, rows of tents and other makeshift shelters lined both sides of the street. The rampant evidence of homelessness, vandalism and crime were shocking to see. Boarded-up windows were everywhere, and graffiti covered every wall. Rough-looking people sprawled on the sidewalks and huddled in doorways.

"You were right, this is nothing like I remember from last time," she said, glancing at the lock on her door to make sure it was engaged.

"It's happening all over," he said, turning left at the intersection. This street was in much the same state as the previous one. Block after block of abject poverty, addiction and hopelessness.

Gradually the area began to improve slightly, but she was definitely glad she would have Donovan with her for this. Not that she was truly afraid of Jean Luc or worried that he would try to hurt her. It just gave her an added sense of security to know she had someone well-trained and trustworthy watching over her.

"It's just up here on the left. Brick building on the corner. The café is on the ground floor," he told her.

"I see it." It looked pretty seedy as well.

He found an underground parking garage a block north toward the freeway and parked near the entrance. Before she'd unstrapped and grabbed her purse, Donovan was opening her door for her.

"Thank you," she murmured, and stepped out onto the concrete. The strong scent of urine hit her, and she had to struggle not to wrinkle her nose.

He stuck right next to her as they walked up the ramp to street level. Her physical awareness of him was acute. He was a lot taller than her, well over six feet, and his powerful build made her feel all fluttery and ultra-feminine. She was also curious about his relationship with Shae. Callum had told her she was Donovan's daughter, but that she lived with her stepdad Walker, who also worked for their company. Did that mean Donovan was single?

On the sidewalk she got lots of curious looks, and wished she'd zipped back to the hotel to change before coming down here. In her pencil skirt suit and heels, she definitely stood out in this rough part of town.

Donovan's silent presence beside her made her feel completely safe in the rundown neighborhood, but he couldn't protect her from the flashes of memories that hit her from her early years in Haiti.

She knew what abject poverty felt like. What gnawing, painful hunger felt like, and was thankful every day that she'd been adopted by an American family who had encouraged her to pursue her passions and go to college. Yet without that awful, scary time in her life as a kid, she would never be where she was today.

"We're a few minutes early," Donovan said, gesturing for her to cross the street in front of him.

They stood side by side in front of the café. She watched the people coming and going, and when she glanced at Donovan, she paused at the noticeable difference in him. He continuously scanned the area, in protective mode. Ever vigilant.

She relaxed a little. "Wonder why he wanted to meet here?" she mused aloud.

His gaze was locked on something down the block. "That him?"

She turned and saw the older black man coming toward them up the sidewalk. Her pulse quickened. She'd only seen one picture of Jean Luc, a selfie he'd taken on his phone and the lighting had been bad. "I think so." She took a deep breath, forced herself not to fidget.

The man drew closer. He had on heavily worn jeans that were too big for him. His jacket was frayed and stained. His hair was in need of a cut, but his beard was trimmed. He flashed a hesitant grin as he approached them, lifting a hand.

She smiled back, anxious as hell and taking solace from Donovan's steadying presence behind her. "Jean Luc?"

He nodded. "Anaya?"

"Yes." Now that he was closer it was a shock to see some of herself in him. Through the eyes especially, and the cheekbones. She hadn't inherited his height though. "Hello."

He stopped in front of her, studying her face raptly for a few moments, then awkwardly held out his hands, palms up. She took them, struck by a sudden and overwhelming tide of emotion that put a lump in her throat. This was her father, and whatever he'd done, whatever crimes he'd committed in the past, she wouldn't be here without him. He was part of her.

His hands were dry and rough with calluses that only hard physical labor could explain. "You are so beautiful," he said in a heavy accent.

"Thank you," she murmured, flushing. He smelled faintly of soap, and she could see a few patches on his jacket where he'd tried to repair damage. "I'm glad to meet you."

"Me too." He glanced past her at Donovan, his expression cooling with obvious suspicion.

"This is my friend Donovan," she explained quickly. "I don't know my way around here at all, so I asked him to bring me."

Jean Luc nodded at him once, his expression thawing as he refocused on her and withdrew his hands.

"Did you just come from work?" she asked.

"*Oui*. I do cleaning at a yard down by the docks."

That explained the calluses. He was almost painfully lean, his clothes shabby and threadbare. And when the scent of cooking bacon wafted toward them, she didn't miss the way his eyes darted to the café door. "Are you hungry? They serve breakfast all day here."

He met her gaze briefly, then looked away. "No, I'm fine."

But he wasn't. Anyone could see that, and she'd bet he hadn't eaten anything substantial for a while. It upset her to think of him going hungry. "Why don't we go sit down and eat together while we visit?" she suggested.

He hesitated, his gaze sweeping over her business attire. "It's not a very nice place," he said, looking embarrassed.

"Is there somewhere else you'd rather go?"

He shook his head, shame tightening his expression.

"Let's give this place a try, then. It's busy, so the food must be pretty good," she said brightly, and looped her arm through his. Her father, she thought in wonder. It seemed too incredible to believe that she'd finally found him. She glanced at Donovan. "You coming?"

"You two go ahead," he said. "I'll grab a coffee and wait until you're done."

"Are you sure? You're welcome to eat with us." She didn't expect him to wait outside at her beck and call like a hired lackey.

"No, you go catch up." He held the door open for her, gave her a reassuring smile that warmed her insides. She could tell that he'd already made a thorough assessment and decided that she wasn't at any risk. And she also knew without asking that he would be posted somewhere nearby with eyes on her the whole time.

That helped ease more nerves. "All right, then I'll see you in a bit."

Jean Luc followed her inside the café. They took a booth near the window and sat across from each other. His stiff body language and difficulty in making eye contact told her this was uncomfortable for him, and she wanted so badly to put him at ease.

She started talking, keeping the conversation light and in French while she asked general questions about him. His answers were a little vague, but it was evident that he was struggling to get by.

"Where are you living now?" she asked as the server poured them both coffee.

"I move around from place to place," he said evasively, stirring four packets of sugar into his drink. "Wherever I can find a room I can afford."

Shelters, he meant, and another pang hit her that he was struggling so much. It couldn't be easy as an uneducated, nearly sixty-year-old immigrant with a former criminal record trying to find his way in this country.

They placed their orders and he finally asked about her. She gave him the basics, starting in Haiti with how the Bishops had adopted her at age six and brought her to West Virginia. "We moved around a lot. I have a big family. After graduating I went to college and became an engineer. Now I work for an aeronautics company, and I'm here for meetings at Boeing."

His eyes widened. "Boeing, the airplane company?"

She smiled. "Yes."

He shook his head in wonder, grinned. "Wow. You're smart, eh?"

"Pretty smart," she said with a smile. Wrapping her hands around her mug, she decided to ask the thing she most wanted to know. "Did you know about me? Or that my mother was pregnant?"

He shook his head again, taking a long sip of his coffee. "No. I never saw her again after I left for Port-au-Prince."

Disappointment hit her. So that topic was a dead end. She'd been hoping he would fill in the holes for her.

"What happened to her?" he asked.

"I don't know. She took me to an orphanage when Hurricane Gordon hit, and I never saw her again. I've tried to find her, but I think she's probably…" *Gone.* She bit her lip, paused to collect herself and cleared her throat. "Sorry." It still hurt. Being abandoned, even though she understood that her mother had done it for Anaya's own good.

"It's all right." He gave her a sad, kind smile, and she had trouble accepting that he was capable of the crimes he'd been convicted of. He didn't seem like a hard, callous man, or a violent one. Although desperation driven by poverty could make people do terrible things. "It's a hard life back home."

"Yes." Devastating, inescapable poverty for too much of the population, exacerbated by corrupt government and a constant stream of natural disasters. "I'm lucky to have had the opportunities I did here." So much of her emotional trauma centered around feelings of abandonment. But if her mother hadn't made the decision to leave her at that orphanage, Anaya's life would have been infinitely harder.

The server brought their food. Anaya had ordered a small snack since she had a dinner in a few hours, but she was heartened to see Jean Luc dig into his full plate of eggs, bacon and pancakes. He ate quickly but she could see he relished every bite.

They talked for another few minutes afterward, but it was clear they'd exhausted the conversation for this first meeting. She paid for their food, then reached across the table and secretly pressed some folded-up bills into Jean Luc's hand.

He froze, a look of astonishment on his face. "No," he said with a sharp frown, shaking his head and trying to give the money back.

She closed her hands around his, forcing him to keep it. "Please. It's not much, but hopefully it will help get you somewhere safe and clean to sleep for a while."

He stared at her, linked by their palms pressed together in the center of the table. Finally he flashed her a grateful, sheepish smile. "Okay. Thank you."

"You're welcome." She wanted to do more.

They left the booth and stepped out onto the sidewalk together. A cool, damp breeze was blowing in from the water. By nightfall it would be downright cold out here. Too cold to be outside overnight, let alone at his age.

It bothered her to know that little bit of money she'd just

given him was the only thing standing between him and sleeping on the unforgiving streets.

Facing him, she put on a smile. "I'll be in town for a few more days at least. Maybe we can meet up again before I leave?"

He smiled back, and it struck her again how much of herself she could see in those features. "I'd like that."

She lifted her arms, gave him a questioning look. His teeth flashed in a grin, and then he drew her to him in a gentle, if awkward hug.

Anaya returned the embrace, her throat thickening. "Well. Goodbye for now."

"*Oui, à bientôt, ma fille.*"

My girl.

He left her standing there battling a rush of tears as she watched him walk away, a tall, wiry figure, shoulders bent from the weight upon them.

"How'd it go?" a low voice said behind her.

She sniffed, swallowed before turning around to face Donovan. The sight of him brought a rush of relief and heated awareness. He was so big and masculine and sexy. A dark guardian angel she wanted to burrow against to soak up the sense of security he gave her. It felt like nothing bad could touch her as long as he was next to her.

"Surreal." She glanced behind her and watched Jean Luc turn the corner and vanish from view. "He's having a really hard time. I wish I could help him."

When Donovan didn't answer she looked back at him. His green eyes held hers, assessing, but she could feel the intensity in him. He was hard to read, his expression giving her zero clues about what he was thinking, and yet for a moment she would have sworn he was tempted to hug her.

"Ready to go?" he said gruffly instead.

She blinked, startled by how badly she'd misread him. He was all business. It made perfect sense of course. He was on the clock right now, and a man like him would need to maintain strict boundaries with his clients in order to do his job properly.

But that didn't make the stab of disappointment any less sharp.

FOUR

Donovan pulled out Anaya's chair from the table in the private dining room and waited until she was comfortably seated before taking the one on her right. The French CEO sat on her left, and the young dipshit was across and one down from her.

Donovan had picked him out within five seconds of arriving at the restaurant. Dressed in an expensive suit, full of himself, his body language as cocky as the rest of him. And since they'd arrived at the table, he'd barely taken his eyes off Anaya.

Donovan had to curb the impulse to drag him out of the room and have a word in private about what would happen if the asshole didn't leave her alone.

When she'd stepped out of her hotel room earlier in that red cocktail dress, his tongue had stuck to the roof of his mouth. The dress hugged every delectable curve of her body to classy perfection while leaving her lower legs bare, the sleek muscles highlighted by the black high-heeled pumps she wore.

Everyone around the table conversed in little groups. Donovan spoke when spoken to, but otherwise remained quiet, keeping his focus on Anaya and the dipshit.

"Miss Bishop, we are being rude by neglecting your guest," one of the French delegates said in heavily accented English.

Anaya glanced at Donovan and offered an apologetic smile. "So we are. This is Donovan. He was good enough to accompany me tonight."

Eight sets of eyes fastened on him, and he could feel their curiosity—or hostility, in the dipshit's case. Anaya hadn't defined their relationship, and he could tell everyone was filling in the blanks with their own theories.

He nodded once in reply, forced a slight smile even as he inwardly groaned. He'd always hated this kind of thing and nothing about this was remotely his scene, but being with Anaya made it bearable. She'd worn her hair down, the tight spiral curls bouncing around her shoulders every time she moved. He had the alarming impulse to bury his face in them, breathe in her scent before skimming his nose down the side of her throat.

"And what is it you do, Donovan?" her boss asked.

Next to him, Anaya stiffened slightly. "He's—"

"Computer security." It wasn't exactly a lie. He knew his way around computers and basic security systems and had to do his fair share of computer work for his job.

"Ah. What company do you work for?"

"I work as an independent consultant."

"Yes, and he's very good at what he does," Anaya said, giving him a secret smile that tugged at something deep inside him. A raw place that hungered for redemption and to be worthy of the admiration in her eyes.

He broke eye contact with her and scanned the rest of the table, a bit shaken by how much she tempted him and challenged his concentration. The secret power she wielded over him was disturbing on several levels, and he had to start blocking all that out.

Normally on a job he was all about maintaining emotional distance from the person he was protecting. Especially since he'd learned the hard way about the consequences of what happened when he dropped his guard and relaxed the boundaries.

A woman had paid for his mistakes with her life. It didn't matter that it technically hadn't been his fault, or that he'd been somewhere else when everything went to hell. He still bore the brunt of the responsibility. Was still dealing with the fallout.

His upcoming meeting tomorrow while Anaya was in meetings of her own weighed heavy on his mind. He always dreaded them. Had thought so many times of cutting contact and walking away from it all for good. But guilt and obligation always stopped him.

Forcing his own shit aside, he watched Anaya while she conversed easily with the powerful men at the table. Answering questions, charming them with her wit and gorgeous smile, and then leaving them hanging on her every word when she spoke about the upcoming new engine project her team was starting on.

Everything about this job was different from the ones he'd done in the past, mostly because of her. This was the first time he'd ever been attracted to a client. And no matter how much he tried to fight it, that undeniable pull he felt toward her only grew stronger as the minutes ticked past.

It was dangerous. *She* was dangerous.

Dinner dragged by while conversation flowed around him. He was used to staying in the background, preferred not to be the center of attention, but he'd never felt so out of place in his life as he did here amongst these high-powered businessmen in their tailored, designer suits. After dessert, everyone left the table to mingle and have drinks while a pianist played in the corner.

Donovan excused himself from Anaya and quickly hit the washroom, knowing she would be safe in the room without him for a few minutes. He was back within three, but the second he walked in he saw the cocky dipshit had managed to catch her in the corner on her way around the room.

Riggs moved in closer to her, his back to the rest of the room. Too close, using his height and size in a blatant effort to intimidate her while he said whatever shit was coming out of his mouth.

Oh, *hell* no.

"Excuse me," Donovan said to the man who had tried to engage him in conversation, and broke away to stride across the room, his attention riveted on Anaya.

To her credit, she remained poised and kept her cool. Donovan saw her lips move, her expression calm. When whatever she said to the dipshit didn't make him back off, she placed a hand in the middle of his chest and pushed him firmly until he was forced to take a half-step back to let her move past.

Donovan's gaze zeroed in on his target. People nearby stopped talking when they saw him coming, and instinctively backed out of his way. The dipshit didn't notice, too busy hassling Anaya, making the mistake of catching her arm to prevent her from leaving.

Something dark and territorial flared to life in Donovan's gut. Her gaze flicked to him, and he read the startled concern there from thirty feet away.

Dipshit started to turn toward him.

Donovan stepped smoothly up to Anaya and wrapped a possessive arm around her shoulders, pulling her into his side, his body angled to place himself between her and the asshole. "Hey, sweetheart," he murmured, kissing the top of her head while he nailed Riggs with a look designed to curdle the prick's insides.

The asshole's face went blank for a moment, then his expression tensed. "I was just—"

"Leaving," Donovan said flatly. There were a lot of other things he would rather have said and done under the circumstances, but this was a professional setting, and he wouldn't embarrass Anaya or cause a scene.

Yet. But if the asshole kept pushing, Riggs was going to get a whole lot more than he bargained for in return.

Keeping her tucked in close to him, Donovan sidestepped the dipshit, making sure to hit him with his shoulder on the way by. The ensuing grunt and the way Riggs stumbled to catch his footing only slightly mollified Donovan.

"You want another glass of wine?" he asked as he steered her through the others toward the bar at the far end, getting her away from Riggs. He probably should care more that he'd just made them into a fake couple for the duration of the weekend, but he didn't.

Curious eyes followed them, but he saw more than a few giving the dipshit disgusted looks and wondered why the hell the law firm would keep on someone like that. Must be related to someone important there.

"I'd love one." Her tone was calm but held an underlying edge of annoyance. "I was handling it, but thank you. That made things a lot easier."

Yes and no. Because now everyone in the room thought he was her boyfriend. "He's such a prick."

"Yes, he is, and he's never going to change. I can't believe they brought him here. But he's the firm founder's grandson, so I guess that gives him a free pass."

Figured. Christ, that kind of shit pissed him off.

At least they were well away from Riggs now. The situation had been handled, so there was no good reason for Donovan not to let her go. Except he didn't want to.

Nope, he wanted to savor the feel of her up against him for as long as possible. The pressure of her side against his tormented him with the question of what it would be like to have all those luscious curves plastered to him. Naked.

Her scent drove him crazy. Something light and clean but sweet. Like a mix of citrus and vanilla. He had to curb the impulse to lean his face close to the side of her neck and breathe more of it in.

He stopped at the bar and ordered her a glass of the white she'd been drinking, expecting her to pull away at any second. She didn't. Instead, she leaned into his side more, her warm weight striking sparks along every inch where their bodies touched—and some where they weren't.

Shit. What the hell was it with her? Everything about her turned him on.

"You're very detail oriented." Her eyes sparkled up at him with a hidden smile as she accepted a glass from the bartender.

"It's my job."

Her expression changed, tensed slightly, and she eased away. His hand itched to pull her back to him. "What'd he say to you?" he asked, wondering at her reaction just now.

She swirled the wine in her glass expertly before taking a sip. "Tried to make it out like he's the victim and I'm a cold bitch for rebuffing him."

Yeah, he kinda wished he'd outright threatened the asshole now. This was the second time the entitled dick had approached her about the "misunderstanding," and it set off more than a few alarm bells. Riggs was way too fixated on her, and obviously pissed off that she'd reported him for his initial behavior. "And what'd you say?"

"That I would tolerate him in a professional capacity while we're here because I have no choice, and I expected him to grow up and be an adult about it."

He chuckled, remembering her expression as she'd faced off with the guy. Looking him dead in the eye while coolly, elegantly telling him to go fuck himself. She was a constant surprise, and so far, he liked every new thing she revealed. A lot.

Too much. And beneath all her poise and confidence, he also detected a hint of vulnerability he'd glimpsed earlier when she'd met Jean Luc. A sweet gentleness that awakened every protective cell in his body and weakened him like nothing else could.

Yet another addition to the growing list of reasons why he needed to keep the boundaries firmly in place both now and after this job was over.

Anaya surveyed the room, smiled at her boss when he waved them over. "Shall we?"

He'd much rather get out of here and take her somewhere private to get to know her better. Find out if she tasted like citrus and vanilla too. But that wasn't happening—ever, and he needed to get his head on straight. "Yeah."

He followed her across the room, resigned to endure more small talk with a bunch of strangers he had absolutely nothing in common with. Fortunately, it turned out to be not so bad.

After his territorial and public claim on her earlier, Anaya's team seemed even more interested in him. He didn't give them much when they asked him questions about his background, just that he was former military and had done security contracting after that.

For some reason it only made them more eager. Five guys converged on him, peppering him with questions about where he'd worked overseas, what types of military aircraft he'd used, what unit he'd served in. He didn't tell them that he'd been SOF, but he didn't see the harm in telling them some things about his service.

"Have you ever done a free fall jump?" one of the younger guys asked, excitement clear on his face.

He shrugged, aware of Anaya watching and listening intently and secretly hoping it impressed her. "I did a few." More than a few hundred, that is.

The guy's eyes widened, and a wide smile spread across his face. "That's so awesome. I've always wanted to try it but never worked up the guts to actually go through with it."

"It's not that bad after the first few times. Jumping out of a flying aircraft isn't comfortable for most people," he added wryly.

The guy nudged Anaya. "You ever skydived?"

"No."

"Would you? Maybe a tandem jump?"

"Maybe." Her gaze slid to Donovan. Held, and he felt the current of awareness arcing between them right to his gut. "Depends on who my partner was."

The trust and admiration in her eyes floored him. And so did the unmistakable spark of desire he read there too. Was it real? Or was she merely playing the part in front of her colleagues to convince them they were a couple?

Her full lips curved upward. They looked so damn soft. It wasn't hard to imagine how they would feel beneath his own, the way they would give to the pressure of his mouth as he kissed and sucked at them. "But you'd have to promise to hold on to me really tight the whole time," she added.

"Oh, I would, don't worry about that." He'd enjoy every second of it. Covering her, the back of her body pressed flat to the front of his while they experienced the rush of plummeting through the air together. Showing her a piece of his world while personally making sure she was safe.

The trouble would be making himself let her go afterward.

With the ice officially broken between him and her coworkers, the rest of the evening was almost enjoyable. Especially since Anaya played up the fake relationship he'd initiated by remaining close all night and acting all attentive, touching his arm, his back, her body brushing his as she moved. A few times she even curled an arm around his waist, and he couldn't help admitting that he liked pretending he was hers.

He was attuned to her on every level, constantly fighting being distracted by her closeness, her scent, the sound of her laugh, and the incredibly sexy sound of her speaking French to the guys from France. She made it damn hard to concentrate, and in a different scenario that would have been dangerous.

Tonight, however, he decided to cut himself a rare amount of slack.

They were in a private room in an upscale hotel restaurant, surrounded by business people. There were no credible threats against her. The only source of trouble was the dipshit, and ever since Donovan had staked his claim earlier, Riggs had kept his distance, lurking alone in the far corner with a sulky expression as he nursed his drink.

He kept watching Anaya but never made a move to approach her. At one point Donovan had noticed one of the senior partners taking him aside, presumably to reprimand him if the sullen expression on Riggs's face was any indication.

Donovan didn't trust him to maintain his distance indefinitely. If he got drunk enough, he might even try to corner Anaya again. And if that happened, Donovan would make sure he regretted it.

The party broke up at just before eleven. Some of the men invited him and Anaya to go to a bar across town but she declined, laughing. "No thanks. I'll see you bright and early in the boardroom tomorrow." She looked up at him with those deep dark eyes he found it hard to look away from. "Ready to go?"

"If you are." It was as natural as breathing to wrap an arm around her and pull her in tight as he guided her out the door into the cool, damp night air. It had showered while they were at dinner. The old-fashioned cast iron streetlamps around the perimeter cast shimmering pools of light on the wet sidewalk and street, and the light breeze held the scent of damp leaves.

"Brr," Anaya said, stopping to pull a wrap from her bag. She shook it out and started to wrap it around her shoulders.

He caught her hands in his without thinking. She stilled, her gaze lifting to his, and he saw the unmistakable flare of heat flicker in her dark eyes.

He should have let her go. Should have stepped back and looked away.

Instead, he tugged the soft material from her fingers and wound it around her himself just as her boss passed by with a few others, holding her gaze the entire time. And he didn't look away when they were gone. Didn't drop his hands.

He kept them where they were, pressed lightly to the wrap now covering her shoulders and upper chest, fighting the urge to trail his fingertips up the exposed column of her throat. To stroke them over the point of her chin and across the satin-smooth curve of her cheek. Cup her face in his palm and lean in to taste those lips that had been driving him crazy all night.

Fuck.

He let go abruptly and turned away, setting a hand on the small of her back instead. He shouldn't be touching her at all anymore, but he couldn't deny himself at least this much as he walked her to the valet parking stand and handed over his ticket. They stood in silence together, the heat of her body searing his palm, the desire he'd just seen in her eyes making his pulse quicken.

Headlights swung around the corner of the hotel as the valet brought their vehicle up. Donovan helped Anaya into the front passenger seat, had to force himself to release her instead of burying his free hand into her hair and kissing her the way he'd been imagining all night.

He clenched his jaw as he rounded the hood. This was insane. Yeah, this job didn't require him to be on high alert like most of his others did, but it was no damn excuse. He was allowing himself to be distracted, and that wasn't okay. She'd hired him to protect her, not seduce her. She trusted him—his abilities and his professionalism.

Mentally reprimanding himself, vowing to be more professional in his thoughts from now on, he got behind the wheel and steered for the exit. "Need anything before we head to the hotel?"

"No." She gave him an unreadable look and didn't say anything else.

The radio played quietly as he drove them across town, a silent, palpable tension building between them. Neither of them spoke on the way up in the elevator, but in the confined space he was intensely aware of how close she was, her scent swirling in his head.

He stole one forbidden look at her in the paneled mirrors on the other side of the elevator, his gaze sliding over every gorgeous curve of her body before he forced them to the front once more.

He walked her down the hall to her room, keeping a few feet of distance between them but keenly aware of her presence, and that a big, soft bed was available just on the other side of this door.

Nope. Not going there.

He unlocked it, started to walk in, then stopped. "Sorry, habit. I always check the room personally to make sure it's secure."

She bit her lower lip to hide a smile, her dark eyes laughing at him. "Probably not necessary in this case, but if you'd feel better, go right ahead."

He would feel better. So he did, making a quick sweep before coming back out. He held the door for her, angling his body to let her by, making sure they wouldn't touch. Tomorrow's meeting was scheduled for oh-eight-hundred. "I'll come get you at seven-forty-five."

"Wait." She stopped him with a hand on his arm, her eyes searching his. "I thought we could have breakfast together first, around seven. Unless you'd rather not," she added quickly, dropping her hand.

Once again, he found himself in unfamiliar territory. And while the sane, disciplined part of him warned that eating together would only blur the already compromised boundaries between them more…

He couldn't summon the will to give a fuck. "Sure. I'll come get you at seven."

Relief flickered in her eyes, but she hesitated, seeming in no hurry to go into her room. Then her gaze dropped to his mouth.

His hand tightened around the door handle, a bolt of lust slicing through him. The arousal he'd been fighting against all night suddenly roared to life, drawing every muscle in his body tight as blood rushed to his groin.

His dick swelled, pushing hard against his fly, the need to kiss her pumping through him, to back her into that room and peel her dress off her body before pinning her to the wide bed and tasting every inch of her.

Nadia's sister, his conscience snapped at him as he struggled against the most intense attraction he'd ever felt in his life. *She's a client. And she doesn't know the real you.*

That last thought acted like a bucket of ice water dumped over his head.

Anaya thought he was some kind of hero because he'd

helped rescue her sister, when he was anything but. And if she knew the truth she wouldn't be interested anymore.

She deserved more than a few orgasms and an abrupt goodbye when this job was done. Deserved a hell of a lot better than *him*.

He pulled in a breath, relaxed his grip on the handle. "Sleep well," he said in a gruff voice, and strode down the hall to his own room.

The sooner this job was over and they went back to their own lives on opposite sides of the country, the better off they'd both be.

FIVE

Donovan arrived at the bar near T-Mobile Park at five minutes to eleven the next morning. Officially he was off the clock. Anaya was in meetings at another hotel downtown until at least three and didn't need him until then.

They'd had breakfast together at a greasy spoon joint a few blocks from her hotel. She didn't seem like the greasy spoon type, but she'd heard good things about the food and wanted to try it.

She'd carried most of the conversation because he'd made up his mind last night to stay detached, but try as he might, he couldn't maintain it with her. He genuinely enjoyed her company, was interested in her and what she did. She was warm and open with a great sense of humor, everything he wasn't. Anaya was the light to his dark, drawing him like a freezing man to the irresistible warmth of a fire.

On the drive to the other hotel after, he'd told her he had to meet someone but would be back to wait for her within an hour. She hadn't asked who it was or what it was about, but he could tell she'd wanted to. He was glad because he didn't want to lie to her, and he certainly didn't want her to know about this part of his past.

The yeasty smell of beer and cooking burgers hit him when he walked in the door. His eyes adjusted to the relative dimness, allowing him to scan the place. The instant he spotted Nick sitting in the corner, the knot in his chest tightened. He started toward the table, prepared to take whatever came and wondering what kind of mood Nick was in this time.

Nick looked up as he approached, and Donovan's steps faltered. In the dim lighting he looked haggard and gaunt, with hollows under his cheekbones and his eyes almost sunken in his skull. At least a weeks' worth of growth covered his face, and his light brown hair looked like it hadn't been cut in months.

"Hey," Nick murmured, seated in a booth with his back to the corner so he could maintain clear sightlines.

"Hi." He sat, automatically keeping tabs on everything happening around them. As veterans, it was ingrained in both of them, something neither of them could shut off. Both had earned a Ranger tab, though they'd never served together.

They weren't friends. More like forced acquaintances linked by a tragic history. Donovan only maintained the link between them out of a nagging sense of responsibility and guilt he couldn't shake. "How you doing?" he asked.

Bloodshot blue eyes met his. "Been better. You?"

"All right." The server came over, giving him a few moments to figure out how to handle this. Nick was obviously in a bad place. Worse than Donovan had ever seen him, with the exception of right after…

"Double cheeseburger with fries, and I'll have another of these," Nick said, lifting his beer bottle.

Donovan ordered a coffee and nothing else, since he was still full from breakfast. The server left, and Nick leaned back in his seat. "So? What's new? You've got a new job, right?"

He nodded. "Started a few months ago. What about you?"

Nick lowered his gaze, jaw tightening. "I haven't worked in a while now."

"What happened?" he asked quietly, growing more concerned.

"Got fired a few weeks ago. Couldn't drag myself out of bed some days to show up. Boss got tired of it."

Donovan studied him. His arms were clear. No sign of needle marks. Maybe he was still clean. Maybe the last stint in rehab had worked. But he could also be injecting himself somewhere less visible or popping pills to escape his grief. "You don't look so good, Nick," he finally said, not seeing any reason to tiptoe around it any longer.

Nick cracked a grin and gave a humorless chuckle that sent a chill over Donovan's skin. "No, I guess I don't. But I'm still here, right? That's the main thing. I'm still fighting."

"Right."

"Anyway, enough about me. You've got a new job. How's your daughter doing?"

"She started college a few weeks ago."

"Bet that feels weird, huh?"

"So weird."

"What's she studying?"

"General first year prerequisites right now. Business admin later."

"Ah. She's gonna be a boss lady."

"Yep." He took a sip of his coffee, not knowing what else to say.

"Glad things are going well for you." The words sounded nice, but the bitter edge to his tone told the real story. Nick's life was shit and he resented Donovan for not being in the same position. "What about a lady? You seeing anyone?" A glint of interest lit his bloodshot eyes.

"No."

"No? No one?"

"No." Even if he had been seeing someone, he wouldn't have told Nick. It would be like rubbing sulfuric acid into an open wound. And this conversation had edged into decidedly uncomfortable territory. "Listen, about the job. Is there something else you're interested in doing—"

"I'm not seeing anyone either. Obviously," he said with another one of those hollow smiles that made Donovan's insides tighten. "And this time of the year makes it all harder, you know?"

He nodded and didn't say anything. Because he didn't know what to say, and wondered for the hundredth time why he'd come here and why he kept doing this to himself.

Because you owe him, his conscience said sharply, *and it's the least you can do for the guy. That's why.*

Every year it was the same. Nick would contact him near the anniversary of the event that had changed their lives forever, usually a few weeks before to arrange a time and place to meet. Donovan always did his best to make it.

The actual anniversary was next week. He imagined Nick would be on a bender from now until the day after. Even if he'd still been employed, he wouldn't have been able to hold down a job right now anyway.

"Are you still talking to someone, Nick?" he asked. Because it was clear he needed help. Big time. And Donovan's sense of obligation toward him only went so far.

Nick pulled a face and took a long swallow of his beer. "Nah. Fired the last shrink months ago. None of them know shit. They all think they have the right answers, think they know what I should be doing. But none of it helps." He shook his head, face tightening as his voice thickened. "Nothing ever helps."

Nick's growing agitation made Donovan's pulse kick up. Last year Nick had gotten drunk and caused such a scene that Donovan had been forced to drag him outside and put him in a cab before he got arrested. He had no desire to repeat that toxic dance again. This was the last time he was doing this.

"It's one day at a time, you know?" Nick went on. "Some days I think I'm finally getting over it. Then, bam. Something will trigger it. Stupid things. Something that reminds me of her. A song on the radio. A show on TV."

The server brought Nick's food. He picked up the burger. "You sure you don't want anything?"

"I'm good." Mostly he just wanted to wrap this up and get out of here without Nick getting drunk and having to be forcibly removed from the premises, as had happened a few times before.

Nick eyed the burger, seemed to have to force himself to take a bite. He chewed slowly, a slight expression of distaste on his face, as if it was disgusting. "Don't have much appetite right now," he muttered, setting the burger down and reaching for a fry. "But I force myself to eat at least once a day even if I don't feel like it. She'd want me to take care of myself." He lifted tortured blue eyes to him. "She'd want that, right?"

"Yes, she absolutely would." Donovan had barely known Caroline, but without question she'd loved Nick. And he had to believe she would hate knowing Nick was slowly destroying himself after losing her.

"I got it," Donovan said, grabbing the bill and reaching for his wallet.

"Thanks, man."

"Sure." He left cash on the table, itching to get the hell out of here. Away from Nick and all the memories he stirred up. "You need a ride someplace?" he asked as he stood. Nick would contact him again around the holidays, giving him a few months' reprieve.

"Nah, I'm good." His burger lay almost untouched on his plate, maybe three bites taken out of it, and the fries didn't have a dent in them.

Donovan nodded, unable to stand it a second longer. "Take care, man."

One side of Nick's mouth lifted in a sardonic, bitter smile. "Yeah. You too."

He stepped outside onto the sidewalk and pulled in a deep breath tinged with a hint of the ocean at the bottom of the hill. Not as clean and strong as it was back in Crimson Point, but that briny smell was unmistakable. It made him think of Shae, and that he missed her already. Maybe when he got back, he could talk her into doing a day hike along the coastal trail together.

He'd just climbed into his vehicle when he got a text from Anaya. *Change of plans. Can you pick me up and take me to The Museum of Flight? I need to try and arrange a tour for this afternoon, but I want to scope it out first.*

Sure, he answered. *Be there in twenty minutes.*

Okay. Thanks.

He smiled ruefully. So polite, and genuinely appreciative of what he did for her. He could count on one hand how many times he'd guarded a client like that, and they'd all been women. Celebrities and relatives of the ultra-rich. Never anyone he'd known personally before acting as their security.

He'd also never wanted to strip any of the others naked and bury his face between her thighs, drinking in the sounds she made while he made her come with his tongue. Only Anaya. And it had to stop.

She was waiting outside the entrance when he pulled up front, her bright smile of greeting hitting him dead in the chest.

"Thanks for this," she said when he popped the door open for her and she climbed in, filling the interior with her tangy-sweet scent. "I hope I didn't interrupt your meeting?"

"No, it wrapped up before you texted."

"Oh, good. Did it go okay?" She was watching him closely.

"Yeah." He didn't want to talk about it. Not even with her. Especially not with her. "How did it go with you? They start negotiations yet?"

"Just." She rolled her eyes. "So not my thing. I promised my boss I'd sit in, but things got tense really fast, and they took a break. I proposed moving our 'field trip' to this afternoon to try and defuse the tension."

"Ah. Negotiation tactics."

She raised her eyebrows at him. "Better than watching a bunch of alpha males get into a pissing contest across the conference table."

A laugh burst out of him, startling him. And it felt good.

She grinned. "I like it when you laugh."

Him too. And God knew he hadn't had much to laugh about for a while now. Somehow she brought it out of him effortlessly.

He found a parkade near the museum, left the SUV close to the entrance and then walked with her up the concrete steps to ground level. The sidewalk was busy, two tour buses offloading their passengers at the corner. Wrapping his fingers around Anaya's upper arm, quelling the quick jolt of awareness even that touch caused, he led her around the crowd to the crosswalk light.

"Have you ever been here?" she asked him, tucking an errant curl behind her ear.

"No."

She glanced at him sharply at his flat tone. "Do you hate museums?"

"Hate's a strong word."

Her lips quirked. "Okay, then do you like them?"

"Not usually."

"Bet you'd like this one if you gave it a chance. I'm serious," she said when he gave her a doubtful look. "There's bound to be something in here you'd find interesting."

"Maybe."

"All right, I *bet* you there is," she said. "Twenty bucks says you find something inside that piques your interest."

No bet, because she would be in there, and she definitely piqued his interest. "I'm good."

"Come on," she insisted. "Twenty bucks." The light turned green and the crosswalk signal lit up. She stepped off the curb, starting across the street. "If you don't have a good time, I'll—"

At the squeal of tires, he whipped his head to the left. A pickup flew around the corner and veered right at them.

Anaya froze.

Donovan grabbed her around the ribs and dove back toward the sidewalk just as the truck hurtled past, close enough that he felt the air punch around him.

They hit the ground hard, Anaya beneath him. He kept her pinned there, his gaze darting to the truck. Its taillights came on as the driver briefly hit the brakes, then it sped off, tires smoking against the asphalt.

He rolled off her. The crowd of tourists were staring at them, women holding hands to their mouths or chests. "Are you okay?" he asked, reaching down to help her up.

"Yeah," she said, wincing as she got to her feet. Her knees, elbows and the heels of her hands were bleeding where the pavement had scraped them. She'd lost one of her shoes. "What the hell? That crazy idiot could have killed us," she said in a shaky voice.

Donovan quickly refocused on the retreating truck, memorizing the plate before it was out of sight. Anaya had said the driver was crazy.

But the way the truck had veered straight for them, and the warning tingle in his gut made him wonder if it hadn't been an accident at all.

SIX

Anaya sucked in a breath when she stepped out of the SUV in the underground lot of her hotel and tried to put weight on her bare right foot. Donovan was right there to wrap a steadying hand around her upper arm. "Is your ankle worse now?" he asked.

"Yeah." The heel of her shoe must have gotten caught on the sidewalk when he tackled her. She'd found it lying snapped off a few feet away. But if he hadn't tackled her, she'd be dealing with a whole lot worse than a hurt ankle right now. She might even be dead.

"Here." He bent slightly, started to slide an arm under her legs like he was going to pick her up.

"Oh, no," she protested. "It's not that bad." Not broken. Probably. She hoped.

He looked at her doubtfully for a moment, then relented and straightened, banding an arm around her waist instead and looping hers across his wide shoulders. She could feel his muscles bunching beneath the supple leather of his jacket as he pulled her in tight to his side to brace her. "Go slow. But if it hurts, stop. I can carry you no problem."

A little flutter curled low in her abdomen at the thought of being swept up and carried in those strong arms. He was sexy as hell just standing there doing nothing. If he picked her up and cradled her against that muscular chest, she wasn't sure she could control herself. "I'm okay." Her head was throbbing where the side of it had smacked into the sidewalk.

She was shaken, sore and bleeding, her raw knees, elbows and palms stinging like hell—but alive. All she wanted at the moment was to get upstairs to her room without causing a spectacle, and if he carried her people would definitely stare. Maybe she needed to go to a walk-in clinic to get her ankle checked.

He pretty much carried her anyway as he helped her the short distance to the elevator, stood bracing her on the way up to their floor. She pressed her lips together on the way to her room, every time she put weight on her right foot sending a sharp pain through her ankle.

He unlocked the door and helped her over to the bed. "Sit down here," he told her, handing her another gauze pad to dab at the blood trailing down the front of her shins from the sores in her knees. "I'll be back in a minute." He rose and left the room.

She sighed and closed her eyes, letting a little shudder roll through her. That had been way too close for comfort. She'd just frozen. Staring at the truck barreling at them like an opossum in the middle of the road. While Donovan had reacted instantly, saving them both.

He knocked a few minutes later and walked in carrying the first-aid kit from the vehicle. Face serious, he knelt in front of her on the carpet, his big hands carefully wrapping around her right lower leg, just above her throbbing ankle. She swallowed a gasp as sparks of sensation skittered over her skin, warmth curling inside her.

He slid his thumb down to probe unerringly at the tender

spot on the outer top part of her ankle. At her quick inhalation, he looked up at her, the concern in those gorgeous green eyes hitting hard. "Hurt here?"

"A bit." More than a bit, but she didn't want to come across like a complete wimp. He had been in the military, would have endured much worse than a twisted ankle and still carried on. "It's not that bad. Maybe we can just wrap it tight and that'll help."

He looked back down at where his hands cradled her ankle, gently tested the joint, moving her foot up and down and back and forth. She winced and he glanced up again. "Don't think it's broken. Probably just a sprain, but you should get X-rays just in case."

"Not right now, but maybe later. I need to get back to the meetings."

Surprise flickered in his eyes. "You sure?"

"Yeah, I mean, it's just a few bumps and bruises. I'll get cleaned up, change, and then head back. But I think the museum trip is out for me. Unless they've got an electric scooter for me to use," she teased.

He didn't say anything as he reached for the kit and took out some things, then began tending to the scrapes on her knees.

"I can do it," she said, a little embarrassed, and reached for the alcohol wipe.

He pulled his hand out of reach. "No, let me. This one's pretty deep," he said, leaning in to dab the wipe gently on the sore.

She covered a wince at the burn. "I'm okay, really. Are you?"

"I'm fine."

She had the distinct impression that he would've said that even if he'd dislocated a shoulder or broken a bone. It was starting to bug her that he was so hard to read. A few times she'd thought she'd seen male interest in his eyes when he looked at her, but now she was second-guessing herself. Other than pretending they were a couple for a few hours last night in front of the others, he'd been nothing but professional and a bit remote.

That's because you're a job to him, nothing more.

It was a sobering reminder, but with him kneeling there in front of her and absorbed in his task, she couldn't stop herself from admiring the view. His dark, thick hair fell over his forehead, the dark sweep of his lashes shadowing the tops of his cheeks as he worked.

There was a little scar at the corner of his mouth, adding to the rugged, masculine landscape of his face. His shirt hugged the muscular contours of his chest and shoulders to perfection.

Cut it out. He's not for you and you know it. Or do you need to learn that lesson again the hard way?

Her stomach muscles tightened as Bryan's face swam before her for an instant. He'd been everything she'd ever wanted. Until he wasn't.

She tore her gaze away from him and busied herself with cleaning up the scrapes on her palms. It was surprising how much they hurt, but it was probably because of all the nerve endings involved. A clean cut would have been less painful.

He put little bandages on her knees and palms, then started on her elbows. "You're gonna be stiff and sore for a while."

"I'll take that over being dead any day."

He glanced up, a slow half-smile tugging at his mouth, making her heart stutter in spite of herself. "Me too."

"I need to call my boss," she murmured, digging her phone out of her purse.

It was just so damn hard to think straight when Donovan was this close. The tender concern he was showing her now, remembering how he had literally dived on top of her to protect her earlier, had her all tangled up and aching inside.

She knew it was stupid of her. Already feeling attached to him when it couldn't lead anywhere.

"Got the field trip all arranged?" Darren answered brightly. "I ordered us in some pastries and drinks from that bakery you recommended, and that broke some of the tension, but I think we could all use a change of scenery and something fun to do together as a group this afternoon."

"Glad to hear you've managed to keep the peace so far, but unfortunately the museum thing's gonna have to wait. We uh, had an incident on the way there." She explained what had happened.

"God, are you okay?" he asked, shocked.

"Yeah, we're both fine. Just cleaning up now, then I'll head over. Make sure you include me in the lunch order because I'm starving. And I definitely need a dessert." She glanced at Donovan, now busy tending to her left elbow. Hopefully he had no clue that he was making her insides go crazy.

She glanced down at herself. Damn. There was blood on her favorite skirt suit. Hopefully the dry cleaners could get it out. "Donovan, do you want anything for lunch?"

"No, I'm good," he answered, all business as he dabbed and bandaged, the feel of his fingers wrapped around her arm causing her to flush all over.

"I'll be there within the hour," she told Darren, and ended the call.

Next Donovan cleaned and bandaged her right elbow, then his long fingers curled around her wrist. She met his gaze, felt that fluttering again deep inside. She still couldn't tell what he was thinking, but she sensed he was hiding a lot beneath the surface. "You hurt anywhere else?"

She shook her head. Her neck was a bit stiff, but she wasn't going to say it. "Just a little bump on my head, but it's no big deal." She touched her fingers to the tender spot on the side of her scalp, froze when he pushed her hand away, his fingertips sliding through her curls.

Their gazes locked. She held her breath, heart rate kicking up as a rush of desire swept through her. His face was inches away, his lips so close to hers.

She could almost feel them on her own. Imagined the way his fingers would curve around her head as he held her still and brought his mouth down on hers.

"I need to make a call," he said in a low voice and abruptly lowered his hand, shattering the fantasy. "Go ahead and clean up."

Feeling a little like she'd just been dismissed, she pushed up from the bed with her hands. He grasped her upper arms, helped her to stand with her weight on her left foot. "Let's get you into the bathroom."

She allowed him to help her into the bathroom and lowered herself onto the edge of the tub.

"I'll be right here if you need anything," he told her, then closed the door behind him. She heard him on his phone as she began to strip.

"Hey," his deep voice said. "Just about got run down outside The Museum of Flight by a pickup." He paused. "Yeah, she's okay, just banged up. Can you run the plate for me?"

She frowned, her fingers a little unsteady as she undid the tiny pearl buttons on her blouse. How had he even had time to see the plate?

"Thanks. Let me know what comes up."

She struggled out of the blouse and skirt, winced at the pain in her elbows as she reached behind her to unhook her bra. Not wanting the hassle of having to bother with the shower, she ran the water in the sink and used a clean facecloth to wash up. She had an abrasion on her cheek too, but it wasn't bleeding anymore.

After freshening up and changing into a pink summer dress that wouldn't touch her throbbing knees, she gingerly stepped out. Donovan looked up from his phone, his gaze sweeping over her from head to foot and back again. It was only an assessing look, but her body didn't seem to care.

Heat suffused her, her nipples pulling into tight points inside her bra.

His phone rang. He checked the screen before answering. "Hey," he said, holding her gaze while his low voice wrapped around her. He listened in silence to whoever it was, his expression closed. "Got it," he said a few moments later. "Keep me posted. I'll be in touch if I find out anything else."

"Who was that?" she asked when he lowered the phone.

"Walker." When she looked at him blankly, he elaborated. "Colleague, buddy and my daughter's stepdad. I had him run the plate on the pickup."

Oh. Wow to all of that. "What did he say?"

"It was reported stolen. Police found it a few blocks away from the museum. So far there's no footage of the driver, but they're looking into it." His expression shifted. Turned somber, even a little angry. "But it was stolen a few blocks from here about half an hour before it almost ran us down."

Staring into his eyes, a chill ran up her spine. That was almost exactly how long it had taken them to drive over there, park and get to the crosswalk. "So…you mean it wasn't an accident? Whoever stole the truck followed us there, waiting for the chance to run us over?" Her voice was tight with alarm. This was getting crazier by the minute.

"It's possible."

Holy shit. She crossed her arms over her chest, suddenly chilled, the discomfort of her scrapes and bruises fading beneath a cold wave of shock. "No one would do that randomly."

"No," he agreed softly.

Looking into his eyes, she could tell they were both thinking the same thing. Riggs.

Grabbing her phone, she called Darren. "Was Riggs there with you the entire time I was gone?" she asked the moment he answered.

"No, why?"

She met Donovan's gaze, tensing. "He wasn't?"

"No. Why, did he bother you again?"

Actually, he might have just tried to kill me. "Where did he go? Do you know?"

"He stepped outside for some air, he said. While I was ordering the stuff from the bakery."

"Is he there now?"

"Yeah, he got back about ten minutes ago. Do you want me to find out where he went?"

She needed to ask Donovan first. "Let me call you back, okay?"

"Anaya, wait, what's going on?"

She sighed. "Are you alone right now?"

"Yes."

She waited for Donovan's nod of assent before continuing. "Donovan had someone run the pickup's plates. Whoever was driving stole it and followed us across town to the museum. So it looks like this might not have been an accident."

"Oh, shit, are you *serious*? You think Riggs was involved?" He sounded stunned.

"I don't know. I hope not, but…" She didn't know what to think right now. Riggs was a predatory, entitled asshole, but would he really want her dead? Though, she had hurt his ego and gotten him in trouble for the harassment. Maybe he was looking to get back at her. "I'll call you in a bit. Don't say anything about Riggs to anyone."

"I won't. Let me know if there's anything I can do, okay?"

"I will." She ended the call and faced Donovan.

"So Riggs was gone during the same period?" he asked.

"Yes." She shook her head, the throb getting worse. "Him wanting to kill me is a stretch. But him actually trying to run me down on a busy street in broad daylight in front of dozens of witnesses is beyond nuts. He's a bully, but a coward at heart."

"But it's not impossible," he pointed out. "People kill for all sorts of reasons, and Riggs definitely has motive here."

She rubbed the center of her forehead, thinking hard. "I guess," she finally agreed. After a moment, she looked back up at him. He hadn't moved, watching her with a set expression on his gorgeous face. "So what now?"

"I take you back to Crimson Point this afternoon."

She blinked, unprepared for that. "But the rest of the meetings, the negotiations. I can't just…" She trailed off at the set look on his face.

"As you said, someone just tried to run you down on a busy street in broad daylight in front of witnesses, and right now Riggs is a potential suspect. Until we know for sure what's going on, I need to get you out of here."

Anaya didn't like it, didn't like anything about this, but she had to admit he might be right to err on the side of caution under the circumstances. "Okay," she said, suddenly tired, not to mention disappointed.

Going back to Crimson Point was the sensible thing to do for now. But it also meant her time with Donovan was about to come to an abrupt end.

SEVEN

Jean Luc paused in wielding his shovel and set the edge of the blade down on the damp pavement to drag his sleeve across his sweaty forehead. Behind him, tall cranes were busy loading and unloading cargo on the huge freighters in port. A ship's horn blew a long, low note, signaling it was about to leave port.

It was just past noon. He'd started his shift at seven and he'd only stopped once a few hours ago for a coffee break. In spite of the cool weather, his shirt was sticking to his back and armpits and he felt every one of his fifty-nine years, the ache in his lower back, shoulders and across his shoulder blades almost unbearable.

Every day he asked himself how much longer his body could hold out with this kind of work. But if he wanted to eat and a place to stay, it was the only option available for an uneducated immigrant like him.

The others had all stopped for lunch, now lounging in the shade cast by the low building on the other side of the yard. Those guys all knew each other, spent their breaks together every day. They were also far younger than him, so they had nothing in common, and tended to stay apart. Jean Luc didn't trust people he didn't know and preferred to keep to himself anyway.

He leaned his shovel against the chain-link fence and walked over to get the paper bag he'd brought. The half-sandwich he'd saved from yesterday was soggy from the tomato and the lettuce was limp, but it was food, and he'd gone without it too many times to be fussy.

Lowering himself stiffly to the ground, he rested his back against the cushion of the chain link, pausing a moment to close his eyes while the murmur of voices floated across the yard to him on the salt-tinged air. The late September sun shone down on his face, drying the sweat on his skin. The weather had been warm and sunny for the past few weeks, but to him it was cool compared to home.

He missed Haiti, missed his family there. But he could never go back. He'd made enemies there who would hunt him down and kill him if they found out he was on the island.

His mind drifted to Anaya. Meeting her yesterday had been the best thing that had happened to him in years. Maybe ever. She looked like his eldest sister had at that age. He remembered Anaya's mother so clearly. Beautiful, just like the daughter they'd made together. Their relationship had been far too brief, and he hadn't even known she'd gotten pregnant.

His daughter was everything he could have hoped she would be and more. Smart, accomplished, successful, and had a kind heart. Ready to forgive and accept him even after he'd been absent from her life until now. And the money she'd given him had both secured a safe place for him to sleep last night and filled his belly, so he didn't have to go down to the soup kitchen for once.

He was proud of how she'd turned out. Wondered if she'd been genuine about wanting to see him again before she left

Seattle. Probably not now that she'd met him in person. He was sure he was a huge disappointment to her.

He was a big enough disappointment to himself.

The break passed far too quickly. A shrill whistle blew, signaling it was time to get back to work. He opened his eyes, wearily pushed to his feet, and paused when he saw a white guy standing just outside the side gate about thirty yards away.

He was sorely out of place in his neat, clean clothing, dark sunglasses and no hard hat. But that's not what made Jean Luc's inner radar go off. No, he was sure the man was staring at him from behind those darkened lenses. How long he'd been there, Jean Luc wasn't sure, but something about his presence and stillness was unsettling.

He didn't move as the man started toward him, but his pulse jumped. He glanced left and right but the other guys had all returned to work, and there was no one else around. The foreman was in his office across the yard, and the security guys were nowhere to be seen.

Jean Luc straightened, watching the man closely as he approached, his suspicion growing. He could be a cop or an undercover government agent. Maybe they'd been watching him. Maybe they knew what he'd done…

He shifted his stance, fighting the instinctive urge to flee. "Can I help you?" he asked, keeping his expression neutral. Life on the streets back in Haiti had taught him never to show any sign of fear or uncertainty.

The stranger stopped a few feet away and glanced around. Jean Luc could feel the others watching them from across the yard. Knew everything was being recorded on cameras around the yard right now. "You Jean Luc?" the man asked.

"Who wants to know?"

The man's head turned toward him, and Jean Luc could feel

his gaze on him through those dark shades. "I heard you might be looking for a side job."

He already didn't like where this was going. "Who said?"

"Heard you're the kind of guy who can get things done."

Jean Luc glanced over his shoulder. The foreman was still in his office, but he might be seeing all this on camera. And the other guys were definitely watching. "What kind of job?" he asked, though he had a bad feeling he already knew.

"Who was that woman you met with yesterday?"

Somehow he managed to hide his shock, even as alarm built in his gut. The question had been worded casually enough, but the underlying threat was obvious. "You been following me?" he demanded.

He shrugged. "Who was she?"

The casual attitude wasn't fooling him. This man was dangerous. "Who are you?" he demanded, his control slipping slightly as his temper spiked.

The guy studied him for a long, tense moment. His whole demeanor made the back of Jean Luc's neck prickle. He was too bold. Too sure of himself. *Merde*, was he undercover DEA? He'd only done a handful of drug runs on US soil, out of desperation. But maybe they knew. "I'm nobody."

Oh, he was somebody all right. Somebody who knew how to follow a person without being noticed. Someone with the balls to stroll in here and do this in plain view of security and anyone else who cared to watch—and possibly overhear.

"I'm not interested," he muttered, and turned away.

"Why did you meet Anaya yesterday?"

He froze, then whipped around, his pulse accelerating. Who the hell was this guy? "Who?" he said, feigning ignorance. And becoming more concerned by the minute.

The man shrugged, one side of his mouth lifting in an unpleasant smile. "Who is she to you?"

"I don't know what you're talking about." Something bad was going on here. He would protect Anaya.

Rather than take the hint and leave, the man closed the remaining distance between them. Jean Luc stayed rooted to the spot, refusing to budge or back down. It was the only way to deal with bullies.

The man stared at him for a few seconds before speaking again in a low voice. "I know who you are. I know what you've done."

A chill spiraled up his backbone at the thinly veiled threat. He kept his expression impassive. "And what is it I've done?"

Another smile. This one pure nasty, assuring him the man had a mean streak and wasn't afraid to turn it loose when it served him. "You've been a bad boy, Jean Luc," he murmured, his expression and tone so smug, Jean Luc's right hand curled into a fist.

The edges of his nails dug into his palms with the pressure of his fists. He longed to punch him. Drive his fist into that smug, pretty face and ruin that smirk permanently by splitting his lips and breaking some teeth. Only his fear of being arrested and then maybe deported held him back.

"I'll ask one more time. How do you know Anaya?"

He forced his anger back. "We only met yesterday. What do you want?"

"I need you to do something for me."

Jaw tight, he listened to what the man said, then shook his head, adamant. "*Non*."

Before Jean Luc could move, the man grabbed his hand. A wad of money met his palm. "Think this through carefully. Because there's more where this came from," the man murmured.

Just for a moment, he hesitated. He desperately needed

more money. He couldn't afford to keep doing this kind of grueling manual labor, financially or physically.

Non. Anaya came first. He would not betray her. "I don't want your money," he spat, jerking his hand free and stepping back.

The man's face tightened. "Careful. You don't know what I'm capable of."

"Get the fuck out of here," he snapped, done with this asshole.

"How's the citizenship application going?"

He paused, his spine going rigid.

"Would be a real shame if something got it denied. Like some certain recent activities you took part in."

His jaw tightened. Had this bastard just threatened to—

"Something like that would get you deported back to Haiti."

Jaw tight, he spun back around to face him. "Say what you have to say and leave," he snarled.

But he wasn't prepared for what the man said next.

"Jean Luc," an angry voice said from behind him.

He glanced back to find the foreman striding toward him from the trailer, his brows lowered in a perpetually pissed-off expression.

The stranger slipped a card into the front pocket on Jean Luc's shirt. "I'll be in touch."

Jean Luc stood there without moving while the man walked away, his mind in turmoil.

"Who the fuck was that?" the foreman snapped when he got close enough.

"No one," he said dully, the half-sandwich he'd just eaten now sitting like a rock at the bottom of his stomach.

"Then get back to work." The foreman spun on his heel and stalked back toward the building.

Dread expanding in his gut, Jean Luc went over to the fence

and picked up his shovel. Glancing over his shoulder, he found the stranger standing in the shadows on the other side of the fence, watching him.

He turned away and resumed his work, desperate to escape what had just happened in the physical work ahead.

But hours later it still hadn't worked. Because he knew there was no escape for him now.

EIGHT

"You sure you don't want crutches?" Donovan asked as he steered Anaya toward the vehicle waiting at the curb out front of the walk-in clinic. She was in obvious pain, and it bothered him.

"No, I'm okay," she insisted.

They'd waited over an hour for her to be seen by a doctor, and then two hours more to get X-rays. The films had confirmed no fracture, but her ankle was swollen and already starting to bruise. They'd wrapped it up with a compression bandage and given her some anti-inflammatories. "You want to sit in the back? You can elevate your foot on the seat."

"No, I'd rather ride up front with you."

That shouldn't have pleased him as much as it did. But he wanted her up front too. Wanted to be able to look at her as he drove.

He helped her into the passenger seat, then steered out of the clinic lot and toward the freeway. "I made some calls while you were in with the doctor."

"To Walker?"

"He was one of them, yeah. Based on what you said about

Riggs, I did a little digging. Because that kind of harassment is never isolated. If he did it to you, guaranteed he's done it before, and that he'll do it again."

"Seems about right."

"It is, and Walker found out Riggs is in a tight spot right now. Rumor has it he's close to losing his place at the firm—along with all his clients and reputation if the partners kick him out."

"And, of course, he blames me for his current predicament."

"You're a convenient target because you were right in front of him."

She shook her head, watching the traffic go by when they stopped at a light. "I still don't see him having the balls to mow me down himself."

"But he's got money to pay off someone. And connections to cover it up."

"And motive," she murmured, almost to herself.

"That too. Anyway, I thought you should know, it's not just you. He's done it to others, but you're the only one who had the guts to stand up to him. Walker's doing more digging on the details, and I'll tell you what he finds out."

"I'm really curious about Walker. What's his background?"

The abrupt shift in topic made it clear she didn't want to talk about Riggs anymore. "Military, and then he worked in intelligence."

She looked over at him, eyes widening. "He was a spy?"

"Not exactly," he said evasively. Though Walker had done a lot of fieldwork in the past and handled intel assets personally, most of his career had been in the decidedly gray area.

"And what about you? Which branch did you serve in?"

"Army."

She narrowed her eyes slightly, considering him. "Not just regular army though, am I right?"

His mouth twitched. "No. I earned a Ranger tab."

"That's impressive. How long were you a Ranger?"

"Eleven years."

"That's a long time. Then what?"

He shifted in his seat, discomfort eating at him. *More like your conscience*, a little voice pointed out. "I was a US Marshal for a while, then went on to security contracting work."

"Wow, that's quite an impressive resume."

"Not really." *Especially since an innocent woman died on my watch.* He was glad Anaya didn't know about that.

He felt protective of her on an incredibly personal level, and it was going to be a big relief for him when they parted ways in a few hours once he dropped her off at her sister and Callum's place in Crimson Point. Because this building attraction between them was something he wasn't prepared to deal with.

He kept careful watch as he got them on the freeway and headed south away from Seattle. Nothing suspicious tweaked his radar. He didn't see any sign that they were being followed.

"I called Nadia and my dad while I was waiting for the X-ray results," Anaya said. "They're both glad I'm leaving Seattle for now. By now my entire family will know what happened. I'm going to be deluged with calls and texts any minute now."

She'd no sooner said it than a series of chimes filled the air. She pulled out her phone and shook her head ruefully. "Right on cue." But she set it in her lap without responding to whoever had messaged her. "What's your family like?"

He made a point of never talking about himself with clients, hated talking about his family in general, but he couldn't shut this conversation down without coming off as a dick, and he understood Anaya was looking for a distraction to temporarily take her mind off all that had happened. "Just my parents and me. They're divorced. I haven't seen either of them in a long time."

"Oh. Sorry."

He shrugged. It was what it was. "I hear your family's big."

She chuckled softly. "Yes, it is. Half of us come from different places around the world and we speak almost a dozen languages between us. And we're also dysfunctional as hell."

The wry humor in her tone didn't hide the pain beneath her words. He felt for her. She tugged at a place inside him that before now was inaccessible to everyone except Shae. "We don't get to pick our family of origin."

"No, but for all our problems, I love them anyway. Especially Nadia. We're really close, as you've no doubt noticed. Both of us are close to our dad too." She glanced over at him, and he could feel the weight of her stare as he drove. Could practically feel her brain working, all the questions tumbling through her mind. "I'll admit, I'm dying of curiosity about Shae. She's your daughter?"

He nodded once, still uncomfortable with discussing his private life.

"Too personal?" Anaya asked.

He suppressed a sigh. Yeah, she was a client, but the job was pretty much over now, and would be officially done in another four-and-a-half hours when they reached Crimson Point.

Anaya was so damn nice. He liked her. She was easy to talk to. He decided to open up to her a bit. "Her mom and I were together for about a month before I shipped out on a deployment to Afghanistan. It wasn't a planned pregnancy, and I only found out eight weeks later."

"How old were you when she was born?"

"Twenty-one."

"That's so young. I can imagine it was a big shock, to find out you were going to be a father."

"Yep, it was."

"So I'm guessing you guys didn't get married?"

"No. Her mom made it clear she didn't want or expect anything from me going forward." He hadn't been ready to be a parent. Jillian had known that and given him an easy out by offering him papers relinquishing parental rights before Shae was even born.

"Is that what you wanted?" she asked after a moment.

"At the time I thought it was." He'd thought it was best for Jillian, and Shae as well. "But I wanted to meet her after she was born."

"Did the mom let you?"

"Yeah, Jillian was great about it. Let me come over the day after I got back." He'd never forget seeing Shae for the first time. Or getting to hold her, a tiny, fragile little bundle with a flower headband in her thick brown hair. That's when he'd found out that love at first sight was real. "I sent some money every month. Spent time with them while I was on leave. Sometimes I'd take Shae while Jillian ran errands or went out with friends."

"That must have been a steep learning curve for you."

He cracked a grin. "Oh yeah. But Shae and I figured it out."

"Were you gone a lot when she was growing up?"

He didn't know why she was so interested in this. "Yeah." Too much, but he'd been too selfish and wrapped up in his own life to see it back then.

"And how did Walker come into the picture?"

"I met him overseas and wound up introducing him and Jillian. They got married about a year later. Shae was still little when he adopted her."

"What happened to Jillian?" she asked softly.

"Died of ovarian cancer four years ago."

"Oh, that's awful. I'm sorry."

"Thanks. She was a good person and a hell of a mom."

Jillian hadn't deserved that shitty, painful fate, and he felt for Shae, who'd been close to her mom. "Anyway, that's the backstory. Walker stepped up and did the heavy lifting with Jillian where Shae is concerned."

"And that's why she calls you by your first name instead of Dad."

"Yeah." He wasn't proud of it, but he knew he didn't deserve to be called Dad anyway.

"You still seem to have an okay relationship with her though. When I saw you together the other night, she seemed comfortable with you and happy to be there."

"It's a work in progress. I've got a lot to make up for."

She was still watching him. He could feel the intensity of her gaze like a low buzz across his skin. "You moved to Crimson Point to be close to her, didn't you?"

He inclined his head, wondering what she was thinking. Fighting back the inevitable shame that came with revealing he hadn't been there for his own daughter. "Walker told me about a job opening at the company and I jumped at it." He didn't look at her. Didn't want to see the disapproval or disappointment he was sure was stamped all over her face.

"You guys seem to get along well."

"He's a good guy, and a helluva dad to Shae."

"I love the way you talk about him."

At the unexpected approval in her tone, he risked a glance at her. "What do you mean?"

"Come on, how many people do you know who talk like that about their kid's stepdad, let alone their ex's partner? I think it's incredible. Shae's lucky to have you both."

He grunted, his hand tightening on the wheel. "You ever been married?" he asked to steer the conversation away from him.

She looked away, focusing out the windshield. "No. Almost, but…no." Her voice was quiet. Flat.

He glanced over, surprised by the sudden change in her. Seeing the stiff way she held herself, he cursed inwardly for bringing it up. The breakup had obviously been hard for her. Whoever her ex was, he had to be the stupidest motherfucker alive to let her go.

He almost said it out loud. Had to clamp his jaw shut to hold the words back.

Her phone rang, ending the awkward silence. "Oh, it's Jean Luc," she said in clear relief, and answered. "*Bonjour.*"

He didn't hear what was said on the other end and spoke only a handful of French anyway. But he loved listening to her voice, loved the sound of the words as she talked.

At one point, he clearly heard her mention Crimson Point as she explained something. And when she ended the call two minutes later, she had a troubled look on her face.

"Everything okay?" he asked, still wishing he could take back his previous question.

"Fine. He sounded upset that I'm leaving Seattle. I told him I might be back yet before the meetings wrap up, but if not… I really wanted to see him one more time before I fly home. He's struggling like hell to carve out a life here, but too proud to admit it or ask for help."

"I'll take you back to see him before you go," he offered before he could change his mind.

She blinked at him in surprise. "You will?"

He made an affirmative noise. "I can check around and see what kinds of social support are available to him as well."

"Thank you," she murmured, her voice a little rough.

He didn't dare look at her. Knew if he did and saw the emotion in her voice mirrored in her eyes, he'd cross the line again.

He shifted his right hand to the wheel so he wouldn't be tempted to reach for hers. "Sure." It was such a small thing but seeing her bio dad again clearly meant a lot to her. He wanted to give her that at least, something for her to look forward to after the scary near miss today. Didn't want that to overshadow everything else on her trip.

And he sure as hell didn't want to acknowledge the hollow sensation that formed in his chest when he thought about her leaving.

NINE

Anaya laughed as Ferhana jumped in alarm when the edge of the wave touched her bare feet and toddled back toward them, eyes wide. "She's just adorable."

"Isn't she?" Nadia tucked a lock of hair behind her ear that the wind had tugged free of her braid, smiling as she watched Callum playfully chase their daughter down the damp sand.

After morning showers, the day had turned bright and gorgeous. A rich blue sky stretched overhead, studded with puffy white clouds pushed along by the breeze. Gulls and other seabirds soared overhead while the waves rolled onto shore. Up and down the beach, other families were out taking advantage of the weather, flying kites, having picnics and making sandcastles.

"What a great place for a kid to grow up," Anaya murmured.

"It's incredible," Nadia agreed.

Callum scooped Ferhana up. The baby's shrieks of laughter floated back to them on the wind as he clasped her tight to his chest and pressed kisses to the side of her neck. "And oh my God, could he be any more adorable with her?" Anaya laughed.

"I know. I honestly don't know how I kept away from him for as long as I did. In hindsight, I never stood a chance." Nadia's whole face softened with adoration, every inch the mom she'd been born to be.

Anaya had to look away, a sharp twinge slicing through her chest. "I'm just glad you woke up and realized how you truly felt about him before it was too late," she said. Nadia was as stubborn as she was loyal and free spirited. She'd almost missed her chance with Callum because she'd been preoccupied with guarding her heart.

Anaya knew something about that now.

Nadia nudged her with an elbow and shot her a grin. "You just love being right, don't you?"

"Well, I mean I don't *hate* it." They'd had a wonderful day so far. Nadia was beyond excited about the freelance job she was about to start for a private nonprofit helping protect vulnerable orphans around the globe. She would be working with Ivy, the insanely badass female operative who had helped pull Nadia out of Kabul, and her sister Kiyomi. Kiyomi sounded even more mysterious than Ivy, and Anaya was dying to find out more after her sister started working with them.

Nadia snickered and offered her a bottle of sparkling pink lemonade they'd picked up from Whale's Tale, along with the rest of their picnic. Buttery and flaky ham and cheese croissants, individual raspberry custard tarts—which they were totally counting as a serving of fruit—and peanut butter swirled dark chocolate chunk brownies. "How's your ankle?"

"Still attached." She gingerly moved her foot a little, stopping when it hurt. The pressure bandage helped a bit, but the ankle was still swollen, painful to walk on, and turning from blue to purple and green. Callum had had to help her walk here over the sand.

Callum loped back to them, Ferhana riding on his shoulders,

a huge toothy grin on her little face. "I'd say this princess is about ready to crash."

Nadia stood and reached up to take her. "Let's get you back to the vehicle before you fall asleep."

Anaya quickly packed away the remains of their lunch into the bags Nadia had brought.

"Come on, hopalong." Callum reached out a brawny arm and helped scoop Anaya up, then held her around the waist as they started back for the sidewalk. The shifting surface of the sand made the trek a lot harder and more painful than a hard, flat surface would have been, but the view and spending time with her sister's family was more than worth it.

On the sidewalk, they paused to brush sand off themselves. Anaya inhaled a deep breath of the clean, salt-tinged air and took a moment to look up and down Front Street, completely charmed by the town.

Wood-sided buildings painted in a rainbow of colors from vivid shades to a weathered silvery-gray lined the waterfront. A bar called the Sea Hag stood on the corner, the bank of windows at the back overlooking the rolling waves. The vet clinic where Ryder's wife worked was about a block north of it, and Whale's Tale was just down and across the street from that.

Shading her eyes, she could see the top of Crimson Point Security, an old brick heritage building built in the late 1800s that had been completely renovated inside with major security upgrades. It was already Tuesday, two days since she'd come back from Seattle. She wondered whether Donovan was there, and if he'd been given a new assignment.

She'd thought about him more than was probably healthy since he'd dropped her at her hotel the other night. She had declined Nadia's invitation to stay at their place because she wanted privacy. But since then, she had spent too much time analyzing some of what he'd told her. By his own admission it sounded like he hadn't been much of a father to Shae when she was growing up, though she understood he'd been young.

That insight into his character gave her pause because it hit too close to home, reminding her of what would have happened if she'd stayed with Bryan.

She shook the thought away, annoyed at herself for thinking about him again. And her past wasn't the same as what Donovan had gone through at all. He'd only been twenty-one when Shae was born.

As she turned back to her family, she paused, heart skipping a beat when she spotted a dark-haired man with Donovan's tall, powerful build coming down the sidewalk. But then he turned toward her, and the bubble of excitement burst. It wasn't Donovan.

"Oh, there's Beckett," Nadia said, lifting a hand to wave. "His wife Sierra owns and runs the vet clinic." Beckett waved back and disappeared into the clinic.

Anaya followed Nadia and the others to their vehicle. Callum read something on his phone before getting behind the wheel. "Boyd's just invited us up to their place for dinner."

"Oh, they're back from their honeymoon already?" Nadia asked.

"Guess so." He glanced back at Anaya. "You wanna come with us?"

Nadia twisted around to look at her. "You'll love them. Boyd's a bit intimidating and slow to warm up to new people, but you'll win him over in no time, and Ember's a sweetheart."

"I've actually got a lot of work I need to catch up on," she said. She *did* have work to do because she was working remotely until they were certain her safety was no longer at risk. Her boss and the others were deep into negotiations with the French team now, and Darren was confident they were close to reaching a deal.

But mostly she just wanted some time to herself to unwind and recharge. And shake off this heavy weight of loneliness she'd been feeling ever since Donovan had dropped her off. "But maybe I can meet them another time before I leave."

"Sure, we can make that happen if you want," Callum answered, and started the engine.

She was dying to ask him about Donovan. Whether he'd said anything or asked about her, and what he was doing now. She vaguely remembered where his house was up the hill north of town, but she wasn't going to just show up on his doorstep again like some stalker.

She'd even toyed with the idea of texting him and inviting him out for coffee or lunch. Something casual. But if he'd wanted to see her, he would have reached out by now. And she was starting to think she must have only imagined the flashes of desire she thought she'd seen from him before.

"You've still got a couple hours before we're due over there," Nadia said as she helped her from the vehicle in front of the hotel a few minutes later. It was a cute, quaint little boutique place a few blocks up the hill from the waterfront and her room had a view of the ocean. At night she could see the wink of the lighthouse up on the point. "If you change your mind, text me and we'll come pick you up on the way to Boyd and Ember's."

"Okay, sounds good." She didn't think she'd be changing her mind though.

Nadia waved at Callum to stay put behind the wheel and helped her through the front door into the lobby. "You're getting around a bit better than you were yesterday."

"Yeah. Thanks for the help, but I can take it from here."

"You sure?"

"Yes. Go get Ferhana home for her nap before she falls asleep in the car seat."

"Good call. She can be a bit of a nightmare when her

schedule gets thrown off." Nadia hugged her and left with a cheery wave.

Anaya stepped into the elevator with a little smile on her face. She and Nadia had been close right from day one after Anaya arrived at the Bishops' house. She'd never seen her sister as content as she was now. In spite of every obstacle, including some that Nadia herself had thrown between them, she and Callum had found their way back to each other, were now engaged, and parents to an incredibly resilient little girl they both adored.

It warmed Anaya's heart to know that true love and happy endings really were possible. And gave her a sliver of hope that maybe she'd still find her own one day as well.

She limped down the carpeted hallway to her room and opened the door to the gorgeous purple suite, the Do Not Disturb sign still hanging from the knob.

Stepping inside, she stopped dead. The weighted door fell shut behind her while she stood rooted to the spot, staring at the sight before her. She'd made the bed and had left everything neat and tidy before leaving the room a few hours ago.

Now everything lay in total disarray.

The covers had been ripped from the bed and thrown on the floor. All the drawers in the bureau were opened, her clothes and other belongings dumped in front of it. She rushed to the bathroom as fast as her sore ankle would allow, heart thudding as she took in the scene there.

My jewelry.

At the last second, she remembered to pull the sleeve of her sweater down to avoid blurring any prints on the handle and ripped open the bathroom drawer where she'd put her jewelry. She sucked in a pained breath when she saw two things missing: the diamond bracelet that had been her university grad present from her family, and the gold pendant necklace, the one and only thing she had left of her birth mother.

The second one hadn't been worth much in terms of monetary value, but to her it was irreplaceable. It had been her mother's. The only thing of value she'd ever had in her life, and she'd put it around Anaya's neck the morning she'd left her at the orphanage.

Remember me...

Devastated and sick to her stomach, she used the phone on the desk to call down to reception. "My room's been broken into."

"Oh my gosh, I'm so sorry to hear that," the young woman said in a shocked tone. "Is anything missing?"

"Yes. Can you verify whether housekeeping let someone into my room while I was gone?"

"I'll call the police, then check with the staff right after."

"Thank you." She put the receiver back in the cradle and went straight to the closet to check her laptop case. The laptop was open and sitting on the carpet in front of the closet.

It made no sense. Why take jewelry and not her laptop? And why *open* the laptop?

She found the answer a few minutes later when she checked the last drawer. The cash she'd left tucked under her clothes was gone too. So whoever had done it must have been after money and the jewelry that could be pawned easily.

A knock came at the door a few minutes later. "Miss Bishop?"

She checked through the peephole before opening it. A good-looking and fit man in his thirties with short brown hair and vivid blue eyes stood there wearing a cop uniform. "Hi."

"I'm Sheriff Noah Buchanan. I understand you've had a break-in earlier."

"Yes, come in." She stepped aside to let him in.

He took it all in with a sweeping glance. "Was anything taken?"

"Some jewelry and cash."

He looked back at her. "How much cash?"

"Around four hundred or so. I can't remember the exact amount. I put it under my clothes in this drawer." She showed the spot to him.

He took out a notepad and wrote it down. "And the jewelry?"

She swallowed past the sudden thickening in her throat. "A diamond bracelet and a gold pendant and chain." She gave a detailed description of both.

He wrote down everything she said, then met her gaze. "Anything else?"

"Not that I've noticed yet. Whoever it was took my laptop out of the case and opened it, then left it on the floor. The person at the front desk said housekeeping hasn't been in the room."

He nodded. "I'll check everything out again once I'm done here. Have you disturbed anything in here since you came in?"

"Just the contents of the drawers when I checked them. I didn't touch the handles with my skin."

"That's good, thank you for thinking of that. Hopefully we'll be able to get some good prints." He tucked the notepad away. "Theft isn't common in Crimson Point, especially with tourist season being over. I'm sorry this happened to you."

"Thank you." The little voice niggling at the back of her mind refused to be silenced. "So, this probably isn't related, and it might even sound a little crazy, but I think I should mention it just in case."

"Okay," he said, and waited patiently for her to continue.

She conveyed what had happened in Seattle, what she'd been doing there and why she'd returned to Crimson Point ahead of schedule. "Like I said, these things probably aren't related. Riggs had an alibi that checked out with Crimson Point Security. He wasn't the driver, though I guess it's possible he could have hired someone to come after me."

If Sheriff Buchanan was shocked by her words, he didn't show it. "Who was the bodyguard assigned to you?"

"Donovan Myers. Do you know him?"

"I've met him once. But I know Ryder and Callum, and your sister."

It made her feel a little better that he knew Nadia and the others. "I was going to call her and let her and Callum know what happened. Is that okay?"

"Yes. And don't feel like you need to stay here while I look into this. I'm going to start with reviewing housekeeping and check the security camera footage, and I'll have a deputy come in to dust for fingerprints."

"Thank you." She called Nadia as soon as the sheriff went downstairs to begin the investigation. Her sister was as shocked as she'd been, and Callum arrived twenty minutes later to pick her up.

She hobbled out the front door and got in the vehicle. "Sorry about this."

"Don't apologize. This isn't your fault." He eyed her as she did up her seatbelt. "You okay?"

She nodded. "Just...tired and unsettled."

"That's understandable. Did you tell Noah what happened in Seattle?"

"I don't think they're linked, but yes. Just in case." She was convinced they were separate incidents. "I bet it turns out to be either an employee or another guest who wanted some fast cash."

Yet that little tickle at the back of her brain wouldn't leave her alone. The two incidents had happened so close together. Either she had really bad luck, or...

Nope. She didn't want to even think it. She was too tired to contemplate the implications.

Nadia met her at the door with a big hug. "Come inside and relax. Noah's thorough. Hopefully he'll find the suspect and maybe even get your things back."

"I don't even care about the cash. Or the bracelet, really. But that pendant is different. It's worth a hundred times more to me than the other stuff."

"I know." Nadia rubbed her back in sympathy. "Come stretch out on the couch and I'll get you some tea."

"Thanks." She was glad Nadia was here with her. It made the loss and sense of violation more bearable.

Callum had canceled dinner with Boyd and Ember. He was in the middle of cooking burgers on the barbecue out back when Anaya's cell rang. A secret part of her hoped it was Donovan, that he'd heard what happened and was calling to check on her. But it was Sheriff Buchanan.

"I've reviewed the security footage," he told her. "It shows a possible suspect running from the hotel about twenty minutes after you left for the beach this afternoon. Can you come down and take a look?"

"Yes, of course. I'll be there soon."

Callum handed over grilling duty to Nadia and drove her back to the hotel. Sheriff Buchanan took them both into a room marked Security and strode to a computer sitting on the desk. "This is the best view of him."

The video showed the back of the hotel and the parking lot. The lot was half full of cars. Ten seconds in, the back door opened, and a man burst out. The angle was bad and he had a hoodie pulled up, concealing his face.

He paused just outside the door, scanning around furtively

before darting left and rushing away out of sight. Tall. Thin. Something about him was vaguely familiar.

Buchanan tapped another feed. "This is from another camera on the side street." He pressed play.

The suspect turned the corner and ran up the street, right at the camera. Anaya's hand flew to her mouth, her insides tightening.

No. No, it couldn't be.

"What's wrong?" Callum asked. "Do you recognize him?"

She could feel them both staring at her. She blinked fast against the sting of tears, disappointment and hurt twisting inside her. "Yes. That's Jean Luc Dumas. My biological father."

TEN

Donovan leaned back in his seat and took a pull from his beer bottle, eyeing Walker across the table. With tourist season now over, the Sea Hag was quieter than it had been in months. He'd missed coming in here. "So? Did I miss anything while I was gone?"

Walker swallowed a bite of his chicken club, the setting sun highlighting the silver at his temples. "Few more jobs came through," he said in his deep Mississippi drawl. "Ryder said we're fully booked for the next few weeks."

Except him, since his contract with Anaya was over, unless she decided to go back to Seattle for the remainder of the meetings.

"Oh, and I also heard a rumor the company's hiring its first female security specialist."

"Really? Who is she?"

"Dunno. How's Anaya doing? Any updates with her?"

"No." He hadn't seen or talked to her since he'd brought her back, to establish some distance from her and reinstate the boundaries that had been blurred too much. "Cops in Seattle think it was a random incident, and Anthony Riggs apparently had an alibi."

"Apparently? You don't think it's true?"

"I'd say fifty-fifty. The guy's an entitled asshole with money and his family's rep behind him. It'd be easy for him to pay someone off to provide an alibi."

Walker frowned and reached for his hard cider. Made by a local company a few miles inland using apples from their orchard and a hundred-year-old cider press. "You really think he'd risk targeting her like that? He's got a ton at stake if he's caught."

Donovan shrugged. "Guys like that think they're untouchable."

He nodded. "She holding up all right?"

"I haven't heard anything from her since I brought her back. Maybe she's decided to spend the rest of her time here until she flies home." He didn't want to think about her leaving. Didn't want to think about her period, because he'd already thought about her way too much. He kept having to stop himself from calling to check on her, or even stop by her hotel to see how she was doing.

"Anyway, how's Shae doing with her classes?" he asked to redirect the conversation.

Walker finished another bite of his sandwich. "Good. She's busy and meeting new people. I think she might be seeing someone."

He set his beer down. "Yeah? Who?"

Walker lifted a well-muscled shoulder. "She hasn't said, but she's been pretty private about her phone when I walk by, and I've caught her with that smile on her face when she thinks I'm not looking."

"The one that makes it look like she's stuck in daydream mode?"

"Yeah." His lips curved into a grin. "So pretty safe bet there's a guy involved."

Shit. "If you find out anything about him, let me know."

Walker's deep blue eyes filled with amusement. "You want me to do a background check on him?"

He grimaced. "No." Yes.

"She's got a good head on her shoulders. I trust her."

"I do too. It's the guy I don't trust."

"That's fair." He smiled around another mouthful of his dinner. "If she works up the guts to introduce him, I'll call you over so we can meet him together."

He chuckled, imagining the look of terror on the kid's face when confronted by the two of them at once. They wouldn't do anything too over the top because that would piss Shae off. Just enough to make it clear their daughter wasn't to be fucked around with.

"Deal." His cell buzzed in his pocket. Pulling it out, he saw Callum's number and answered, wondering if they'd tapped him for a new assignment already. "Hey."

"You still in town?"

"Yeah, why?"

"Anaya's room was tossed and robbed while she was out with us this afternoon."

What? "Shit, really?"

"Yeah, but it gets worse." He paused. "Her biological dad was caught on camera fleeing the building in that same time window."

"What the hell?" He went rigid in his chair. "Is she okay?"

"She's pretty upset."

Yeah, no shit. "Where is she?"

"With me at the hotel. I tried to get her to come to our place, but she refused. I think she's worried about bringing trouble to our doorstep. At a minimum we need to move her to a different hotel."

Donovan didn't doubt that she would want to try and protect her family from any collateral damage, but she probably also wanted to be alone right now. "I'll head over now."

"Thanks."

He stood and told Walker what was happening as he put on his leather jacket and reached for his wallet.

"No, I got this one," Walker said. "Go. Make sure she's okay."

He intended to.

His truck was parked in the lot beside the Sea Hag, but it was only a few blocks to the hotel and parking there was always at a premium because it was small. So he pocketed his keys, jogged across Front Street and then up the hill. Callum met him in the lobby.

"You're sure it was him?" Donovan asked.

"Positive. Anaya ID'd him herself."

Damn. "What did he take?"

"Cash and some jewelry. But it's weird. He wasn't careful at all. He tossed the room like he'd been short on time and frantically searching for something. I'm thinking he didn't find it, panicked, then grabbed the money and a couple easy things he could pawn before taking off."

"There was no one else with him? Nobody waiting on the street or in a vehicle nearby?"

"Not that any of the cameras in the area picked up. Come see the footage we got from here." He took him into the security room and showed him the video.

"What the hell was he thinking?" Donovan said as he watched Jean Luc run up the street and out of view around the corner. "Why target his daughter? She'd have given him the money if he'd asked for it. Hell, she gave him some when they met without him asking." And he'd have had to come all the way down here from Seattle by bus or catching a ride from someone.

"Maybe he's an addict or owes someone money. Anyway, Noah's done up his report and has deputies out looking for him. They dusted for prints. So far Anaya hasn't noticed anything else missing."

"She in her room?"

"Yeah, 309. Nadia's with her."

Donovan loped up the stairs and knocked on her door, driven by the need to personally ensure she was okay. Nadia pulled it open, Ferhana perched on one hip. "Hey," she said, looking surprised to see him.

"Hi." He stepped inside. Anaya was on the other side of the room folding some clothes at the dresser. She seemed to relax when she saw him but pressed her lips together for a moment as if fighting tears. "Hi," she finally managed hoarsely, making him ache with the need to pull her into his arms.

He glanced around the room. "Callum told me everything. Have you noticed anything else missing?"

"No."

Ferhana started fussing. Nadia bounced her slightly, glanced between the two of them. "I need to get her home to bed. Did you want me to stay?" she asked her sister. "I can have Callum take her—"

"No, I'm okay. Really," she said, putting on a smile. "You go on home. I'll see you tomorrow."

Nadia studied her for a moment, then relented. "Okay." She walked over, drew Anaya into a hug. "We're here for you."

"I know. Love you."

"Love you back. Ferhana, say bye to Auntie Nay-Nay."

Ferhana brightened and reached out her plump little arms.

Anaya melted visibly and hugged the baby gently. "Night, sweetheart." She kissed the top of the toddler's curls.

Donovan got the door for Nadia. "You'll make sure she's okay?" she murmured, glancing back at her sister with worried eyes.

"Of course." He let them out, then shut and locked the door before turning around to face Anaya. She was busy folding the last of the clothes that had been dumped on the floor. "I'm sorry," he said. She didn't need this shit on top of everything else.

She met his gaze. "Thank you." Turning away to resume her work, she shook her head. "I still can't believe it."

Him either. When she'd mentioned Crimson Point to Jean Luc on the phone the other day, Donovan would never have dreamed he would follow her and do something like this. "Noah's got people out looking for him."

"I know." Her normally silken voice was flat.

She and Nadia had obviously been working on getting everything back in order in here, but Callum was right. Why toss the place like this unless you were up against a tight deadline and desperately searching for something? It made no sense. Jean Luc must have been in one hell of a hurry to be so careless. "Did you tell him where you were staying?"

"I mentioned it yesterday when we texted. That was stupid. He must have followed me and been watching."

"You didn't know he would do this."

"No. But I'm so damn mad at myself for not being more careful. I don't know him. I had this stupid fairytale idea in my head that he was a good man, that he cared about me and had my back because we're blood. That necklace meant the world to me. I—" She broke off and put a hand to her mouth.

He moved without thinking, closing the distance between

them. She looked up at him at the last second, and the devastation in her eyes tore him up.

He drew her to him without a word, something hitching in his chest when she wound her arms around his waist and buried her face in his shoulder, seeking solace.

Wrapping her up tight in his arms, he buried his nose in her curls. She flattened against him, pressing every luscious curve to his front, her shoulders hitching as she fought back tears. He breathed in her scent, closed his eyes and held her in silence, hit with a mix of relief and an overpowering urge to take care of her.

She felt like heaven. He wanted to comfort her and make her feel safe, but he also wanted to kiss away her sadness. Peel her jeans and sweater off, then lay her down on the wide bed behind them and make her stop thinking altogether while he wiped everything else away with his lips, tongue and hands. Until she was twisting beneath him and begging for release, and he finally drove his cock as deep inside her as he could get.

She took a shuddering breath and then sighed, turning her head so that her cheek was cushioned against his right pec. "It's worse because it was him," she murmured.

"I know," he said, giving into temptation and stroking a hand over her hair. The tight curls were soft against his palm, springing back at the end of each stroke.

"But it's mostly the necklace. It's probably not worth more than a hundred bucks, but it belonged to my mother. She gave it to me the day she…" She stopped, drew a shaky breath. He lowered his hand and ran it up and down her back, hating to see her so upset. "The day she left me at the orphanage."

It wasn't what he'd expected her to say. "You remember it?"

"Yes. Vividly. A major hurricane had hit the day before. I guess it was the proverbial straw on the camel's back, because she walked me all the way to Port-au-Prince in the middle of the night and left me at the Catholic orphanage. The necklace was the only thing of value she'd ever had in her life, and she put it around my neck before she left."

Jesus, that was heartbreaking. "How old were you?"

"Six."

He gathered her closer, wishing he could go back in time and somehow protect her from the fear and pain that must have caused her. "Damn."

"She was desperate and must have thought she had no other choice, that she was doing me a favor by giving me a chance at a better life. A life she knew she would never have." She tipped her head back, stared up at him with big, sad brown eyes he could fall into if he wasn't careful. "Do you think there's a chance I can get it back? I'm guessing he'll try to pawn it. Maybe if I check with all the pawn shops between here and Seattle over the next few days, I can get it back."

It was a long shot, but damn, he could see why it meant so much to her. "I'll help you look for it."

The grateful smile she gave him squeezed his heart. "Thank you. I really appreciate it."

"Sure." She was still pressed against him, their faces inches apart. "You can't stay here anymore."

"I know. I already booked a room at the Sand Dollar."

A less fancy place at the opposite end of town, higher up on the hill overlooking the water. "Good." He managed to keep his eyes on hers, but when her gaze dropped down to his mouth a second later, a torrent of desire ripped through him.

He tightened his arm around her waist. Slid his free hand up her spine, up her nape and into the thick mass of her hair, his eyes locked with hers.

She stilled, her pupils dilating. And God help him, any remaining resistance in him evaporated like mist in the sunlight.

He dipped his head, pulse thudding as her eyes closed and

she tipped her face up to him. His lips settled over hers. They were even softer than he'd imagined. He sank into them, and the rest of the world fell away.

There was only Anaya, the feel of her, her arms and lips cradling him while he learned the shape and textures of her before delving his tongue inside to taste. Her soft moan sent heat flooding into his gut. He'd been half-hard since he'd touched her. Now he was instantly erect, his cock pressed to her abdomen.

His fingers tightened in her hair. The curls clung to him the same way she did, wrapping around his fingers. He could feel the prick of her elegantly manicured nails in his back through the thin fabric of his shirt. Wished they'd both been naked so he could feel the sting of it and explore all her smooth skin with his hands.

Her tongue touched his almost shyly. He bit back a groan and moved forward, pressing her up against the wall beside the dresser. She gave a low hum of arousal and flicked her tongue against his more boldly, nails digging harder between his shoulder blades as she arched her back, pressing her breasts more firmly into him.

He reined in the wild hunger she unleashed in him and kept her pinned there, slowly caressing her mouth with his tongue while he spread her thighs and wedged his hips between them. Anaya made a choked sound and rolled her hips, rubbing her center along the length of his erection.

Pleasure streaked through him, his heart racing with the raw need flooding his body. He shifted so his cock was nestled nice and tight against the center seam of her jeans, then began rocking with slow, measured movements.

"Oh," she whispered, her head falling back.

He dropped his mouth to the edge of her jaw, licked her earlobe. "You feel so damn good," he murmured. "I want to—"

He stopped himself before he blurted out something raw and sexual.

"Want to what?" she whispered breathlessly, gazing into his eyes with so much heat it almost snapped his control.

Eat you up. Make you come against my tongue. See the look on your face as I bury my cock in you and make you come again.

He kissed her again, flicking his tongue against hers. Teasing. Pushing. Reveling in the way she whimpered and rubbed against him, wanting more.

He'd give her more. Enough to take the edge off and wipe that sad, lost look from her eyes.

Enough to make her want him with every single breath she took.

He slid a hand up her ribs to cup the curve of her breast. She made a hungry sound and pushed into his palm. He tugged the low neckline of the soft sweater down to reveal the purple satin and lace bra she wore. Stared at the dark nipple hidden beneath the lace as he swept a thumb across it.

She sucked in a breath as it tightened. He did it again, watching her face this time. Tugged the material down until it cupped the underside of her breast, pushing it up toward him, the tight, dark nipple begging for his mouth.

His hands clamped around her waist and rib cage to hold her still while he dipped his head and touched the tip of his tongue to the hard nub. Anaya clutched the back of his head, pulling him closer. He obliged, taking her nipple into his mouth, giving it little flicks of his tongue as he sucked.

Her long, liquid moan set him on fire. His cock throbbed in time with every wild beat of his heart, hard and aching. He rolled his hips against her center, his mouth busy at her breast.

One of her hands shoved between them to undo the button at the top of her jeans.

Hell yes.

He eased his hips back enough to allow her to put her feet flat on the floor again, grasped the top of her waistband and shoved her jeans halfway down her thighs to reveal a pair of black lace panties. He ran his fingers over the front of them, looked up into her face when she drew in a quick breath. Her eyes were half-closed, lips parted, shiny and wet from his kisses.

On a groan he kissed her again, unable to help himself. He couldn't get enough of her. Couldn't control the tide of desire she caused in him.

Tongue tangling with hers, he pushed the lace aside and cupped her with his palm. She was all slick heat against his hand, his fingers sliding easily through her wet folds and up to the soft tuft of hair at the top of her sex. He paused there a few seconds, tugging gently at it. Playing with her folds before sliding deeper to find the swollen bud of her clit.

"Oh, God, Donovan," she panted, her fingers digging into the back of his neck.

He dropped another kiss on her luscious lips, watched her face while he caressed the sensitive knot. Slow, soft circles at first. Dipping in for another kiss when he eased a finger into her slick heat. Drinking in her breathless moans for a few heartbeats before lowering his mouth back to her breast, closing his lips around her hard nipple while he drove her out of her mind with his fingers between her legs.

She was so fucking gorgeous and uninhibited in her pleasure. She leaned back against the wall and arched for him, giving him total access to her body, needing the release he was about to give her. He wanted to drop to his knees and bury his mouth between her thighs, get her off with his tongue, but she was so close already, and he was enjoying sucking her nipple too much to stop now.

He shifted his hand, buried two fingers in her and stroked in and out while he rubbed his thumb along her clit. She hitched in a breath, a tremor rippling through her, and then she went off, clutching him with desperate hands as she rode his fingers, her sexy, throaty cries of release almost making him come in his jeans.

He caught her mouth with his, drank every last sound of her pleasure until she went lax and sagged against him. With effort, he ripped his mouth free and buried his face in the curve of her neck, breathing hard, his muscles strung taut, cock an aching, painful pressure against his fly. He forced himself to ease his hand from her slick core, allowed himself one last fleeting caress before he gripped her hips and straightened.

Anaya gazed up at him with drowsy, sated brown eyes that looked a little stunned, her bare breast still exposed, panties partway down her thighs and the delicate folds he still wanted to kiss and lick all over glistening from her orgasm. "That was..."

Yeah. It fucking was. And he needed to get the hell out of here before he pinned her flat to the bed and buried himself as deep inside her as he could.

His eyes went back to her lips. His cock flexed as he imagined pushing her to her knees right now, burying his hands in her curls and pulling her down until those sexy lips enveloped his cock.

Unable to help himself, he went back in for another taste. Kissed her slow and deep, craving her with every cell in his body, the fantasy of her sucking him off dragging a groan from deep in his chest.

He tugged her panties and jeans back up instead, then her bra and sweater. Only when she was fully covered did he risk breaking the kiss to look down at her again.

She stared back at him, eyes still a little dazed as she

reached a hand between them. His abs went rigid when her palm made contact with his belly. She slid it down slowly, watching him with pure arousal.

He snagged her wrist and stopped her, closing his eyes for a brief moment. "I can't," he said, his voice deep and guttural, the most intense arousal he'd ever felt still pumping through his system.

She blinked in surprise. "Why not? I want to touch you. Suck—"

He covered her lips with his before she could say it, repressing a shudder. "Get your stuff packed up," he murmured against the corner of her mouth, ready to come out of his skin. "I'll take you to the other hotel." He could spend hours just kissing her. Hours more exploring her and discovering all the things she enjoyed. She was so fucking soft, her skin so gorgeous and smooth, and she needed comfort and reassurance after what she'd just been through.

But if he stayed even a minute longer, he wouldn't stop at just kissing, and there was no way he could lay down with her on the bed and just hold her. So he needed to get his ass out of here before he lost his grip on the last remnants of his control.

"Because it's your job?" she asked, watching him carefully.

"No. Because I want you safe." He wrenched himself away from her, suppressing a groan at the incredibly sensual picture she made with her lips swollen from his kisses, curls tumbling around her shoulders.

She licked her lips, dark eyes heavy with satisfaction…and a hunger that almost destroyed his willpower. "All right. Give me a few minutes."

"I'll be outside." Because he sure as shit couldn't trust himself in here right now.

He was waiting in the hall when she emerged a few minutes later, and took her bags. "Let's go."

He called a cab, escorted her to the Sand Dollar and saw her up to her room. Checked it himself to make sure everything was secure, then turned to her. "Are you sure you won't stay with Cal and your sister?"

"No. I'm okay here."

She wasn't okay. Not emotionally. But she would be in time, because the adversity she'd already lived through had made her strong.

He reached for her once more, gave her a tight hug in an effort to soothe her and soften his abrupt withdrawal. "Try to get some sleep. I'll call you in the morning, but I've got my cell on me if you need anything." He brushed his lips over hers, unable to help himself, and stepped back before she could deepen the kiss. "Lock the door behind me," he said, then made himself turn around and walk out of her room.

ELEVEN

"Sweetheart, I'm so sorry this happened to you," her dad said.

"Thanks." Propped up against the cushioned headboard in her hotel bed, Anaya raised her leg and gingerly circled her ankle. It didn't hurt as much today and the swelling had gone down, but she wouldn't be doing any running or returning to the gym anytime soon. "It just sucks."

"Yes, it does. I can't believe he would do that." He sounded equal parts shocked and disgusted.

"Me neither. I would have given him money if he'd asked." Why would Jean Luc have done this?

"I know you would have. You have such a big heart. Both you and Nadia, but yours is hurt more easily."

It was true. "I can't help it."

"No, and that gentle spirit is one of the things I love most about you."

That made her smile a little. "Thanks, Dad."

"Anytime, kiddo." He paused. "Have you…spoken to your mother about this?"

She groaned. Things were complicated with her mother.

"No, and I won't for a while yet." Her mom was…a lot, and Anaya didn't have the mental or emotional bandwidth to deal with any snide comments or guilt-trip attempts right now. That seemed to happen most times she called to say hello.

"Okay, no judgment. I'm just so sorry you're dealing with all this."

"Me too. But on the bright side, things are going well at work at least. The French CEO has called me three times to make sure I'm okay. He likes me."

"Of course he likes you. Maybe you should go work for him if he'll give you a raise and a good position."

She laughed. "No. I'm happy with my boss and my team." She'd informed her boss last night about moving to the new hotel. "And besides, back home I'm only a few hours' drive from you. Just wish I wasn't so far away from Nadia and the baby."

"How is my granddaughter, anyway?"

She rolled her eyes. "You're ridiculous. I know you video call her every day."

"Yeah, but that's not the same as seeing her in person. Is she just as cute in real life?"

"Uh-uh. Way cuter."

"I thought so." He sighed. "I'm gonna have to get my hermit ass on a plane and fly out there, aren't I?"

"Yep, and better get on that quick. She's going to grow up so fast, you'll regret not making the effort now."

"I know, I know," he grumbled, his gruffness all a front. His heart was every bit as soft as hers, he just didn't want anyone outside the family to know it. "Are you sure there's nothing I can do to help you?"

"You're doing it right now." Just hearing his voice made things seem better. Bearable.

He grunted. "How about a big hug, then?"

"I'd love one." Her dad was such a good, kind man. He'd provided her and all her siblings with a rock-solid foundation and unconditional love even in the midst of his turbulent marriage and chaotic household.

Yet as wonderful as a dad hug would feel right now, she wanted another one from Donovan more. What had happened last night still felt like a dream. He'd brought her to orgasm so easily, but then backed off and retreated when she had wanted him to stay.

What was up with that? He wasn't her bodyguard anymore. She couldn't see what the issue was, or why he'd left. She wasn't going to call him, however, and look desperate. And if he was playing mind games or testing her somehow, she wasn't interested in that.

"You'll call me again if you want to talk some more?" her dad asked, pulling her out of her thoughts.

"Of course. Thanks for listening, Dad. Love you."

"Love you too, kiddo."

She set the phone down in her lap and sighed, turning her head to look out the window. A pure blue sky stretched out as far as the eye could see, the ocean a sparkling blue-gray as the sun glinted off the white crests of the waves rolling toward the beach.

A knock on the door startled her. "Who is it?" she called out, frowning. Damn, she'd forgotten to put the Do Not Disturb sign on the door after Donovan left.

"Janie from the front desk, Miss Bishop. I have a delivery for you."

"Delivery," she muttered as she got up, pleased when there was no sharp spike of pain as she set her right foot on the floor.

She checked the peephole just to be sure, then opened the door. The young woman beamed at her as she rolled in a room service cart bearing a large vase of flowers. A huge rainbow burst of violet-blue irises, coral gerbera daisies and yellow roses.

"Oh, wow," Anaya said, reaching for the card tucked into the flowers. A smile curved her mouth when she read it. It was from Maurice, the French CEO, and he'd typed the short note in French.

A small gesture to show my concern and support. Get better fast.

There was a teddy bear too, with dark brown fur wearing a blue T-shirt emblazoned with a large pink heart in the center, from Darren and her team. Maurice had also sent a bottle of champagne in a bucket of ice and a box of chocolate-dipped strawberries—and better yet, nothing at all from Riggs.

"This is a surprise," she said on a laugh, touched.

"I know, they're beautiful," Janie said. "Can I set the cart over by the window?"

"Sure, please." Sunlight poured in through the windowpane, making the flowers glow. The bear was adorable, and she couldn't wait to bust into those berries. It was lovely to know her work colleagues valued and cared about her.

But as tempting as those berries were, she was craving a real breakfast. So after showering and changing into a butter-yellow fit-and-flare dress, she grabbed her purse and used a ride app to go down to the waterfront, keeping a wary eye out for any sign of Jean Luc on the way.

When she stepped out of the vehicle a strong breeze laden with the salty scent of the ocean whipped around her, tugging some errant curls from her ponytail as she pulled her sweater closed across her body. Front Street was quieter than it had been on the weekend, but there was a lineup outside Whale's Tale. She headed straight for it, her stomach grumbling.

"Is it always like this on weekday mornings?" she asked the man in front of her.

"Pretty much. Especially Wednesdays, because that's caramel pecan sticky bun day."

Oh, *sold*. "If there's only one left in the display case when we get there, I'll arm wrestle you for it."

He laughed. "If you want it that bad, I'd split it with you."

"Very kind. I—"

"Anaya?"

She glanced behind her and broke into a smile. "Shae, hi."

Donovan's daughter tucked a lock of windblown hair behind her ear, a friendly grin on her face. "I didn't know you were still in town."

"Yeah, my plans are sort of up in the air right now." She guessed Donovan hadn't mentioned anything about what had happened in Seattle or yesterday.

"How'd things go in Seattle? I talked to Donovan last night. He sounded preoccupied, so I didn't bother asking about how it went."

Preoccupied about what? Her? And if he hadn't said anything, Anaya wasn't going to. "They went okay. Just popping in for breakfast?" she asked to take her mind off him.

"It's caramel pecan sticky bun day, so yeah." She eyed both Anaya and the man in front of her. "And I'll wrestle you both for it if there's only one left when we get in there."

Anaya laughed. "Man, these must be really good sticky buns."

"The *best*."

"Are you on your way to class?"

"No. I've got a night class at seven. Thought I'd come down and grab something to sustain me first before I go back home and get my laundry done and start hitting the books." She made a face.

"Well, that sounds fun," she said dryly.

"Doesn't it?" Shae laughed. They chatted while the line

moved slowly, and thankfully there were enough sticky buns for everyone when they finally reached the counter.

Poppy came out of the back carrying a tray of something, looking awkward as she balanced it over her pregnant belly. The tall young guy working behind the counter stopped what he was doing and rushed over to take it from her. "You shouldn't be carrying stuff like this," he admonished, and Anaya liked him instantly. "Let me or Rylie do it," he said, gesturing to the young brunette manning one of the coffee machines down the counter.

Poppy laughed. "You sound like Noah. Okay, here then," she said, handing him the tray.

"Thank you. Now go sit down in the back and call us if you need something else carried. Or, you know, go home and *rest*. We've got this."

Poppy reached up to pat his cheek. "You're a sweetheart, and I know you do." Turning, she spotted Anaya and Shae. Her face lit up. "Hi, guys! How are you this morning?"

"We're good," Shae answered. "How are you?" She looked pointedly at Poppy's prominent belly.

Poppy rubbed a hand over it. "Oh, you know, still hanging in there. Enjoy your breakfast. I'm gonna head to the back before I get in trouble again." She winked and walked away in what was closer to a waddle.

"Morning, ladies," the young man behind the counter said to them with a charming smile. His nametag read Finn. "What can I get you?"

Shae was all smiles as she and Anaya ordered, chatting away to him with a slight flush in her cheeks.

Anaya insisted on paying, and Shae invited her to join her at a table while they ate. Anaya asked her about college, her aspirations, but Shae was distracted, glancing continually toward the counter where Finn was helping an elderly lady, his bright white smile gleaming as he laughed at something she said.

Anaya raised her eyebrows at Shae as she took a sip of her latte, not bothering to hide her smile.

"What?" Shae said, blinking.

"You like him," she whispered, just loud enough for Shae to hear.

Shae flushed, shot him a covert look and lowered her voice. "He's Danae's son, and we're just friends."

"Oh." Sure looked like Shae wished it was more than that.

She stole another glance at him. "It would be too awkward, with my dad and Donovan both working for Ryder," she mused, but the longing in her eyes gave her away. "Doesn't matter anyway, because I don't think I'm his type." She glanced down at herself, grimaced. "Ugh, and of course I show up in sweats with zero makeup on the morning he's on shift."

"You look fine. You've got an effortless kind of beauty, and you have incredible skin, hair and eyes."

Shae ducked her head. "That's…really nice of you to say."

"No, I mean it sincerely."

She dug into her sticky bun. "My closet's a disaster. Half the stuff in there doesn't fit me anymore, and the other half I never wear. I meant to get a new wardrobe over the summer but I'm not great with that kind of thing and time just got away from me."

Anaya considered her for a moment. She had some emails to answer and a couple of files to read, but nothing that couldn't wait until this afternoon or even tonight. "I've got some time this morning. Feel like hitting the mall with me? Not to brag, but I'm pretty good when it comes to fashion." She really needed a break from everything going on. If Jean Luc was still in the area there was no way he would follow her to a mall and attack her in public.

Shae's eyes lit up. "Really?"

"Absolutely. I'm always up for a little shopping." She deserved to have a little fun after all the crap that had happened lately.

"Then *yes*," Shae said, eyes shining with excitement. Donovan's eyes. She had his hair color too, but otherwise didn't much look like him so she must take after her mom.

"Good," Anaya answered, already looking forward to it.

Finn came over to chat just as they were finishing their breakfast. Shae blushed and babbled a bit, but he didn't seem to mind. In fact, from where she was sitting, Anaya was pretty sure the interest between them was mutual.

Shae stepped outside onto the sidewalk with her after, a little smile on her face. "So, do you have a car here?"

"No, but I'll order us a ride." She got on her cell and pulled up a ridesharing app.

"Oh, there's Donovan," Shae said as Anaya was finishing.

She glanced up and, sure enough, there was Donovan's SUV coming down the street. Her pulse picked up instantly as she remembered last night and hoped this wouldn't be awkward.

He slowed and stopped next to the row of parked cars in front of them and lowered his window. "Morning," he said, his eyes hidden by dark sunglasses. Lord, he was sexy.

"Hi," she answered, feeling as giddy as Shae had while talking to Finn.

"You heading into the office?" Shae asked.

He nodded, and Anaya could feel the force of his gaze on her through the shades. "How are you feeling?" he asked her.

"Good, thanks for asking." She was staring, couldn't help it. That mouth had been on hers last night. On her breasts. And those big, talented hands had stroked her in ways that—

Shae linked her arm through Anaya's. "Were going shopping together."

His eyebrows lifted over the tops of the sunglasses. "Are you?"

"Yeah, I've got a night class later."

Anaya immediately wondered if he was concerned about her and Shae's safety, given the incident with Jean Luc. She wasn't sure if he'd told Shae about it. Doubted he would have. "Is that okay? We'll stick together."

He hesitated a moment, then nodded, easing her mind about the decision. "Yeah, of course. You got a ride?"

"Anaya just ordered us one," Shae said.

He glanced in the side mirror, saw the car coming up behind him. "Okay. I'll have my cell on if you need me to come get you. Have fun." The slight grin he aimed at Anaya made her heart flutter. "Talk to you later." He pulled away, leaving her all tingly inside and unsure what—if anything—was happening between them.

"Wow, he's in a good mood," Shae murmured, and stole another look over her shoulder.

Finn was back at the counter, laughing with a customer. Anaya set a hand on top of Shae's forearm where it linked with hers. "Just for the record, based on what I saw from Finn? I'd say you very much *are* his type."

Shae's eyes snapped to her, the flare of hope there tugging at Anaya's heart. "Yeah?"

"Oh yeah. So don't be so quick to count yourself out." And even though she knew it was stupid, Anaya was starting to hope that she was Donovan's type too.

TWELVE

Shae turned this way and that, studying her reflection in the mirror with a critical eye. The dress was pretty, for sure, but a drastic change from anything she'd worn before. She was having a great time though.

"Well?" Anaya asked from outside the changing room.

"I don't know. I like it, but…" They'd spent the past few hours picking out fairly basic pieces for her to build a wardrobe around. Things Shae honestly wouldn't have thought to look at, like cardigans and different kinds of shirts she could layer and either dress up or down. All in black or another neutral color.

This dress had been on a mannequin in the window of another store as they'd walked by. It had caught her eye immediately, but she would never have gone in to try it on if Anaya hadn't pushed her. It was the polar opposite from the rest of the things she'd already bought. Bright, flirty and feminine. But was it too much?

"Come out here and let me see."

She frowned a bit at her reflection, smoothing her hands down the front of the pale lilac dress. The hem was ruffled and came to a few inches above the knee. The halter neckline tied around the back of her neck in a big bow that dangled between her shoulder blades. Oh, it was so damn cute. But she wasn't sure whether she looked stupid in it.

"Girl. Come on, get out here and lemme see."

She gave the waistline one last tug and opened the door. Anaya sat up straight in her chair across the small, octagonal room, smiled and nodded in approval. "It's *lovely*, Shae. Sweet and pretty and oh so feminine."

"Yeah?" She twisted to look at her profile and back in the three-way mirror mounted on the walls. She had more than enough money saved up for it, and it wasn't that expensive.

"Definitely." Anaya stood and crossed to her, reaching for the back of Shae's hair. "Look." She gathered the mass in her hands, gave it a deft twist and plucked a clip out of her purse to secure it at the back of Shae's head before tugging a few wisps free around her face and neck.

Anaya met her gaze in the mirror, eyes sparkling. "There. What do you think? A simple necklace, pair of earrings, and some cute shoes and you're ready for a night out."

Shae couldn't help smiling too, excitement fizzing in the pit of her stomach. She liked Anaya a lot already and trusted her judgment with this. Anaya had style. "It is pretty."

"Gorgeous," Anaya agreed, stepping back. "With that length skirt you could wear flats or heels. Maybe a little sandal with a bow on the toes, or a flower."

She grinned. "I totally need to get some new shoes." This was so damn fun. The most fun she'd had in… Well, too long. Her small circle of trusted girlfriends were all back east and she hadn't made any close friends here yet, as she and her dad had only moved here in June. She tried to think of the last time she'd done a girls' shopping day, realized it hadn't been since—

Her smile faded, a stab of grief hitting her.

"What's wrong?" Anaya asked.

"Nothing." She angled herself again to check out her other side in the mirror.

This dress was definitely coming home with her today, along with a new pair of pretty shoes to go with it. And maybe she'd get her hair cut too. A new, updated style with some layers that was feminine but low maintenance and still long enough to be pulled up in a clip or ponytail when she didn't feel like being bothered with it.

This new look was symbolic. When her dad had taken the job with Crimson Point Security and dragged her to the opposite side of the country with him a few months ago, at first she'd hated it. And resented him.

Now she understood why he'd done it, and why he'd timed it for right after her graduation. He'd wanted to give them both a fresh start in a new place without constant reminders of her mom everywhere. To help them both move on in a decisive way.

Now she so desperately wanted to throw off the sadness of her past, shed it like a cocoon and emerge as a butterfly, ready to spread its wings. It was time.

"I was just thinking about my mom," she said softly. Anaya was easy to talk to, even about this. "We used to do special shopping days together every so often. I guess I didn't realize how much I've missed it." Missed *her*.

Anaya's deep brown eyes filled with empathy. "I bet you do. I'm sorry she's gone."

"Thanks. Me too. Are you close with your mom?"

"Not really. My relationship with her is …complicated, and I'll just leave it at that."

Now she felt bad for asking. "Oh. Sorry."

"That's okay. So, what do you think of this dress?"

She pushed out a breath, shoved aside the weight of grief before it could take hold and ruin the day. Her mom wouldn't want her to be sad all the time. She reminded herself of that constantly. "Okay, so this one's definitely a winner?"

Anaya nodded and curled an arm around her. "Definitely."

Shae leaned into her, resting the side of her head on Anaya's shoulder. Anaya gave off such a warm, maternal vibe. "Thanks for doing this with me."

"It's my pleasure." Anaya gave her a squeeze, causing something to tighten in the middle of Shae's chest.

Shae decided to wear the dress out of the store. "Next stop, shoes. And then I was thinking maybe I should get my hair cut. If you have time," she added quickly. "You've already given up so much of your day—"

"No, that sounds great. Do you have a regular salon you go to here?"

"No."

"Not a problem." She whipped out her phone. "Let's see if we can find you an appointment somewhere this afternoon. And if there's time before you need to go to class, maybe a pedicure too?"

Yep, Anaya was awesome. Shae would love to have a half dozen friends just like her. "I'd love that."

"Good. Then it's happening." Anaya hooked her arm through Shae's as they wandered through the mall, busy on her phone. "You keep your eyes peeled for a shoe place while I track down a salon."

Just over two hours later, Shae walked out of a salon near the mall with a brand-new haircut, sporting an angled bang and layers that made her hair bounce around her shoulders with every step, and some light eye makeup and lipstick courtesy of Anaya. In her pretty dress with her bright pink toenails peeking out through the open-toed pumps she'd bought at a discount shop, it felt like a giant weight had suddenly been removed from her shoulders.

"I feel like a new woman," she said as they hit the sidewalk. Different than she'd been a few hours ago.

"Still the same woman, but coming out of her shell more," Anaya said, giving her a friendly nudge. "And maybe feeling a bit more self-confident too, I'm sensing?"

"A *lot* more," she answered with a grin. "Just gotta say, you're really good at all this."

Anaya laughed. "With so many sisters, I've had lots of practice. I used to drag Nadia to the stores with me. We're different, especially when it comes to our personal styles—she's a flower child to the core—but it sure was fun buying outfits together when we saved up enough money to go shopping."

"I can imagine. I've had fun with you."

"Good. Now I don't know about you, but I'm starving. Want to grab a bite before we head back to town?"

"Sure. What do you feel like? I know a great Greek place a block from here." She glanced down at Anaya's foot. Her limp had become more pronounced as the day progressed. "If your ankle can take it."

"It can take another block of walking if there's some kickass souvlaki waiting at the other end."

Shae laughed and tossed her hair over her shoulder, loving her new look. "It's definitely kickass. How'd you hurt it, anyway?"

Anaya looked at her in surprise. "Donovan didn't tell you?"

"No. Why, what happened?"

"Well, we—" She paused, seemed to consider her words carefully. "There was an incident in Seattle. A truck nearly ran us down as we tried to cross the street."

"Oh my gosh, I didn't know."

"I would've been hit if Donovan didn't dive on top of me and knock me out of the way."

Pride burst inside her. Donovan was badass. He hadn't been

a big part of her life until her mom got sick. Now he'd moved here to be close to her, made an effort to be there and spend time with her. He was trying hard, and she loved him for it. "I'm glad you're both okay." She shook her head. "It's been an unspoken rule that he and my dad won't tell me about things like that. Dangers they face and whatever. It's frustrating. I'm not a little kid."

"No, but you'll always be their little girl," Anaya said with a gentle smile. "They want to protect you."

"I know." It was still frustrating. She pointed up ahead. "There's the restaurant just there."

"Ooh, I can almost taste the pita bread from here."

They sat at a table by the window and enjoyed their meal together, chatting away and laughing like old friends. There was something about Anaya that Shae instantly gravitated toward. She was genuine and kind, and Shae admired her polish and poise as much as her professional accomplishments. "Did you always know you wanted to be an engineer?"

"Sort of. I knew in high school that I would pursue sciences, and engineering seemed like a natural fit. What are you going to major in?"

"Business admin, I think. Unless something else comes up that really grabs my interest. I don't feel as passionate about it as you did with your degree, so maybe it's not the right path for me." She shrugged and ate another prawn dipped in drawn butter.

"You'll know in time," Anaya said in a confident tone. "If it doesn't feel right when you get into it, you can always change course and do something else. And the business background you build up in the meantime will always be a solid base for you no matter what you do later on."

"You're probably right." It felt so great to talk about all of this with a professional woman she respected.

Anaya winked. "Course I am. Now pass me another piece of baklava."

After they ate, Anaya insisted on paying the bill and then ordered them a ride back to town. She was limping more noticeably as they stepped outside to wait on the sidewalk. "Is it really bad?" Shae asked, glancing at her ankle with a frown.

"I'll live. Just need to go put my feet up for the night."

The driver picked them up a few minutes later and drove them to Crimson Point with Shae's shopping bags piled on the seat between them in the back. She checked the time on her phone when they reached the town limit.

"Perfect. My bus will be here in under ten minutes. You sure you don't mind keeping my stuff for me?" There wasn't time to drop it off at home, so Anaya had offered to take it to her hotel so Shae wouldn't have to haul it with her to class and back.

"Not at all."

"If Donovan can't come grab it tonight, I'm sure my dad can."

"No rush. Tomorrow works too."

"Okay, let me text Donovan." Dusk was falling when they got out of the car and stepped onto the sidewalk near the bus stop on Front Street. This close to the beach, the roar of the surf echoed up from the sand.

The main hub of the town was quiet, most of the businesses now closed for the night, and Shae only spotted one couple out walking a couple blocks down from them. A far cry from how crowded it had been here just a few weeks ago before tourist season ended.

"It's so beautiful here," Anaya said, tugging the halves of her sweater more firmly around her to ward off the chill of the evening air.

"It really is." She loved it here. Especially loved that she had both her dad *and* Donovan here.

They crossed the road together and stopped at the bottom of the street Anaya's hotel was on. Shae checked her phone when a new message came through. "Donovan says he can swing by and grab my stuff from you tonight if that works."

Anaya's expression tightened ever so slightly. "Oh, sure. Hand over your loot." She reached for the bags.

Shae hesitated. "Are you *sure* you don't want me to take them up to your hotel for you? It's a pretty steep climb, and your ankle—"

"Nah, it's only a few blocks. You go ahead. I don't want you to miss your bus."

"All right." Shae handed them over, then threw her arms around Anaya's shoulders. "Thank you for today. I really needed that."

Anaya returned the hug, the bags bumping into Shae's back. "You know what? I needed it too."

"I'll call you tomorrow. I've got class until two, but maybe we could get together after that for a snack or something."

"Sounds good to me."

Shae let her go and stepped back with a grin. "It's not too much? Showing up to class like this?" She looked down at the hem of her dress, her bare legs and cute shoes that showed off her polished toenails.

"Not if you don't mind turning heads."

"I don't know if I do or not, because I've never done it before," she said wryly.

Anaya gave her an approving smile that boosted her confidence. "You look beautiful in a fresh, girl-next-door way. The outfit is sweet, and the makeup is subtle. It's not too much. Trust me."

She did trust her. "Okay, thanks. Go put your feet up."

"I plan to. Night."

"Night."

Shae turned left for the short walk up Front Street to the bus stop, while Anaya turned right to head up the hill. She'd only gone a couple of steps when the sound of a speeding vehicle behind them made her glance over her shoulder. She stiffened in alarm when it jerked to a halt at the curb right behind them.

Then a man in a hoodie jumped out and ran straight for them.

Shae went rigid, a warning cry sticking in her throat.

"Shae!"

Before she could move, Anaya was in front of her, shoving her back and flinging out an arm to ward the guy off. The attacker seized Anaya's wrist and wrenched her toward him. A choked scream split the air as she tumbled off the curb with him onto the road.

"Let her go!" Shae yelled. She fumbled in her bag, couldn't find the bear spray canister and came up with the tactical flashlight instead.

Whipping it out, she switched it on and aimed the beam straight in the asshole's face, following him with it when he threw an arm up and wrenched his head away to avoid having his retinas seared by the intense light.

Anaya threw an elbow, managed to hit him in the jaw with an audible crunch. His head snapped back, and he snarled a curse as she wrenched free and scrambled away from him on her hands and knees.

Shae ran the few steps to her and dragged her to her feet, still holding the light steady in her other hand. "Help! Fire, *help*!" she yelled to attract the attention of anyone who might overhear, the hairs on her nape standing on end. Her heart pounded like a bass drum in her ears, her hand shaking a bit as she held the beam aimed right at the attacker's face.

"Hey! What are you doing?" someone shouted from down the street. Maybe the couple she'd seen earlier.

The attacker spun around and raced back to his truck, then wheeled it around and took off in the direction it had come from with its tires squealing.

Shae sucked in an unsteady breath and lowered the flashlight, turning back to Anaya. "Oh my God, are you okay?"

"Y-yeah," she mumbled, face twisting in a grimace as she tried to find her balance on her sore foot. "What the hell? Did you recognize him?"

"No." She glanced back at the retreating truck. Dammit, she'd been so focused on chasing him away she hadn't even gotten the freaking license plate.

They glanced right as running footsteps approached. An older man, his expression full of concern. "Are you both all right?"

"I think so." Anaya's voice sounded thin and breathless as Shae put an arm around her to steady her.

"My wife's on the phone with 911. Here, come sit down." He looped an arm around Anaya's waist and helped her hobble over to the bus stop bench Shae had been heading for.

Shae shoved the flashlight away and grabbed her phone to dial her dad. Before she could hit the button, a familiar vehicle appeared at the stop sign and turned toward them.

"It's my dad," Shae said, relief sliding through her so hard and fast that her voice wobbled. She raced down the sidewalk toward him.

He pulled over instantly and undid the passenger window. "What's wrong?" he demanded, his normally soothing southern drawl erased by the whip-like tone.

"Some guy in a truck just tried to attack Anaya and me," she blurted out. She was almost panting now, her knees weak.

"He grabbed her, and I aimed my flashlight in his eyes. He took off, but I didn't get the plate…"

She trailed off, the look on his face sending another wave of cold through her. He was always so calm and unshakable. Her rock. But right now, he looked like he wanted to track down whoever had just attacked them and put a bullet in him.

"Get in the truck," he commanded, his jaw tight.

"But Anaya—"

"I'll get her. Get in the truck, Shae."

She scrambled to do as he said, jumping in the front passenger seat and locking the door for good measure. God, her heart was still racing, her skin crawling as she wrapped her arms around herself and watched her dad go to Anaya.

She shuddered, trying to process what had just happened. And what might have happened if they hadn't managed to scare that psycho off.

EVERLEIGH PUT on her coat and grabbed her bag from her locker, anxious to get home. It had been a long day working back-to-back appointments with patients at the physio clinic attached to the hospital. She hadn't been sleeping enough lately, mostly because she wasn't feeling her best.

She laid a hand to her still-flat abdomen, smiling to herself as bittersweet excitement rippled through her. A little piece of Will lived on inside her.

He hadn't known. She'd found out the week after he died. No one knew yet except her parents and her best friend. She was waiting to get past the three-month hurdle before telling anyone else.

She waved at one of the doctors on duty and the nurses at the station on her way to the rear exit, stopping briefly at the café to grab some soup. The cook made a daily creation from scratch every morning, and chicken noodle with veggies sounded good to her queasy tummy.

"Everleigh."

She turned around to see Grady, an L&D nurse from the mat ward, striding toward her, and smiled. "Hey."

A little over six feet tall, fit as hell with short black hair that was longer in front, deep golden skin and amber eyes, he would make any straight woman's pulse triple. And while she couldn't deny that he was good-looking, she was still too numb from everything to appreciate the view fully.

He smiled back, his dimples creasing his lean cheeks. He looked tired. "Just leaving?"

"Yep, heading home to put my feet up. It's been a busy week." It was a good thing that she'd finally returned to work. She needed it, something else to focus on besides her grief and the overwhelming mountain of things she needed to get done. "You look beat. Just finishing?"

His warm amber eyes glinted with humor. "Just starting. Had a few long days and late nights this week, that's all."

"Military stuff?"

"Yeah." He nodded at the bag in her hand. "Dinner?"

"Mariah made her famous chicken noodle. I had to grab some."

"If it's that good, I'll have to try it."

"And I highly recommend the white chocolate macadamia nut cookies, too." She eyed his fit, muscular frame. "Not that you probably eat much of that kind of thing."

He laughed. "Are you kidding? I *live* for that kind of thing."

Sure wouldn't know that by looking at him. "Okay, then get at least three. Try one at room temp, one warmed up in the microwave for ten seconds, and one ice cold from the freezer. I'm just saying."

"Noted."

"Well, have a good night."

"You too. Drive safe, it's a bit wet out there. Roads'll be slippery after being dry for so long."

"I will. Bye." She went out to the parking lot and started for her vehicle. Grady was nice, always making time to say hi. Everyone she worked with at the hospital was great, but Grady was her favorite.

He was right about the roads. She could see a sheen of oil on some of the little puddles she passed.

Warm and dry in her little car, she pulled out of the lot and headed south toward the coastal highway. She and Will had bought a place just outside Crimson Point, hoping to save up enough money to buy a house with an ocean view in the next few years.

At the thought, a heavy wave of sadness hit her. She shook it off, focusing on the blessings in her life to push it aside. Will wouldn't want her to stop living and mope around. And he would have been over the freaking moon about the baby.

She put her hand to her abdomen again, rubbing gently. Just a few more days and she could tell everyone her news, then get the nursery decorated.

There was hardly any traffic on the highway heading south. She turned off it several miles north of Crimson Point, taking the longer scenic route down the hill. Without a moon it was too dark to see the ocean, but on clear nights the view up here was spectacular.

An old favorite song came on the radio. She turned it up and started singing along to the lyrics. She couldn't sing worth a damn, but she didn't care because it felt good and there was no one to hear her.

The song reached the crescendo as she neared the crest of a hill. On the other side the road curved right. She was in mid-note when headlights suddenly swung around the corner, a big truck headed straight for her.

At the last moment, she wrenched the wheel to the side, a shrill scream tearing from her throat a split second before impact.

THIRTEEN

His heart slammed against his ribs as he raced the truck away from the scene on Front Street. He took a sharp left with his truck, glancing in the rearview mirror to make sure no one was chasing him.

Jesus. That should have been easy.

Grabbing an unarmed, untrained woman off an almost deserted street when she wasn't expecting it was child's play for someone like him. He hadn't expected much resistance, or that someone else would interfere so quickly.

He squinted at the curve ahead in the road, black spots still impairing his vision. That bitch had almost fucking blinded him. He could barely see what was coming up ahead.

They probably hadn't seen his face. His hood had stayed on, and he'd made his move in a dark spot between the streetlights. But they would have at least gotten a description of the truck, and possibly the license plate too.

The truck had to go.

He pressed down harder on the accelerator as the road straightened out. The highway was less than a mile away. He needed to get onto it, put some distance between him and Crimson Point before he found a place to ditch and torch the truck. After that…

He needed to regroup and plan his next move. Because this wasn't over. Not until he killed her in front of his target. That's how it had to be.

The road wound to the left. He squinted harder, focusing on the spot just ahead of the truck's hood. The painted centerlines were faded. The solid single line had changed to a broken line a half-mile back. Now he couldn't see it at all.

He moved farther left, unsure where the shoulder was, and kept speeding along, his mind spinning. He couldn't get caught. Not now. He would just have to be more careful. Watch and wait for exactly the right time to strike.

Suddenly the road bent left. He blinked fast to try and clear the spots away. Saw the headlights coming at him at the last second.

Cursing, he hit the brakes and veered right.

Too late.

The other car turned the same way. He wrenched the wheel harder right. Caught a glimpse of a woman's pale face through the windshield.

Metal screamed as the two vehicles sideswiped each other. He grunted at the impact, his hands clenched around the steering wheel, fighting to steady it as the truck hit the shoulder. The smaller car didn't fare as well.

It spun past him, flipped onto its side and crashed hard into the ditch on the other side.

He didn't stop. Didn't hesitate.

He hit the gas and took off again, the evidence of what he'd done marked by the red taillights standing in the air from the ditch behind him.

"*Fuck*," he yelled, slamming a fist on the dash. Every goddamn thing had gone wrong, and this might be the thing that did him in. What if the other car had a dash cam?

He had to ditch the truck now and find somewhere to hide before the cops arrived at the accident scene. No time to lose.

He'd waited a long time to get his revenge. Nothing was going to stop him now.

∽

SHERIFF BUCHANAN'S vehicle was already parked out front of Walker's house by the time Donovan got there. He went straight in through the back door without knocking and stopped short when Shae appeared around the corner, looking completely different in a pale purple dress and her hair all done up.

Relief hit him hard, pushing out a breath he hadn't realized he'd been holding since he got the call.

She came straight to him without a word, reaching her arms up to wind around his neck.

He hugged her tight, every protective cell in his body lit up. He'd been doing paperwork at home when he'd gotten the call from Walker saying that someone had just tried to kidnap her and Anaya off Front Street.

"You all right?" He could hear the low murmur of voices coming from the next room. Walker had said Anaya was okay, but Donovan wanted to see it for himself.

"Yes." She didn't let go.

He squeezed her harder, more of the remaining tension inside him easing as he held on. He hadn't realized how much he'd needed this, the physical reassurance that she was okay. She hadn't sought him out for comfort like this since she was little, and something deep inside him knitted back together now that she had come to him.

Maybe he wasn't completely shit at being there for her after all. "Tell me what happened," he said after a minute. He could hear Anaya's voice in the background now. She had to be shaken up too.

Shae stayed in his embrace as she recounted everything. And he didn't like what he heard. None of it. "Was he targeting you or Anaya?"

"I don't know, it all happened so fast. Anaya jumped in front of me before I could move, so he got to her first. I thought he was trying to mug us, but now I'm not so sure."

Yeah, he was willing to bet it hadn't been a mugging. And he was also willing to bet it had been targeted. But he wasn't going to scare her by telling her that.

He kissed the top of her head, fighting a surge of rage at the image she painted. "You did exactly the right thing. I'm proud of you." She'd held it together in spite of her fear and had the presence of mind to use the tac flashlight he'd given her before she'd started college. If she hadn't…

She sighed, her cheek pressed to his shoulder. "It would've been way different if Anaya hadn't jumped in when she did." She looked up at him, the worry on her face tearing at him. "Do you think it's linked to what happened in Seattle?"

Anaya must have told her. "I don't know." But he was going to find out. "You sure you're okay?" he asked, gently easing a hand over her back. Shit, he didn't know what the hell he would do if anything happened to her.

She nodded. "Anaya got banged up though. She hurt her ankle pretty bad again fighting him off."

Another surge of anger hit him. But it could have been so, so much worse than getting banged up. "Is she in there with Walker and the sheriff?"

"Yes." Shae stepped back, swiped the heels of her hands under her eyes.

He gently wiped away a smudge of mascara with the pad of his thumb, overcome with love and a fierce burst of protectiveness. "I like the dress, by the way. You make a beautiful badass."

A weak laugh escaped her. "Blinding him with a flashlight wasn't badass."

"Yes, it was." She might have saved her and Anaya's lives tonight. And shit, it put him in a cold sweat thinking about that.

"I'm gonna go take a shower," she mumbled.

"Sure. Take your time. I'll go talk to the others."

The second he entered the room, his gaze zeroed in on Anaya. She was on Walker's sofa in a pale yellow dress with an ice pack on her ankle. The relief that bled into her expression when she saw him made his chest constrict. It took everything in him not to go over there and haul her into his arms.

"I heard what happened," he said. "You okay?"

She nodded, a haunted look in her eyes that he wished he could erase. "We were lucky."

"Yes, you were." He nodded at Walker and Noah before crossing the room to sit next to Anaya's feet and gently lifted the ice pack off her ankle to take a look. The joint was more swollen than it had been when she'd first injured it and turning a deep purple. She'd have to get more X-rays taken. "So, what'd I miss?" he asked the guys.

"We don't have much to go on," Noah answered. "The description of the suspect is vague, and we don't have a plate number. I'm having my people check with anyone in the area at the time it happened, to see if anyone saw anything or if any security video caught it."

"He came at us at an angle," Anaya said, wincing as she shifted her leg. "It was too dark to see his face clearly, but I heard him swear and he didn't have an accent. And he moved like a younger guy. So it wasn't Jean Luc."

But that didn't mean he wasn't working with the attacker. "Anything else?"

"Nothing that would help identify him." She huffed out a breath, her distress clear. "I saw him coming at the last second and didn't think about anything except protecting Shae."

Oh, fuck, she had no idea what that did to him, that she'd put herself between Shae and the attacker without hesitation. "Thank you for that."

She shot him a frown. "You don't need to thank me for it."

Yeah, he really did. "Was there anyone else in the truck?"

"I don't know. It was too dark to see clearly, and it all happened so fast."

He turned his attention to Walker. "Shae's taking a shower. Don't know if she plans to come back down after or not."

Walker nodded, chiseled features grim. Someone had messed with their baby girl, and they would pay. "She's shaken up. I'll give her some space for a bit, then go check on her."

Noah was texting someone. "You need anything else from Anaya?" Donovan asked him.

He seemed distracted, frowning slightly at his phone before he looked up. "Not at the moment, no."

Donovan turned his attention to Walker. "I'll take her to get X-rays, then back to my place." She didn't argue, and that was for the best, because he wasn't giving her any other option.

Walker nodded. "Let me know if you guys need anything."

"I will." He faced Anaya, who was watching him with those deep, dark eyes, and a wave of desire and protectiveness crashed over him.

She'd gotten deep under his skin already. He'd made up his mind to keep his distance from her, but this changed things.

Until they knew what the hell was going on here, she was safer with him than anywhere else.

So long as he kept his hands to himself and his dick in his pants.

"Come on," he murmured, bending to slide an arm around her back and the other under her knees.

"I can walk," she protested, grabbing her purse.

"No, you can't." He scooped her up and headed for the door.

Walker held it for them. Donovan eased Anaya into the front passenger seat of his SUV and glanced up. The corner room window was lit up. Shae was safely tucked in her bedroom, and he knew that Walker would lay down his life to protect her if necessary.

He was just opening the driver's door when Noah burst out of the house. "Poppy's in labor," he said as he ran. "I gotta get to the hospital."

"Congrats," Donovan answered, glad something good had happened tonight. "We'll see you up there."

He got in, started the engine and pulled out of the driveway. Noah was already halfway up the road, his taillights quickly disappearing over the crest of a hill. Anaya was quiet, and it was more than just fatigue and shock. What had happened last night hung between them, thick in the quiet interior.

He didn't want to talk about it. It shouldn't have happened. He should have walked away before temptation got the better of him. "You warm enough?" he asked when he couldn't stand the silence any longer.

"Yes. Look, I'm really sorry."

"For what?"

"I shouldn't have asked Shae to go out with me today. I would never have asked if—"

"I know, but don't even go there, because this wasn't your fault."

She didn't answer, but he could tell she was still blaming herself. He gripped the wheel with both hands to keep from reaching for hers.

An ambulance was parked in front of the Emergency doors when Donovan drove up. Two paramedics were lifting a gurney down with a patient strapped to it.

He found a parking spot close to the doors and came around to the passenger side, where Anaya was standing on one foot, holding the door handle for balance. "I can hop there if you don't mind being my crutch."

"Carrying you's easier." He bent and lifted her again, ignoring her protests as he shut the door with his leg and shifted her in his arms. Truth was, he liked holding her. Liked the feel of her snuggled into him, her scent wrapping around him. It soothed something primal inside him.

Light raindrops fell as he carried her to the entrance. Inside he set her down in a chair to wait while he got the paperwork from the admin desk and handed it to Anaya to fill out. He glanced up when someone strode around the corner. "Travis."

The PJ stopped and gave them a smile. "Donovan. Everything okay?"

"Just need to get some X-rays on Anaya's ankle. By the way, we just saw Sheriff Buchanan. Poppy's in labor. They'll be here soon."

"Yeah, I heard and came down to meet them." He nodded at Anaya. "Hope there are no fractures."

"Me too," she answered, then turned to him when Travis left. "Who was that?"

"You heard of Boyd? Callum's former CO."

"Yes, Nadia's told me about him."

"Travis is his son. He's a physician assistant and a PJ with the Air National Guard." He handed the paperwork in, then helped Anaya into a waiting area down a hallway outside the X-ray room.

"This could be a long wait," she said apologetically.

"It's fine. I want to make sure there are no fractures."

And then he wanted to make sure no one ever came after her again.

FOURTEEN

"Ah, here's your nurse now," Grady heard Travis saying as he turned the corner with the wheelchair.

The look on Poppy's and Noah's faces when they saw him pushing the chair toward them at the main entrance doors was priceless. A bit dazed, maybe even a little skeptical.

It happened so often Grady had gotten used to it long ago and didn't take offense. People took one look at him, a young, tatted guy in scrubs, and their eyebrows shot up.

"They're waiting upstairs for you," he told them, quickly turning the wheelchair around for Poppy. "Hey, Trav."

"Hey." They shared a private smile, both of them operating on fumes at this point.

Their unit had been at base training all this past weekend and then again last night. They hadn't left Portland until oh-two-hundred hours this morning, meaning both he and Travis had grabbed two hours of badly needed sleep before coming in to start their shifts. Whereas Whit and Groz were both probably still crashed out at home.

"This is my good buddy Grady," Travis told Poppy and the

sheriff. "He's the most experienced L&D nurse here, and also a PJ in our unit, so you couldn't be in better hands."

Clear relief bled into Noah's expression at the news. "That's good to hear."

Grady grinned. He loved what he did, was lucky to do this *and* Pararescue. Best of both worlds. "Let's get you upstairs," Grady said to Poppy, helping the sheriff ease her into the chair.

Poppy nodded and didn't answer, busy breathing hard through another contraction, her knuckles white as she gripped her husband's hand.

"That's perfect, just concentrate on your breathing," he told her, wheeling her quickly to the elevator down the hall.

"It's happening fast," Noah said in concern.

"How long ago did the labor start?"

"I'm not sure. She said about five hours ago, but I'm betting it was before that." He shook his head at her in consternation as they stopped at the elevator. "She didn't want to call while I was on duty."

"Nothing you…could've done," Poppy managed between gritted teeth. Her face was flushed, drawn tight with the pain.

Noah shot him a look that said he had a choice comeback for that, but wisely kept his mouth shut. "The contractions are about seven minutes apart or so, but some are closer together than that."

She was definitely in active labor. It was just a question of how far things had progressed. "We'll check everything and see where we're at when we get her into her room."

He helped coach her through another contraction on the way upstairs, mentally keeping track of its intensity and how long it lasted. "Here we go," he announced, steering her into one of the private birthing rooms on the mat ward.

Two other nurses were standing by. They got Poppy up and changed into a gown while Grady gloved up and grabbed the equipment he needed. A few minutes later, he finished his exam and stood back to peel off his gloves. "You're eighty percent effaced, and almost four centimeters dilated. And the baby's doing great," he told them with a reassuring smile. "Everything's going exactly as it should."

Noah groaned and leaned his forehead against his wife's. "Thank God." His head came up. "So...how much longer?"

"Hard to say, but if she keeps progressing like this, it could be just a few more hours."

"*Hours*?" Poppy said in distress. "When do I get my drugs? There's still time for the drugs, right?"

He grinned, feeling for her, and glad he was a guy. "Absolutely, the anesthetist will be in shortly. In the meantime, I'm going to go check with the doctor on duty."

He was partway to the nurse's station when Travis stepped out of the elevator beyond it. One look at his team leader's face and he knew something bad had happened. "What's up?"

"It's Everleigh."

His pulse jumped. She'd just left the hospital a couple hours ago. He'd seen her on the way out the door to the staff parking lot. "What about her?"

"She was involved in a hit-and-run on the way home. Other driver took off, but she wound up trapped upside down in a ditch. Fire crew had to cut her out of her vehicle."

Jesus Christ. "How bad is she?"

"Looks like she's gonna be okay, but…" He shook his head sadly.

But what? He broke into a jog. "You get hold of Poppy's doc?"

"Yeah, she's on the way. I'll stand in until she gets here, and you go down to the ER." He held the elevator door for him. Grady rushed inside and hit the button before meeting Travis's gaze again.

"Do what you can for her," his buddy said.

He nodded as the doors shut, thinking of Everleigh. The physical therapist had started working here three months before he'd been hired on the mat ward early this year. Everyone liked her. Him more than he should, given that she'd been engaged up until two months ago.

And while she might technically be single now, after the loss she'd suffered she wasn't even close to being interested in a new relationship. Didn't change the way he felt about her, however.

Down in the ER, Molly looked up from the computer at the nurses' station and saw him. The sympathetic look she gave him made his stomach drop.

"Everleigh," he said. "Is she—"

"She's in bay five, and I'm glad you're here, because she could sure use a friend right now."

He was her work friend. But if things had been different, he would have done anything to be a whole lot more to her than that.

He hurried straight to her, stopped a moment outside the drawn blue curtain to take a breath and center himself before entering. The instant he did he caught sight of a blue hospital gown and a swath of white-blond hair falling over the edge of the bed. They'd put her on a spine board and in a neck brace, so she couldn't look over at him.

He stepped into her line of sight. "Hey—"

His words cut off like they'd been severed by a scalpel when those smoky blue eyes locked on him. Full of a grief so stark, it felt like he'd just taken a roundhouse to the gut. Bruises were forming on her face and tear tracks ran from the outer corners of her eyes and into her hair.

But his attention went straight to the blood staining the sheet where she had a pad pressed between her thighs.

His gaze snapped back to hers, his heart sinking. Oh, fuck... He hadn't known.

She blindly flung out a hand. He caught it, wrapped his fingers around it and held tight as he stepped closer. Her skin was cold. "What happened?" he murmured.

"I w-was almost h-home," she whispered, pausing to swallow before she continued. "I came around the corner and a truck was right in front of me. I swerved, but..." Her face crumpled, her free hand going to her belly. "The baby..."

He went down on one knee beside her, stroked her hair back from her forehead with his free hand. He didn't care if it crossed a line. Didn't give a shit if it wasn't professional or if it gave him away. "How far along are you?"

Her lips and chin quivered, those pain-drenched blue eyes pleading with him. "Ten weeks. Someone went to get a Doppler."

To check the fetal heartbeat. Although judging from the amount of blood she was losing... "Are you hurting anywhere?"

"Just some cramping." Her fingers clamped around his, a desperate look crossing her face. "I can't take this, Grady, this is all I have left of him. Oh, God, please help—"

"I will," he promised, even though he knew he and everyone else on staff here was powerless to stop this. "Is there someone else I can call to come be with you?"

She sniffed. "N-no."

Her parents were in Arizona, and she didn't have any other family. "I'll stay with you." He needed to be upstairs helping the delivery team with Poppy and the other mother in labor a few doors down from her. But there was no fucking way he was leaving Everleigh to face this alone.

"Thank you," she choked out.

He'd subtly rested the pads of two fingers on her radial

pulse point. It was fast, well over one hundred bpm. Blood was leaking onto the sheet beneath her, the pad already saturated. "Let's get you cleaned up and make you a bit more comfortable in the meantime, okay?" he said gently. This was her worst nightmare, and he didn't know how to make it any more bearable for her.

She tried to nod.

He gathered what he needed from the cabinet behind him and put on gloves. Tried to think of something to say. She'd been through absolute hell the past two months. This on top of everything else was too fucking cruel, especially when she was so sweet and kind.

"What's taking them so long?" she whispered, voice catching.

"I'll go check in a minute," he promised, gently removing the saturated pad from between her legs.

He put the clean one in place, placed her hand on it to hold it there and covered her back up, keeping his body in position to block her view of how bad the bleeding was. She didn't need to see that after everything else she'd been through.

After putting a clean sheet beneath her and getting rid of his gloves, he covered her with another blanket, tucked it around her and then laid a hand on her shoulder, bringing those pain-drenched eyes back to him. "I'll go find out what's going on and come straight back."

Outside in the hallway, he saw Molly coming toward him carrying the fetal Doppler. "Where's Dr. Anderson?" he asked.

"In the trauma bay with a rollover victim. He's already ordered an ultrasound, and said he'd be here as soon as he can, but he's going to be a while. What's the situation like on the mat ward? Can we get an OBGYN down here to do the exam?"

"No, they're slammed, two moms in active labor right

now." Shit, he didn't want Everleigh to have to lie there waiting for a minute longer than absolutely necessary. "I'll do it."

Molly handed over the Doppler, eyes full of concern. "You want me to go in with you?"

"Please." Everleigh liked and trusted Molly, and she was going to need all the help and support she could get right now.

"Sure."

Everleigh's face was pale and tense when they stepped into the room. Her gaze dipped to the device in his hand and stark fear flashed in her eyes.

"Hey," Molly said with a soft smile, moving to stand beside her and take her hand. She was a mother, would know exactly how distressing this must be for her. "You warm enough?"

She gave a jerky nod and stared resolutely at the ceiling. "Please just do it," she blurted to him.

"All right."

Already certain what he'd find, dreading the moment when it was confirmed, Grady eased the blankets down to her hips, then gently drew her gown up to expose her abdomen. Transvaginal Doppler was more accurate at this stage of pregnancy, but this way was far less invasive and should still be able to tell them what they needed to know.

Without speaking, he put some gel on the rounded head of the probe and settled it low over her abdomen, adding pressure as he switched it on and began slowly moving it over her belly. He really, *really* wanted to be wrong about this.

Everleigh was completely rigid. Eyes squeezed shut. Barely even breathing as they all listened, straining to hear that little swish-swish-swish of the fetal heartbeat.

There was nothing but silence.

He kept moving the probe around, praying he was just in the wrong spot. "Dr. Anderson's ordered an ultrasound. We'll take you down there next and—"

She grabbed his hand holding the probe, stilling it. He met her gaze. The devastation there made his chest constrict. She knew.

"Stop," she whispered. She was trembling now. A fine, rapid tremor that was spreading throughout her whole body.

He stopped and removed the probe. Didn't know what the hell to say to her and glanced at Molly.

"I'm going to make sure the ultrasound tech's ready for you," Molly murmured, squeezing Everleigh's hand before shooting him a tormented look on her way to the door.

He set the fetal monitor aside and quickly covered Everleigh back up, maintaining his professional demeanor. "Everleigh—"

"No," she choked out, grabbing for his hand. She clenched it tight, tears flooding her eyes as her face crumpled. "My baby's dead. I've lost everything, I…"

He was on his knees beside her in an instant, leaning over her and wrapping his arms around her as best he could with the cervical collar and spine board in the way. Trying to comfort her. Wishing there was a way to shield her from this latest loss.

All the while knowing there wasn't a fucking thing he or anyone else could do to ease her pain.

After a few minutes, her sobs subsided. Her slender frame was wracked with little shudders as he eased back on his heels to study her, feeling helpless. He got a clean cloth and gently washed her face.

"Thanks," she murmured, her voice hoarse. She looked exhausted. Fragile. Like this latest blow had shattered her completely.

It killed him.

"Sure." Her eyes were swollen, face blotchy as she met his gaze squarely.

They both knew what would happen after the ultrasound

confirmed the loss of the fetus. That she would be prepped for a D&C and have to undergo that as well.

"Will you stay with me until they take me into the OR?" she whispered, her acceptance of what would happen twisting something in his chest.

He stroked a hand over her hair. "Of course I will."

Wild fucking horses couldn't drag him from her side right now. Even while the protective alpha male in him demanded he hunt down the reckless, cowardly son of a bitch who had done this to her.

FIFTEEN

Donovan rolled over in the darkness to grab his buzzing phone from the bedside table, surprised to see Noah's number on the display. "Hey," he answered, still wide awake because Anaya was just down the hall, and he couldn't stop thinking about her or fantasizing about sliding into bed next to her. Sliding deep into *her*. "Everything okay?"

"Yeah, Poppy had the baby two hours ago. It's a boy, and he's perfect."

"That's great, congratulations. So why are you calling me at three in the morning?"

"A local reported a burning vehicle about a half mile from the coastal highway. Crews put out the fire and my deputies brought in forensics. The make and model match the description of the truck involved with Shae and Anaya. And from the location and damage, we also think it was involved in the hit-and-run earlier."

"What hit-and-run?"

Noah explained. "It'll be a while before we can confirm all that, but given the state of the vehicle, it's not likely we'll be able to pull any prints or DNA."

"Got it. No tips coming in about the driver?"

"Not yet."

"Okay. Thanks for letting me know. Go enjoy your new family and get some sleep while you can. Trust me, you're gonna need it." The military used sleep deprivation to break people. It was no joke, and babies were masters of it.

Noah huffed out a laugh. "Will do. Bye."

He set the phone in its spot and rolled onto his back to stare up at the darkened ceiling. The house was quiet, the rain showers that signaled the end of summer pattering against the roof and windows. It should have been soothing.

Instead, all he could think about was Anaya curled up alone in the guestroom down the hall. Along with everything he'd like to be doing to and with her in that bed right now.

There was no way he was getting back to sleep now, so he got up and quietly walked toward the kitchen, surprised to see Anaya curled up on his sofa with a blanket draped over her. He'd been quiet but she woke anyway, pushing up on one elbow to reveal her bare shoulders, the tops of her breasts pushed up by the nightgown Walker had brought with the rest of her things from her hotel room earlier.

"Sorry," he said, pausing at the end of the hallway.

"It's okay." She rubbed a hand over her face. "What time is it?"

"Almost three." He lowered himself onto the loveseat across from her. "Noah called. Poppy had a baby boy, they're all fine. And they think they found the suspect truck from last night."

She listened to him in silence while he filled her in on the latest. "Was anyone hurt in the accident?"

"Yes. They brought her in while we were waiting in the ER. Noah said she's going to be okay though."

"So, more proof that it wasn't a random mugging attempt."

"Right."

She sighed and wrapped the blanket around her as she stood. "I need a drink. Should we crack open the champagne?"

"Really?"

She shrugged. "Why not?"

He followed her into the kitchen, flipped on the light over the range and took down two wineglasses while she got the champagne out of the fridge. "Might as well eat these too. No sense in letting them go to waste." She set the chocolate-dipped strawberries on the counter.

He watched while she expertly opened the champagne and popped the cork, the blanket gaping open in front of her, exposing the valley of her breasts and the sexy outline of her body hugged by the thin nightgown. Dragging his eyes away, he pushed the glasses across the counter, waited as she filled them.

She passed one to him then held hers out in a toast. "To being alive and living in interesting times that might make me rich if I ever write a book about it," she said, the way she lifted her chin and the determination on her face striking a chord deep inside.

It was so damn hard to stay detached with her. They had incredible chemistry, he also admired and genuinely liked her as a person, and bonus, her witty sense of humor made him laugh. She stirred feelings in him that no one else ever had, and he didn't know what the hell to do with them besides lock them down.

He tapped his glass to hers and took a sip, thinking. Lining up all the pieces involved. The timing of it all. "Your boss sent this to you at the hotel?" he asked.

"And the French CEO. The front desk clerk brought it up to my room yesterday morning, right before I headed down to Whale's Tale." She reached for a strawberry.

He snatched the box away before she could touch it.

"What?" she said, staring at him with wide eyes.

He set his glass down and turned toward the light above the range to study the fruit more carefully. The berries had begun to weep moisture around the edge of their chocolate coating.

There was nothing overly suspicious about them. No obvious holes or needle pricks. But when he raised the box to his nose and inhaled, they didn't smell right. He even thought he detected the faintest trace of a sweet almond scent.

Jesus Christ.

Box in hand, he turned and strode for his bedroom. Maybe he was being paranoid. But better safe than sorry at this point.

"What's the matter?" Anaya called after him.

He retrieved his phone and came back to her, pulling up Callum's number. "Who gave these to you?"

She frowned, thinking. "The French CEO. Why?"

"I want to get them tested."

"For what?"

"Poison."

She gasped, her eyes going even wider as she looked at the box, then at him. "You don't really think…"

He called Callum, who answered on the third ring. "Sorry to wake you, but I need to get hold of one of our forensics people."

"Why, what's going on?"

He told Callum about the hit-and-run, the burned-out vehicle, the delivery Anaya had received and now his suspicion.

"Cyanide?" Callum said. "Are you serious? That's hard to come by."

"I don't know for sure." He sure as hell hoped he was wrong. "But I want them tested for anything just in case."

"Okay, I'll get on it. Let me make a call, and I'll come get the box. Did you guys drink the champagne?"

"Just a few sips." He took Anaya's glass away and set it aside for testing. "How long you going to be?"

"Twenty minutes."

"Okay. See you soon." He ended the call and faced Anaya, who hadn't moved. "Callum's gonna come take the berries to get them tested. Just in case. I could be wrong."

She wrapped the blanket tighter around herself, staring at him. "Why would the CEO want to poison me? Or my boss, for that matter?"

"Maybe they weren't the ones who actually sent it. Maybe someone only *wanted* you to think it was them."

"Riggs?" She shook her head in disbelief. "How? I mean, how would he get hold of poison and pull this off? He's smart and manipulative, but this is crazy."

"He's got money," he answered simply. "A guy with that kind of money could easily hire someone to do it."

She eyed the gifts doubtfully for another second then backed away from the island and walked back into the living room to sink onto the sofa. "I'll sign a new contract to rehire you until this is over," she said into the quiet, her voice dull. Tired. Completely devoid of the brightness and wit he'd come to expect from her. "Under the circumstances, my company might even pay for some or all of it."

And she was serious. "You don't need to rehire me," he muttered, vaguely insulted, "and I'm not taking any more for this. You can stay here with me until this is all dealt with." *Until I know you're safe.*

"That's really kind of you, but—"

"Stay, Anaya."

She looked over at him. Measuring his answer.

He held her gaze, meaning every word. He wanted her here. Under his roof. Under his protection.

Under *him*.

Dammit, having her here made it a hundred times harder to do the right thing and keep his hands off her. "You should go to bed and get some sleep," he said more gruffly than he intended. "Tomorrow's going to be busy."

She stood slowly, watching him with clear confusion on her face. "What about you?"

"Callum will be here soon, and I've got some things to get done after that." He nodded toward the hall. "Go on and get some sleep. I've got this." *I've got you. Won't let anything more happen to you.*

She hesitated a moment, then relented, looking disappointed. "All right." She walked past him and disappeared down the hallway, leaving him inhaling her scent that hung faintly in the air.

He shoved out a breath, battling the urge to go after her. To hold her. Comfort her. Because he knew damn well he couldn't trust himself to stop there, and he was unofficially back on the clock.

He was going to get to the bottom of this and make sure she was safe.

SIXTEEN

Anaya tossed and turned in Donovan's guestroom bed, too sore and full of turmoil for her mind to rest. Callum had come and gone well over an hour ago now. She hadn't heard Donovan come down the hall after that, so he must still be in the kitchen or living room.

So much had happened. She'd been shaken after the attack last night, but now she was outright scared.

Were those strawberries poisoned? Had Riggs sent them? Had he been behind last night's attack, and the hit-and-run? She was starting to believe it had been him all along.

If Donovan had been lying next to her, she might have been able to relax a bit. But he'd pulled away from her to the point that it was like an invisible wall stood between them now.

The only time he'd touched her was when he'd carried her to and from his vehicle on the way to the hospital. Since then, he'd maintained a careful distance, and his actions made it clear he didn't want to talk about or acknowledge what had happened between them in her hotel room the other night.

It saddened her. She didn't regret what had happened. No,

her only regret was that he'd walked out before she could take things further. He'd made his feelings on the matter clear, and she wasn't going to beg.

It wasn't until the darkness outside her window began to lighten to a deep gray that her eyelids grew too heavy to keep open. When she woke next, a steady patter of rain was drumming against the window beside the bed. Blinking groggily, aching all over from her tumble on the pavement, she pushed up on one forearm to check her phone on the bedside table and found it was already after nine.

She got up, wincing when she put weight on her sore ankle. It was swollen and bruised when she took the wrapping off and got into the en suite shower to wash the lingering fatigue away. The hot water helped a little but did nothing to alleviate her exhaustion.

Scrubbed, dressed, teeth brushed and some eye makeup on, she put on the hard plastic walking boot and limped into the kitchen. Donovan looked up from the laptop he had open at the island, a mug of coffee at his elbow.

His green eyes snared her as he gave her a quick visual sweep, causing a flutter deep inside. "Get any sleep?"

"Some. You?"

"Not yet. Want some coffee?"

"I'd kill for some."

One side of his mouth kicked up, the few days of dark growth shadowing his face making him irresistible. "No need for that kind of extreme violence so early in the day." He rose and filled a mug for her, adding some cream.

He remembered. "Thanks," she murmured when he handed it over, sparks dancing under her skin when their fingers touched.

He resumed his seat in front of the laptop, seeming

completely unaffected. It threw her. He'd had his fingers inside her and his tongue in her mouth two nights ago, and now they were like polite strangers.

"Donovan."

He looked up at her, and being the sole focus of his attention threw her for a moment. The man was magnetic and powerful as hell. "I really appreciate what you've done for me, and the offer to let me stay here. But I can't help feeling that you're not comfort—"

"I wouldn't have made the offer if I didn't want you here."

All right, but she wasn't letting this go. "You obviously don't want to talk about the other night."

He lowered his gaze to the computer screen. "Nope."

"Why?"

"Because it shouldn't have happened, and I want to let it go." His tone was final, no give to it.

But I don't. She bit the words back, frustrated. And she didn't get the chance to push him about it anymore because her phone rang. She'd hoped it might be Nadia or their dad, but it was their mom.

She sighed heavily, debating the wisdom of answering, or if she even had the energy to. But the longer she put this off, the worse it would be, so might as well do this now. "Hi," she answered, trying to sound chipper.

"Hi to you too," her mother said in a flat tone Anaya knew all too well. "Were you planning to call me and tell me about any of what's been going on yourself, or was I just supposed to hear it from everyone else? I'm your *mother*, Anaya."

Yeah, that's right, make this all about you. She shoved aside her annoyance and kept her voice even as she smoothed things out. "I was going to tell you. I've just had a lot on my plate. But I'm fine."

"Are you?" Her mom tutted, switching from annoyed and passive aggressive to dramatic. "I can't *believe* all of this. What happened now?"

Anaya took a deep breath and told her everything as succinctly as possible, already feeling drained. Talking to her mother was often draining to some extent. "No suspects yet." Not formal ones anyway. Riggs would be looked at more closely if the toxicology report came back positive.

"Are you staying with Nadia?"

"No. I'm at…" Her gaze darted to Donovan, who was watching her. His stare was unnerving, making her feel like he could read her every thought and expression. "A friend's place," she finished.

"What friend? You can't have any friends out there yet. I think you should—"

"I'm taking care of it, Mom." Her mother knew zero about security in this kind of situation, and Anaya didn't want a lecture right now. Or ever, really.

"I'm just saying, you need to—"

"I said I've got it." This time she couldn't keep the bite from her voice.

A beat of silence followed. "No need to get angry with me," her mom said with an edge to her voice. "I'm only trying to help."

"I know. But I'm okay." *And I don't want your help.*

The revelation caught her off guard. That she legit didn't want her mom involved with any of this and had already made the decision not to include her now. Because she was sick of the stress and emotional manipulation and guilt, and this entire situation had finally crystalized that for her.

"Fine then," her mother snapped. "I guess what I think doesn't mean anything to you, so I'll just sit here and wait for updates about what's going on from one of your siblings, since you and Nadia are both apparently not going to bother calling me anymore."

Anaya closed her eyes, praying for patience. Her mother tested it around half the time they talked, but right now, Anaya's tolerance for the emotionally manipulative bullshit was at an all-time low. Even knowing some of the awful things Anaya was dealing with, her mother once again twisted it around to be about herself. "Well, thanks for calling, but I need to go deal with some things."

"All right. Just remember that I love you and I'm always here for you."

Are you though? Anaya knew her mother thought she loved her. But it wasn't real love. Not the kind of unconditional love and support a mentally healthy parent would give their child.

"I know. Love you too. Bye." She ended the call before her mom could say anything else.

Donovan was watching her, muscular arms folded across his sculpted chest. "Is she always like that?"

The question took her aback. He must have overheard her mom's responses. "Pretty much, yeah."

He shook his head in annoyance as he picked up his mug. "Mine too."

She slid onto a stool and wrapped her hands around her own mug, her interest captured. "Too as in…?"

"Nadia's told me some stuff about your mom."

"Oh." A sharp twinge of embarrassment hit her. She could imagine the things Nadia had said, and they wouldn't be complimentary. "Your mom was the same?"

"Sort of. Different sort of toxic. Both my parents were." When she kept watching him, he lifted a shoulder. "My dad was a goddamn mean drunk, and she enabled it because it was easier."

That had to have been rough. At least she'd had her dad and Nadia to lean on. "How did you handle it?"

"Tuned it out for the most part. Until I couldn't anymore. Took me a long time, but I finally cut the ties and walked away."

"How long ago was that?"

"Nine years. About ten years later than it should have happened."

Ouch. And out of loyalty and gratitude, she felt the need to defend her mother. "My mom is…an interesting individual," she said dryly. "She had a tough upbringing, and she's got lots of issues because of it—"

"You don't need to make excuses for her."

She shot him a frown, annoyed. "I'm not."

He gave her a knowing look. "I get it. I did the same for a long time. Misplaced loyalty."

She broke eye contact and studied her finger as she traced it around the rim of her mug. "Nadia went low contact with her not long after she got back from Kabul. I know my mom's hard to deal with, but she has issues and she's alone. I'm the youngest, so I guess I…feel responsible for helping her." Another revelation, one she'd never spoken aloud before.

A vehicle pulled up into the driveway, breaking her out of her thoughts. Donovan got up, checked out the front window and frowned. "It's Noah."

Anaya stood and limped toward the door as Donovan opened it. "What the hell are you doing here?" he said. "You guys just had a baby last night."

Noah gave them a tired smile. "I know." He was dressed in jeans and a T-shirt instead of his uniform and looked like he was about ready to drop. "But this can't wait."

Donovan stilled for an instant and then stepped aside. "Come sit down and I'll get you some coffee."

"Thanks." Noah nodded at her, gave her a weary smile. "How are you feeling?"

"Okay." Why was he here? More bad news? The toxicology tests couldn't have happened yet. "How are Poppy and the baby?"

His eyes shone with pride. "They're both fantastic. Here, look." He held out his phone and pulled up a picture of Poppy, looking way too fresh and beautiful to have just given birth, her blond hair fanned around her shoulders, pretty face wreathed in a joyous smile as she held her tiny newborn son swaddled in a pale green blanket.

"They're both just gorgeous," Anaya said, melting inside. *One day. One day that will be me.* "But how the hell does Poppy look like that after she just had a baby?"

He laughed. "She'll love you for saying that. But honestly, she was born for it. You should've seen her, I'm in awe."

The love and admiration in his voice made something hitch in Anaya's chest. Everyone said Nadia was the natural mother in the family, but Anaya had wanted that for herself for as long as she could remember. "I'm so happy for you guys."

"Thanks." He nodded at Donovan when he handed Noah a cup of coffee. "This won't take long, but we should sit down for this."

Not liking the sound of that, Anaya took one end of the couch while Donovan took the other, both of them watching Noah expectantly. The sheriff took a few sips of his coffee, set the mug on the table between them and sighed as he dragged his gaze to her.

"We don't have any leads yet on the suspect from last night, but the prints we took from your laptop are Jean Luc's."

"Oh," she said softly. So he'd been trying to access her files, looking for something. "Everything is password protected, so I doubt he got anything he was looking for."

Banking info or a list of passwords maybe, so he could try to steal more money from her? Though Jean Luc didn't seem like the kind of guy who knew his way around computers or any kind of tech. It made his involvement in this even more odd.

"Okay, good to know." He paused. "I also got a call from an FBI contact this morning. They got an alert when his prints were tagged in our system."

"An alert for what?"

Noah's blue eyes filled with sympathy. "He's the main suspect in a double homicide two years ago in Chicago. Apparently they found new evidence with his prints on it a few months ago and have been trying to locate him since."

Everything funneled out around her, a strange ringing filling her ears. She was aware of Donovan sitting a few feet away, watching her. She couldn't seem to process what Noah had just said. Jean Luc had murdered two people? No. He had to be wrong.

But what if it's true? God, and what if she'd been there when he broke into her room? Would he have hurt her to get what he wanted? Maybe even killed her to stop her from going to the police?

She knotted her fingers together in her lap, cold sluicing through her.

"They want to talk to you about your contact with him," Noah continued. "His possible whereabouts, all your communication with him, et cetera. And they want to do it today."

She wrapped her arms around her middle in an attempt to ward off the sudden chill creeping into her bones. "It wasn't him last night. He wasn't the one who tried to mug me."

Noah gave a grudging nod. "But he could be working with someone else."

She slumped back against the sofa, sick all the way to her soul. "Yeah, maybe."

The truth was, she didn't know what the hell to think anymore.

SEVENTEEN

Jean Luc pulled the strings of his hoodie tighter around his face and hunched over to shield his face from the rain as he walked toward the glow of the neon sign on the façade of the motel just off the highway, a few miles north of Crimson Point. A bell jingled softly when he opened the office door.

The elderly woman behind the desk stiffened, her gaze raking over him in clear suspicion and concern. "Can I help you?" she asked in a wary tone.

"I would like a room for the night."

She eyed him again, and he wished he had a change of clothes. He no doubt looked homeless at this point. "It's sixty-five dollars. How are you going to pay?"

"Cash." He took the roll of bills out of his pocket and counted out the sixty-five he owed her. There was pitifully little left over. The remainder wouldn't last him much more than three or four days at the most, and he was already down to one meal a day.

She handed him a key with a large plastic tag attached to it, her expression still suspicious. "Number eight is upstairs to the right. Check out's at eleven."

He nodded and walked outside. It had been a few days since he'd had a decent night's sleep. Staying in a real bed for eight hours seemed like a luxury.

Light rain continued to patter on the ground, the drops sending out ripples in the puddles that reflected the glow of the motel sign. Partway to the concrete staircase, he paused, the back of his neck prickling.

He reached behind him, his hand automatically going beneath the hem of his hoodie to the old pistol tucked into the back of his pants as he scanned the parking lot. Several vehicles were parked against the building, otherwise it was empty and quiet, the tapping of the rain the only sound other than the sparse traffic swishing by on the road fifty yards away.

Nothing moved in the shadows. No one called his name or approached him.

That didn't mean he wasn't being watched.

Lowering his hand, he turned and hurried up the steps to number eight, locking the door the moment he walked inside. He pulled the curtains shut over the window facing the parking lot before allowing himself to relax.

He took off his soaked hoodie and laid it over the back of a chair to dry, then pulled the covers down on the bed and stretched out on his back with a low groan, placing the gun on the nightstand. His body was stiff and sore, exhaustion pulling him down like a weight.

But he couldn't allow himself to sleep. Not yet.

He took his phone from his jeans pocket, hesitated another moment before turning it on. He'd kept it off all day, knowing it would only buy him a temporary reprieve.

When he turned it on, messages popped up. He braced himself, knowing what he would find. And he was right.

We had a deal. You have until tomorrow night to get it done or face the consequences.

The latest one had been sent less than an hour ago. *You can't hide from me. Wherever you go, I'll find you.*

He shut the phone off and set it down on the bed, staring up at the circle of light the lamp made on the ceiling. Knowing he was trapped.

He hadn't finished what he'd started. Because he'd lost his nerve at the last moment, and now his time was running out. But the threats he faced weren't empty. He believed the man behind them was more than capable of destroying his life forever.

He didn't dare go back to Seattle. Couldn't run because he didn't have enough money.

Lord, he was so tired of running. Tired of this so-called "life" he was living, and his conscience grew heavier every day.

The only thing keeping him here was Anaya. And it seemed his only way out of this new mess he was trapped in was to betray her.

BY THE TIME Anaya limped back through Donovan's front door, she was nearing the edge of her emotional limit. Her interview with the FBI had been grueling and now she felt exhausted and hollow inside.

On top of everything else, her biological father was a wanted killer. And he'd been after her just a few days ago. What would he have done if she'd been there? How far would he have gone? Would he have killed her too?

"You hungry?" Donovan asked behind her. Pretty much the first time he'd spoken to her since leaving the police station, back in silent protector mode.

She shook her head. She hadn't eaten anything except a

stale muffin before the interview, but food was the last thing on her mind.

However, dwelling on the shitty things in her life wasn't the way she operated. Early on she'd learned to try to look on the bright side, to make the best of any situation. God knew she'd had enough practice at this point.

Be a good girl.

That toxic phrase was carved deep into her psyche, at some point had become part of who she was, becoming entwined with her very makeup as a person. Both from her final memory of her birth mother, and then reinforced by her adoptive one ever since.

Be a good girl. Don't make waves. Make the best of things. Smooth it over. Forgive and forget. Support and love your mother even though she's impossible.

But you know what? She didn't feel like being a good girl anymore. Was sick of it. Sick of holding things inside because she didn't want to create waves—or even ripples. Sick of putting up with other people's shit because it was expected of her, and because she'd taken on the role of family peacemaker as a kid.

Right now, she was angry and hurt and scared, and she was tired of repressing her intensifying feelings for Donovan just because he didn't want to face them.

He stood leaning against the corner of the living room wall, watching her. "Can I get you anything else?"

Yep. A naked, full-length body cuddle followed by a long make-out session and a mind-blowing orgasm should cover it for now. "No." She sank onto the sofa and elevated her sore ankle on the end cushion. The plastic boot they'd given her to protect it was clumsy but gave it stability. "I gotta say, I really didn't anticipate this trip turning into such a shit show. Aren't I exciting?"

The corner of his mouth lifted at her dry tone. "You're definitely not boring."

"I'll say." She rubbed her forehead and sighed, trying to sort through all her feelings and gauge how much she was willing to rock the proverbial boat right now.

She could call and vent to Nadia, but that wasn't going to help much, and her sister had her hands full looking after Ferhana. Her dad was worried enough about her as it was without adding this on top of everything, and she didn't feel like talking to any of her other siblings about it. "Did you talk to Shae this morning?"

He nodded. "She's doing well, all things considered. Walker verified it, and he's keeping a close eye on her."

"From what I heard she sure seemed glad to see you last night."

His expression changed, guilt flickering over his features before he glanced away and headed to the kitchen. "Yeah."

"That must have felt good."

He opened the fridge and started taking things out. "Yes. I just wish I could have protected her last night. And you."

"It wasn't your—"

"She was really appreciative of you hanging out with her yesterday. She said it's the best time she's had in a while."

He was really touchy about discussing personal things with her. "Good, because she's great. I enjoyed her company, and her quick thinking with that flashlight saved the day." She watched him start cutting things on the counter. "You, Walker and her mom did a great job with her."

He made a face and kept working. "I can't take any credit for that."

She could feel the guilt and self-loathing seething inside him. Wished she knew how to peel back the layers and get him to let her in more. "Ever been married?"

"No."

"Close to married?"

"No."

"Really? Nothing serious since Shae's mom?"

"Not really. Nothing that lasted very long." He stopped slicing and looked up at her, holding her gaze for a long moment before speaking. "When I asked you before, you said you'd almost been married."

She'd started this, should have expected he would turn it around on her, so it was stupid to tense inside.

He watched her with those gorgeous, clear green eyes. "What's that mean?"

"I was engaged once," she said quietly, her stomach pulling tight as the old memories hit her.

He set down the knife, giving her his full attention. Maybe relieved to have the spotlight shifted to her, or maybe he was genuinely curious. "What happened?"

If she wanted to get past the wall he hid behind, she was going to have to be vulnerable first. "You really want to know? Or are you just making conversation to fill the void?"

"I really wanna know. What happened?"

She took a moment before answering. "His name was Bryan. And the short version is, I got my heart shattered."

He added some crackers to the board in front of him and brought it over, placing it on her lap before sitting beside her, carefully easing her booted foot into his lap. He'd sliced some fruit and cheese and added cold cuts and crackers to make a charcuterie board of sorts.

"Okay, maybe I am hungry after all," she said, picking up a little clump of red grapes. Eating gave her something to do besides bare her heart and gave her an excuse not to look at him.

"You were saying?" he prompted, making a little cracker sandwich for himself.

She popped a grape into her mouth. It was crisp and sweet and crunchy, refreshing. "We'd been together for over two years, living together for eight months when we got engaged. We had everything planned out. Wedding, a year or two more of work for both of us before we started trying for a family. Two kids, maybe more later."

"What did he do?" he asked in a dark tone.

"Few months before the wedding, he came home and announced that he'd changed his mind and didn't want to have a family anymore. As in *ever*. I was stunned. We'd talked about it at length before getting engaged, planned it all out together."

"So what happened?"

She ate a strawberry. "He wanted to stay together. Didn't see the change as a big deal and couldn't understand why I didn't want to go through with the wedding anymore. But for me it was a deal breaker. I want a family of my own. So I ended it, and now he hates my guts."

"Ouch. That's rough."

"Yeah. And you know what's even rougher? I found out a few months ago that he married someone else, and they just had their first baby. So apparently, he *did* want to have a family, just not with me."

He winced. "Sorry."

"His loss. But that kind of thing leaves one hell of a mark."

"Sounds to me like you dodged a bullet."

"Agreed." She ate a few more nibbles and turned the tables back on him. "Did you ever think about having more kids? After Shae?"

He snorted. "Shit no. I messed up badly enough the first time."

It shouldn't have stung as much as it did, but the conviction behind his answer made her flinch inside. His words underlined an insurmountable difference between them, telling her point blank that there was no chance whatsoever of a future with him.

And yet it still didn't stop her from wanting him. Even though their short time together could only be physical, and she wasn't capable of staying emotionally detached.

"I don't know the history of what happened with you guys," she went on, "but Shae sure loves you now. She talked about you constantly yesterday. She idolizes you even if you don't realize it." He wasn't nearly as bad a father as he seemed to think.

He glanced at her, and the hope and hint of vulnerability she read in his face tugged at her heart. "Yeah?"

"Definitely. It was pretty sweet. And based on what you've told me before, it sounds like both of us know what a toxic parent is. Sorry to disappoint you, but you're not it." She nudged him with her knee. "So maybe don't be so hard on yourself where she's concerned, huh?"

The hint of a smile played around his lips. "I'll try to bear that in mind, thanks."

"You're welcome." She ate a cracker, considering her next words carefully. In the end, she decided to just be honest while injecting a little humor into the conversation. "Is that why you're keeping your distance from me now? You're afraid I'm going to get clingy and try to convince you to have a family with me one day?"

The look on his face would have been priceless if it hadn't been so heartbreaking. Surprise. A little dread. And more of that self-loathing she didn't understand but wanted to help ease. Whatever was going on for him, it was clear something deep was at work inside him.

He glanced away, his jaw tightening. "I shouldn't have done what I did. There are rules—"

"You weren't technically my bodyguard when it happened, so you didn't break the terms of our contract, and I hereby absolve you of any wrongdoing."

She'd meant it to be funny, but he didn't react, still wouldn't look at her. "There are things about me you don't know. Things that would change your mind about me if you knew."

"I wouldn't bet on that. I like what I've seen of you so far."

He shook his head. "I'm not the hero you and Shae seem to think I am." He didn't elaborate.

"You are to us. And you're also only human. We all make mistakes."

"Yeah, well, I bet you never made a mistake that cost someone their life." He shifted her leg and started to rise, stopping when she gasped in pain. "Sorry." He sat back down and cradled her foot in his lap, looking contrite. "You okay?"

"I've been better."

At her honest reply, he softened and relaxed back into the sofa. "Yeah. I bet." He hesitated, then slid a hand up to capture hers, and given what they'd just talked about, that small intimacy felt significant. She got the feeling that he thought he didn't deserve to have someone in his life, but he was wrong.

Let me in, she coaxed him silently, gliding her thumb across the back of his hand. She knew what it was to be hurt too. *Let me in just a little.*

She read the battle in his face. In the tense lines of his jaw and shoulders as he sat there while the undercurrent of tension built between them. The unspoken hunger in his eyes.

He wanted her. As badly as she wanted him. But he wasn't willing to go there again.

Taking a chance, Anaya sat up straight and curled into him to rest her head on his shoulder. She nuzzled the side of his neck with the tip of her nose.

He hissed in a breath and wrapped his arms around her,

whether to still her or hold her tighter, she didn't know. "You don't know what you're doing," he said.

"No?"

He shook his head, the motion as tight as his grip. "I'm no good for you, Anaya. You deserve someone who—"

"I'll decide what I deserve," she murmured, capturing his cheek in her hand and turning his face toward her. She was done with living according to the expectations of others. This was her goddamn life, and she was going to *live* it, take what she wanted, starting right now.

He stared back at her, the volcanic desire burning in his eyes making her breath catch and her heart trip.

She leaned forward an inch, her gaze on his lips. His arm tightened around her, one hand sliding up into her hair, his fingers locking tight.

He erased the remaining distance, and the punch of desire when their lips touched went through her like lightning. He was less gentle this time, less finessed, holding her in place while he angled his head and took possession of her mouth. She drew in a sharp breath, her entire body coming to life.

Heat raced over her skin, every point of contact sending out shivers of sensation that coalesced into the hot throb building between her legs. She pressed harder against him, twining her fingers in his hair, a whimper of need and frustration escaping. The hard plastic boot made it awkward to move into the position she wanted.

Donovan paused a moment, easing back to stare at her, his expression absorbed as he drew his thumb across her lower lip. "You make me lose control so damn easily."

"Not sorry," she whispered back, tugging at his shoulders.

He relented, giving her what she wanted as he laid her down and wedged himself between her thighs, coming down on top of her to trap her beneath his muscular weight, his kiss muffling her plaintive moan. The feel of him on top of her, the instant security and arousal it triggered, combined with the needy ache where his erection rubbed against her core with every sensual surge of his hips.

She was on fire, so lost in the moment and everything he was making her feel that it took several seconds for the sound outside to register. A vehicle pulling up out front.

Donovan broke the kiss and muttered a curse under his breath, shoving up on his hands to look out the front window. "Damn. It's Walker."

Anaya bit back a protest as he climbed off her, sitting up and running a hand through her mussed curls. Walker had the *worst* timing. Her whole body ached with unfulfilled need, and she had a feeling that when Walker left, Donovan would put that wall back between them—immediately and stronger than before.

"Want me to kill him?" he said as he stalked to the door.

She let out a startled laugh, some of the tension draining out of her. "No, I think you should probably let him live—just for Shae's sake." But whatever Walker had come here for, she hoped to hell it was good news.

EIGHTEEN

It took one second after Walker came through Donovan's front door to tell him something was off. Anaya was over on the couch, looking a little rumpled, and Donovan was anything but happy to see him. He glanced between them, read the tension in their postures, and it didn't take a genius to figure out what was going on.

"I called you, but you didn't pick up, so I headed over," he said by way of explanation, feeling awkward.

"It's fine," Donovan muttered, his tone broadcasting that the interruption was anything *but* fine. "You want something to drink?"

"No, I'm good." He strode over to the loveseat and sat down, holding a folder containing the documents he'd just printed off at the office. "I heard about the latest development with Jean Luc. Twenty minutes after, this hits my inbox." He slid the folder across the table to Anaya.

Donovan stepped behind the couch to peer over her shoulder as she looked at the files. "Police reports? Of the murders Jean Luc is suspected of?"

"Yeah, along with detective notes and lab reports."

"What the hell?" Donovan said, frowning down at the files. "How'd you get your hands on these? They're supposed to be sealed until—"

"Ivy."

Anaya's eyes widened. "As in the Ivy who helped rescue Nadia from Kabul? That Ivy?"

"That's the one." The one and only, and the one who was currently living rent free in his head. Light brown hair, sharp hazel eyes a mix of amber and green that seemed to look straight into his mind. A fit, toned body that filled out the black cargo pants and long-sleeve T-shirt she'd been wearing to perfection on the day they'd met in Germany, after the mission to rescue Nadia. And a skill set that would have been impressive for any SOF operative.

Whoever she was, he'd never met anyone like her.

He leaned forward, pushing her image from his mind as he braced his forearms on his thighs. "I don't know how she even found out about what's been going on here—"

"Maybe Nadia told her."

"Possibly." Or Ivy was keeping tabs on them all personally for some reason. He was more than curious about her, and determined to find out which it was. "Anyway, I thought you should see what she sent, so you know exactly what happened and what Jean Luc is accused of."

Anaya nodded and resumed reading with a troubled frown as Donovan came around the couch and sat beside her to take a look. "Is she a hacker or something?"

"Or something," Walker said. He still hadn't been able to find out anything about her. Not a trace. And no one aside from Alex Rycroft seemed to know her personally. It was driving him bat shit.

Anaya winced and pulled in a breath as she read. "It says the killer stabbed one of the victims five times and slashed his throat before shooting the other one." She set the papers down and looked away, visibly upset.

Donovan took them from her, quickly scanning the contents. "He was trying to access something on Anaya's laptop the day he broke into her hotel room."

"What would a laborer want from her laptop?" Walker said.

"I've been trying to figure that out," said Anaya. "I can't think of anything. All my files on there are password protected anyway."

"Well, at any rate, I'm glad you weren't there," Walker told her. Jean Luc might be her biological father, but that didn't mean he wouldn't kill her if it came down to it.

She and Donovan looked at each other, and there was no mistaking the intensity in his friend's gaze. Donovan had it bad for her, and Walker wondered if he even let himself acknowledge it.

Donovan set the contents on the table and closed the file. "Shae going to class tonight?"

"Yeah, I'm going to drive her up to campus in a little bit."

"You're okay with her going after what happened?"

"She won't be alone. She's meeting a friend there and taking the bus home with her after." He stood and nodded at the folder. "You want to keep that copy?"

"No," Anaya said, quickly handing it back. "I've seen enough."

He got it. Felt bad that she was finding out about Jean Luc's history this way, but better she know exactly what Jean Luc was capable of and get any unrealistic notions or sympathy for him out of her head now. "Sure. Let me know if there's anything else I can do for you guys."

"We will," Donovan said. "Thanks for bringing this by."

He nodded and left, glad to get out of there. It was obvious that things between Donovan and Anaya had crossed the line at some point. He hoped Donovan knew what he was doing, getting involved with a woman who had recently been his client. That he'd crossed the line at all told Walker just how strongly Donovan felt about her.

Driving down the hill toward town, his kept his eye on the horizon. Light rain fell from a solid gray cloud cover, dulling the color of the waves broken up by slashes of white marking the crest of each breaker in the distance. His house stood on a half-acre lot set back from the street on a hill above town, the two-story country craftsman sided in slate-blue shingles.

Shae got up from the kitchen table when he walked in, gathering her books. He stopped in the doorway, staring.

"What?" she asked, filling her backpack.

"Nothing." Her drastic, sophisticated new look was going to take some getting used to.

The sweats and yoga pants she favored had been replaced by form-fitting jeans and a snug sweater that he wanted to cover with a long, shapeless coat. She'd even put her hair up in a fancy twist and done her eyes and lips up. He was seeing her as a grown woman for the first time.

Those perverted kids on campus better keep their damn hands to themselves if they knew what was good for them.

She laughed at him. "Seriously, what?"

"No, it's nothing. Got your bear spray?" He'd reviewed how to use it last night, along with some self-defense moves she knew but hadn't practiced in a while.

"Yes, I'm good to go."

They got into his vehicle. He let her pick the music for the drive to campus, enjoying the sound of her voice as she sang along. "You sound like your mom," he told her between songs. "She could really carry a tune too."

"Yeah, she had terrible taste in music though. But great taste in men." She reached over to pat his shoulder affectionately.

He smiled. "I still don't know how I got so lucky to have you both in my life." He wasn't a mushy, talk-about-your-feelings kind of guy, but with Shae it was different. It was important to him that she know exactly how he felt about her.

She gave him an adoring smile, melting him completely. "Pretty sure we were the lucky ones."

At campus, she hopped out and slung on her backpack, her short leather jacket doing little to nothing to hide her figure-hugging outfit beneath. "Okay, thanks for the ride. See you tonight."

He bit back the instinctive order for her to text him when she left class and then again as she was about to get off the bus. They'd already discussed everything. She was an adult now, like it or not, and after last night she knew to be even more careful. "Call me if you change your mind about the bus. I'll come get you."

"I'll be fine. Bye, Dad." She gave him a sunny smile and a wave, then walked off.

Watching her walk away, he noticed the male attention she drew from the guys who passed her and did double takes. Had to restrain the impulse to jump out and walk her to class personally to warn them away.

Parenting wasn't for the faint of heart. But this having to let go of your baby shit was *hard*.

The rain picked up on his way home, a steady rhythm against his windshield. When he walked into the empty house, he paused to glance around, suddenly struck by the quiet stillness.

Jillian had never lived in this house. He and Shae had moved here in June, right after she finished high school. Yet for just a moment, he half expected Jillian to walk into the kitchen, flash him a smile and start telling him about her day while she pulled out ingredients from the fridge so they could make dinner together.

Not so long ago, the thought would have twisted the knife lodged in his heart. Now the image of her standing there was comforting rather than painful.

The realization startled him, but he couldn't deny he'd felt a little more at peace about her recently. Time hadn't taken away the pain of her loss. It just gradually made it more bearable.

He opened the fridge to figure out what to make for himself, pulling his phone from his pocket when a chime indicated a new email. He tensed when he saw a new one from Ivy, and clicked on it.

Heard you've been asking around about me and thought I'd save you some time. Here's all you need to know.

Seconds later, a black and white jpeg popped up below it.

A raven with outstretched wings, holding a sword in its talons, then a scroll beneath it bearing the word *Valkyrja*.

He frowned, not understanding the significance. What the hell was it supposed to mean? She was toying with him. Playing some kind of game he didn't understand. And there was clearly something wrong with him, because he was secretly enjoying the hell out of it.

After looking for clues about the image online for the better part of an hour, he was still in the dark. There was only one person he could go to about this.

Rycroft was three hours ahead of him back east. He shot off a text. *Ivy just sent me this. Any idea what it means?*

The whole time, he couldn't shake the eerie feeling that she might have eyes on him right now, watching his reaction and enjoying his confusion.

Maybe even through his phone's camera.

He put his thumb over it just in case, refusing to give her

the satisfaction. If this was a game, he wasn't going to make it easy for her to win it.

Three dots appeared on the screen a few seconds later as Rycroft typed a response.

Well, that's interesting, the former NSA agent answered.

Was it? *What's it mean?* Walker pressed.

It means you and I need to have a beer next time you're in town.

He frowned at the response, then made a disgusted sound and shoved his phone into his back pocket. "Meet for a beer?" he muttered, pulling out some chicken breasts and veggies. He didn't much feel like cooking at the moment, but he'd get these going in the oven, feed himself, and have a plate waiting for Shae when she got home.

If Rycroft wasn't willing to tell Walker what Ivy's story was, there had to be a good reason. And now he had a dozen different theories about what it was.

In the meantime…

He couldn't wait to find out what clue she sent him next.

NINETEEN

The vehicle's tires bumped over the lane, splashing through the puddles in the growing darkness. Myers's black SUV.

He kept out of view in his hiding place, heart beating faster as he squinted to see better. Coming to this area again so soon was a risk, but he had no choice. He had to go through with it. There was no other way to make this end.

His pulse thudded in his ears as he waited, hidden from view while he watched Myers step out and glance around. He ducked down lower, froze, and for one terrible moment he thought he'd been spotted.

Myers stood there for several moments, looking around him. Then finally turned and walked away.

He let out a slow breath, relief washing over him. If Myers was here, it meant he wasn't guarding the target. She might even be alone.

He got up and hurried down the gravel lane to where he'd left the vehicle he'd taken less than an hour ago. He'd been hiding here ever since. To make sure Myers wasn't near the target.

Driving up the hill, his breathing turned shallow. *Almost over.*

Myers loved her. But killing her in front of him wasn't going to be easy.

He chose his parking spot with care, hiding the car behind a large laurel hedge, then took the pistol out of the console. It had a full mag and a round in the chamber, but he was only going to need two bullets.

Killing her was the only way to make things right.

"WHAT DO you think of our English prof?" Shae asked Clara, who sat next to her on the bus back to the coast. The evening class had flown by, and she was excited about the first big assignment they'd just received.

"He's sexy as hell."

Shae laughed. "He's like, fifty."

Clara eyed her. "And? He's halfway to being a silver fox, and you can't deny the man's beautiful."

"Okay, I can't deny that he's a very attractive man. But I meant what do you think of his teaching style?"

"I like it. Especially when he reads to us in that *voice*. That passage in Jane Eyre tonight?" She sighed and rolled her eyes heavenward, giving a little shiver that made Shae giggle.

"I know, he should narrate audiobooks. I'll be hearing his voice every time I read another chapter." They had a month to read Jane Eyre because it was so long. She already knew the story because she'd seen a movie adaptation over the summer, but she was enjoying the book a lot. "I like Charlotte Bronte's writing style. More than I thought I would. And I'm pretty sure English is going to be my favorite class this semester."

"What else are you taking?"

"Economics, stats, and business communication." She made a face. "I know, first and second year are dull and you kind of just have to hold your nose and swallow to get through it—"

"Not in Mr. Denyson's English lit class," Clara said with a sly smile.

"No, that's true," she said on a laugh. "So far it's the highlight."

"Good." Clara patted her hand and leaned into her so that their shoulders touched. "I'm so glad you sat beside me on the first day. I was so nervous, didn't know *anyone*."

"You didn't seem it." Clara came across as totally confident in herself and no-nonsense, completely unafraid to voice her opinion and speak her mind. Shae respected that. Clara reminded her a bit of Anaya that way. That reminded her, she needed to text Anaya in a bit and check on her.

"Because I was too distracted by my hot English prof to be my shy, awkward self," Clara said.

"That's fair."

They chatted all the way to Clara's stop a few miles north of Crimson Point. Clara stood, shouldering her backpack. "You want to get together this weekend sometime? Maybe we can buy some treats and watch Jane Eyre together or something."

"I'd love that." It was so great to be making friends again. Crimson Point was small, and Clara only lived fifteen minutes away. "I'll text you."

"Perfect. Have a good night."

"You too." Shae sat back as Clara stepped off the bus. The driver continued on the route. There were only two other people on board now, an elderly man and a thirty-something woman.

Shae gazed out the window as the bus carried on down the hill toward the water. Fall was closing in around them now, a layer of mist rolling in from the ocean along with the rain-laden clouds in the growing darkness. She was looking forward to getting home and cuddling up in front of the fire with Jane Eyre and a mug of hot chocolate, but also a bit nervous about waiting at the bus stop after the incident on Front Street.

Her dad was coming to pick her up. She took out her phone to text him and found some messages from her friends back east. Busy replying to them all, she lost track of time and almost missed her stop, barely pulling the cord in time to get the driver to pull over.

Stepping down, her foot slipped on the edge of the metal step. She lurched, managed to catch herself on the handrail in time to avoid a face plant on the sidewalk, but dropped her phone with a clatter.

"Are you all right?" the driver asked.

"Yes, fine. Thanks," she said, embarrassed. Her phone was lying facedown on the sidewalk a few feet away. She picked it up as the bus rolled away, her heart sinking when she saw the screen was shattered.

She tried to pull up her texting app, but couldn't see anything through the damaged screen, and she couldn't tell whether she'd wrecked something inside the electronics as well. Annoyed at herself, she tucked her phone into her back pocket and glanced around. She couldn't contact her dad or Donovan now.

All the businesses on Front Street were closed, their interiors dark. Even Whale's Tale. Crimson Point Security was an easy walk from here, but everyone had probably gone home for the night at this point. And she wasn't going to wait out here alone a minute longer than necessary.

She hitched the straps of her backpack up higher on her shoulders and pulled her hood up, resigned to walk home up the hill north of town in the dark. Her footsteps echoed slightly on the damp pavement, blending with the rush of the waves along the beach to her left. It was eerie to be out here when it was deserted. She felt exposed. Vulnerable.

She was doing okay until she reached the north end of Front Street, where the bright lights of the historical streetlamps ended. Less than a block up the darkened section of road, the sense of foreboding she'd managed to quell thus far began to grow.

Her pulse accelerated, and not merely because of the steep uphill grade she was walking. Every little noise had her eyes darting into the shadows, a prickling sensation at the nape of her neck adding to her unease.

She glanced around, telling herself to calm but not quite able to shake that awful tingling sensation.

As if someone was watching her from the shadows. Following her.

Unnerved, she picked up the pace and kept going. It was only twenty minutes to home from here. But this area had no houses or buildings, bordered by forest on both sides, a popular area for joggers and people walking their dogs. Except no one else seemed to be out here right now.

At the moment, it seemed like a really bad place to be a woman walking alone in the dark.

She grabbed for her phone and tried to access the light. No good.

Right now, she sorely regretted her decision not to do her road test and get her license so she could have driven herself wherever she needed to go. Crimson Point was small and awesome, and the people were friendly, but at the moment, all she could think about was how alone she was out here, and of all the bad shit that had happened in this area over the past few years.

She dug in her bag for her bear spray instead, clutching it

tight in her hand. If anyone did spring out of nowhere and try to grab her this time, she'd make them freaking sorry.

Her steps and rapid breathing mixed with the steady patter of the light rain. She could smell the damp leaves in the strip of dark forest that ran parallel to the road, the rich, spicy scent of the earth and cedar.

Then, in the background, she heard it. A car approaching up the hill behind her.

Her heart rate kicked up. She upped her pace and glanced over her shoulder, on guard. The car swung toward her, the glare of the headlights momentarily blinding her. She flinched and ducked her head just as the driver's silhouette became visible through the windshield.

A man.

She faced front and walked faster. There was a house another block or so up the hill. She could see its lighted windows—

The car sped up suddenly.

She broke into a run, racing for the house.

The car came up beside her and braked hard.

She sucked in a breath and whirled around, canister of bear spray poised in her grip.

"Hello, Shae," a male voice said as her finger found the trigger.

DONOVAN LEANED back in his chair and folded his arms, regarding Callum and Ryder across the Crimson Point Security conference room table. They rarely met in here, but there were too many unknowns happening and he'd wanted total privacy for this meeting. Anaya was more than a former client to him.

Way more.

"She offered to rehire you?" Ryder asked to clarify after Donovan explained everything.

"Yeah, but I told her forget it. She's staying at my place until the suspects are in custody and I know she's safe." He'd left her cuddled up under a blanket on his couch in front of a movie and activated his security system on his way out.

"The FBI have decided to fly her out tomorrow," Callum said quietly.

Donovan stared at him. This was news to him. "Since when?"

"They just called here before you arrived. I got the tox report back on the berries, by the way. It's negative."

"For cyanide? Or any toxin?"

"No toxins whatsoever. Apparently, the chocolate coating had almond extract in it. That's what you smelled."

Yeah, sometimes cyanide had a bitter almond scent to it. But sometimes it didn't smell like anything at all.

He dragged a hand over his face. Shit. It should have been a giant relief, but it wasn't. There were too many other things going on that might all be connected. The question was, who was behind them all? "Riggs could still be involved. The Feds need to—"

"They interviewed him this afternoon. His alibies all check out, although my contact did say that the one covering the window before and during the almost hit-and-run in Seattle is a bit shaky."

"Shaky?" He wanted to punch something. "They're the fucking FBI, and the best they can do is say his alibi is *shaky*?"

Callum and Ryder exchanged a look before Callum continued in a level voice. "They're keeping an eye on everything. But there's no way Riggs was the one who grabbed her last night."

"Then it could be someone working for him. He's got money, and his family has even more."

"They're aware of that."

He folded his arms, not caring if it made him look defensive. He fucking felt defensive right now. He wanted answers. Wanted Anaya and Shae safe. "Does she know about the flight?"

"She will by now," Ryder said.

He had to unclamp his jaw to respond. She was leaving tomorrow. And even though her safety was paramount, he didn't want her to go. Wasn't ready to *let* her go, and she was being taken out of his hands. "What time does she leave?"

"Flight's at noon. I told the agent in charge that I'd drive Anaya to the airport," Callum said.

Beneath his folded arms, he clenched his hands into fists. As far as he could tell, Callum and Ryder didn't yet suspect that anything had happened between him and Anaya, and that's the way he wanted it to stay. They had both taken a chance on him after the serious mark on his resume, and the last thing he wanted was for them to have reason to see him as anything but a dedicated, capable professional.

Getting it on with a former client—Callum's future sister-in-law—could cost him dearly.

"All right," he made himself say. Logically he knew it was best for both of them if Anaya left tomorrow. A clean cut. Quick and merciful, taking the decision out of both their hands and ending things fast.

On the other, he wanted to keep her close. Much too close. Even though he knew he shouldn't. Even though he knew that she deserved way better than getting involved with him when there was no future for them.

They were too different, wanted completely different things

out of life. He wanted to stay here with Shae. Anaya's life was back east, and she wanted a husband and family of her own.

He couldn't give her that. Definitely not the second part.

His phone buzzed on the table, drawing his gaze to the screen where a green message bubble lit up.

I've been waiting for this.

He grabbed it, something stilling inside him. Then more appeared.

Waiting for too damn long.

He stared, his heart thudding. Who the hell was this?

"What?" Callum asked from across the table.

He couldn't answer, riveted to the screen as another message popped up.

I'm going to take away the one you love most.

"What the fuck?" he snarled, exploding from his chair as he dialed the number back. It rang and rang and rang before a digitized voice announced that the voicemail box was full.

"Myers, what the hell's going on?" Ryder demanded.

"It's him," he said. "The hit-and-run driver."

The threat hit home. *The one you love most...*

"Shae," he rasped out, all the blood rushing out of his head.

He threw the door open and raced down the hall, dialing Shae's cell. She should be on her way home by now. Walker was going to pick her up at the bus stop.

"Hi, this is Shae," her recorded voice said. "Leave a message."

"Fuck," he breathed, panic licking up his spine.

He dialed Walker and raced down the stairs to the parking lot door. "Where's Shae?" he blurted when Walker picked up. "Is she with you?"

"No, I haven't heard from her—"

"We have to find her *now*."

TWENTY

Holding her phone to her ear, Anaya rubbed her forehead with her free hand and sank onto the sofa to prop her foot up. She'd just taken some pain meds because the ache in her ankle had gotten pretty intense again. But this latest pain in the ass was way worse.

"Is this really necessary?" she asked the female FBI agent on the other end of the line.

While being flown home tomorrow made sense to her in some ways, the stubborn part of her also didn't want to give whoever was targeting her the satisfaction of seeing her run. Not only that, her sister was here. And Donovan. She didn't want to leave when things were still unresolved between them. Before she left, she wanted some sense of closure.

"I'm afraid so. The Bureau thinks it's in your best interest to remove you from the area until everything's resolved."

Who the hell knew how long that would take? "Do I have a choice in the matter?"

"Yes. But again, we think—"

"Yeah, got it." She sighed and laid her head back onto the arm of the sofa. Donovan was out at a quick meeting with

Callum and Ryder at the office and should be back any time now. He'd locked and set the alarm at the house before leaving her, had showed her where he kept a canister of bear spray in the kitchen. "The flights are already booked?"

"Yes. Portland to Chicago at noon, and then Chicago to D.C. My office will send you the flight details shortly. If you need anything in the meantime, just call me, but I'll be in touch in the morning and throughout the day in between your flights."

"All right." What else was there to say? "Thank you." Ending the call, she gave herself a few minutes to process everything before dialing her sister. It went to voicemail. Nadia must have Ferhana in the bath.

Her stomach rumbled. Donovan had promised to call her after the meeting to see what she wanted him to bring back for dinner, but she was too hungry to wait. She got up and hobbled to the kitchen. In the pantry, she found a box of spaghetti and a jar of sauce.

Good enough.

She filled a pot with water and set it on the stove to boil, turning the burner on high. She stilled when she heard the back door open quietly. "Donovan?" she called, turning. He hadn't texted.

There was no answer. No beep to indicate the alarm needed to be disarmed.

She set the jar of sauce down and limped toward the hallway. "Donov—" She sucked in a sharp breath, her entire body going rigid when she saw the man slipping inside.

Jean Luc appeared in the faint light at the end of the hall and stopped as he met her gaze. Staring at her with a set expression.

She turned and ran, a wave of terror breaking over her.

"Anaya! *Attend*!" he yelled.

No way in hell. She raced back for the kitchen as fast as she could, her bad ankle and plastic boot slowing her down.

He cursed and charged after her. "Just wait!"

Pain lanced through her ankle and up her leg with each step, but she couldn't stop. She ran into the kitchen, reached for the drawer handle where Donovan kept the bear spray.

Jean Luc's shadow appeared on the floor just outside the kitchen, coming closer with every heartbeat. "No, wait, you must listen—"

No time.

She darted for the door off the kitchen, her fingers fumbling with the lock for a moment, then burst outside into the backyard, flinging the door shut behind her. The grass was wet, rain hitting her in the face as she tried to run for her life.

Donovan had armed the alarm. She'd seen him do it. How had Jean Luc gotten inside without triggering it?

"Anaya, no!" he shouted after her.

Fear drove her, self-preservation and adrenaline dulling the pain in her foot. She kept running, heading for the detached garage, intending to race past it and get to the neighbor's house for help.

The wooden gate in the fence was right ahead. She could make it. She had to make it and get help before Jean Luc caught her.

Her fingers flew to the latch at the top of the gate. She swung it open, stepped through just as Jean Luc's running footsteps sounded behind her on the lawn.

She slammed the gate shut and took off, aiming across the driveway.

A figure burst out of the hedge to the right.

Strong, cruel hands grabbed her before she could draw the breath to scream. Bit into her shoulders.

She turned on him like a cornered animal, screaming and

clawing, fighting to break free. He hissed in a breath when she raked her nails across the side of his face but didn't let go. His arms locked around her ribs, frighteningly strong, and started to lift her, already carrying her with him.

"No!" she yelled, bucking hard, trying to rip the hands off her.

She caught a blur of motion out of the corner of her eye, then something slammed into them. They hit the ground with a bone-jarring thud, driving the breath from her lungs. The side of her head bounced off the mulch at the edge of the driveway, making spots burst in front of her eyes.

She rolled with the force of the impact, managed to throw out her hands to stop herself and shoved up. Yells and grunts blended with the sound of a scuffle as she scrambled to her feet and threw a glance at what was happening behind her.

Jean Luc was fighting the man who had grabbed her. He was Caucasian, mid-thirties with light brown hair.

Not Anthony Riggs. She'd never seen this stranger before in her life.

The two men rolled over and over on the pavement as they exchanged vicious blows. Jean Luc got the upper hand for a moment, managing to pin the other man beneath him. He glanced up, met her gaze for a heartbeat, his expression full of alarm. "*Couris*," he rasped out.

Run.

She broke free of her paralysis and did just that, jumping and swallowing a scream a second later when a shot rang out behind her. Risking a look over her shoulder, she saw Jean Luc clutching his stomach as he dropped to the driveway.

She didn't even have time to process what was happening before the stranger turned on her, a gun aimed at her as he stalked closer. "Stop right there, bitch, or I'll shoot you too!"

Anaya lurched to a halt, her heart knocking against her ribs, eyes locked on the deadly black gun in the man's gloved hand. Twenty feet away from him, Jean Luc groaned in agony and rolled to his side on the driveway.

The shooter kept coming at her. She cringed, cowering as his arm came up, locking around her throat. She choked and shoved up on her toes to try and relieve the terrifying pressure, both hands fighting to ease the restriction across her windpipe.

"You're coming with me," he snarled, and wrenched her backward.

She had no choice but to go with him, his grip unbreakable and the ever-present threat of the weapon in his hand making resistance impossible. Her sole focus was suddenly narrowed to the arm across her throat and her struggle for air as he wrenched her around and forced her back down the driveway.

Jean Luc was nowhere to be seen.

Her eyes darted toward the hedge, picking up the trail of blood on the driveway slowly fading in the rain. She didn't know what the hell was going on, who this man was, or what had just happened.

Jean Luc had fought him as though he was trying to protect her. Is that why he'd begged her to wait? He'd known someone targeting her was outside? Now he was dying in those bushes.

"Move it," the man snarled, shoving her forward.

She stumbled, let out a throttled scream of rage and tried to sink her teeth into the man's arm but all she got was the sleeve of his coat.

He slammed his elbow into the back of her head, stunning her. He adjusted his hold in an instant, allowing her just enough room to suck in a pained breath as he marched her toward the backyard gate.

His rough, rapid breathing rasped in her ear, the excitement in his voice when he spoke turning her stomach. "We're going to give Donovan a little surprise when he gets home."

WHERE THE HELL *WAS* SHE?

Donovan scanned the dark, rainy street as he raced his truck up the hill. Shae wasn't answering her phone, and Walker didn't know where she was. He'd apparently been on the way to pick her up when Donovan had called.

It wasn't like her, not at all, and she should have been back from class by now.

He'd already checked the bus stop and the area around it. Walker, Callum and Ryder were out looking elsewhere.

He grabbed his phone the instant it started ringing, disappointed when he saw Walker's name on screen instead of Shae's. "You find her?" he demanded.

"Yeah, she's here."

He took his foot off the gas, sagging in the seat as he pulled to the side of the road and willed his heart to slow down. *Shit,* he'd thought… "Where?" he managed.

"Home. She got in a few minutes ago."

"I'm sorry," Shae said, her voice becoming clearer in the background. "I'm really sorry I scared you guys. I dropped my phone getting off the bus and broke it. So I started walking home. Finn drove up behind me while I was going up the hill at the end of Front Street and scared the crap out of me. I almost bear sprayed him when he pulled alongside and offered me a ride home."

Donovan let out a deep breath and ran a hand over his mouth, suddenly shaky as hell. He'd withstood enemy fire and stared death in the face more times than he wanted to think about. But just the thought of something happening to Shae had turned him to jelly inside. "Okay. Just as long as you're safe." At least his voice sounded a hell of a lot calmer than he felt.

"Donovan, what the hell's going on?" she asked. "Dad wouldn't tell me."

"I don't know. I'm just glad you're all right. But do me a favor and—"

"I know, Dad's already told me I'm on lockdown until whatever's happening is over."

"Good. Gotta go now, sweetheart, okay?"

"Yeah. And just…be safe."

"I will. Call you later when I can talk. Love you."

"I love you too. Bye."

He ended the call and took a slow, deep breath. Then another. Holy fuck, his hands were unsteady on the steering wheel.

He took a couple minutes to get himself together. When he could breathe properly again, he pulled a U-turn and started for home, calling Anaya on the way. He'd promised to get dinner, but he was going to move her somewhere else right now, a random location just in case. Those messages he'd gotten weren't something he could ignore.

Her voicemail picked up immediately, signaling she was likely on another call. Probably with the FBI or Nadia.

His wipers swished back and forth in a soothing rhythm as he drove down the rain-slick streets. Who the fuck had sent him those messages? Callum had reached out to Ember, Boyd's wife, to see if she could trace the number for them. It would save a lot of time if they didn't have to wait for Noah's department or the Feds to do it.

He pulled into his driveway, a sense of gratitude and resolve filling him when he saw the kitchen light on through the front window. Shae was okay and Anaya was safe here waiting for him. Now he would take added measures to ensure she stayed that way.

He put his key in the lock and opened the door, automatically reaching up to punch the code into the alarm keypad as he stepped inside.

There was no warning beep.

He glanced at the display, frowning. There was no red light to signal it had been armed, but he'd definitely armed it before walking out the door earlier. "Anaya?" he called, shrugging out of his leather jacket.

No answer.

He walked down the hall, the house eerily quiet. Her bedroom door was open. No light on inside, and her en suite was dark too. "Anaya?" he called a little louder. Where was she?

He stepped into the kitchen and stopped dead, as if his feet had been suddenly nailed to the floor.

Nick stood in his kitchen with his arm locked around Anaya's throat, his other hand holding a pistol to the side of her head.

Nick smiled at him, his battered face filled with pure hatred. "Hello, Donovan. Welcome home."

TWENTY-ONE

Nick's heart thudded out of control as he locked stares with Myers across the silent kitchen. His hostage dug her nails into his forearm as he held her tight to the front of his body, his left arm locked around her throat.

The hand gripping the pistol pressed to her head shook slightly. He was breathing fast, a little dizzy from the rush of triumph and euphoria flooding his system. After all this time, this was finally happening. He could hardly believe it.

And the look on Myers's face. The blissful moment of beautiful, soul-satisfying shock followed by that flash of horror. "You sent the messages?" Myers said in a low voice, the resentment in his eyes sending another thrill through Nick. He knew he was fucking helpless right now.

"I did, and you fucked up." He backed up a step, taking his hostage with him. "I thought about taking Shae initially, for about five minutes. But even I'm not enough of a monster to do that. And it wouldn't have been the same anyway. *This* isn't the same either, but it's close enough." Myers loved her. It would rip him to shreds to watch her die and not be able to stop it.

"Don't do this."

It was too late for begging, although Nick couldn't deny he was enjoying this part. "I followed you. Watched the two of you together in Seattle. Saw the way you were with her." He upped the pressure on the woman's throat. She made a high-pitched sound and came up higher on her toes, the tips of her nails digging through his shirt sleeve hard enough to draw blood.

The pain only heightened everything. Sharpened his focus.

Myers's expression tightened, his body tensing as if he wanted to attack. But he couldn't do shit. He was unarmed. Had let his guard down when he'd walked into his home just as Nick had hoped, and wouldn't risk jeopardizing the woman's life.

Because he didn't yet understand that she was about to die anyway.

"Let her go," Myers bit out.

"Not a fucking chance," he spat, revved up and ready to see this through to the end. Whatever price he paid for his actions once all was said and done, it would be worth it to make Myers suffer. To avenge Caroline. He was already dead inside. Locking him away in a cell for the rest of his life was nothing.

"Let her go. She has nothing to do with our history."

"She has *everything* to do with it."

Myers shook his head. "She's innocent."

His heart raced, his breathing ragged in his ears. "So was Caroline. It was your job to keep her safe. But you didn't. And she died in fucking *agony* because of your incompetence. So now you're gonna stand there and watch this happen. See how it feels to watch the woman you love die in front of you."

"No," the woman rasped out, trying to shake her head.

"Christ, Nick, let her *go*," Myers said, edging to the right, fists clenching and unclenching.

"Stop right there," he snarled, digging the muzzle of the pistol into the woman's temple. Myers halted, looking like he wanted to rip Nick's throat out. "You think I'm bluffing? You think I won't do it?"

Myers shook his head and slowly raised his hands, palms out. But it wasn't a gesture of surrender. Merely a concession that Nick held the upper hand, and a futile attempt to try to defuse the situation. "This isn't you. Anaya is innocent and killing her won't bring Caroline back."

"Yes, it *is* me!" he screamed, rage blasting through him like a firestorm. Even now, even after Myers had seen the epic downward spiral that Nick's life had become, he still didn't grasp the whole truth of it.

Myers's jaw tightened. "I know you loved her."

The words hit him in a place he hadn't known still existed. The one spot that was still vulnerable to pain.

He stilled for an instant, his voice failing him as a bolt of grief so raw and powerful blindsided him, stole his breath. Caroline's face flashed before him. She was smiling at him. But her smile faded, replaced by horror and distress at what he was doing. That he was about to take an innocent woman's life.

It wasn't her fault, love.

He heard her voice so clearly in his mind.

But it was only in his mind. Because she was dead. He'd watched her die. And though the woman he held now was innocent, she was the instrument he needed to make Myers hurt as much as Nick was.

On the other side of the small table that served as an island in the middle of the kitchen, Myers held his gaze. "It's not too late, Nick. Stop this now and let her go. It's me you want to punish. Let her go. Take me instead."

He sucked in a breath, his vision going hazy for a moment as another wave of raw fury slammed over him. It was too late to stop now. He was past the point of no return, and besides, he'd already killed that man in the driveway. He would go to jail for that regardless of what else happened. Killing this woman, then Myers, serving a life sentence was worth it so long as Myers suffered first.

"When she died, I lost *every*thing," he choked out. "This is who I've become—because of—"

The woman suddenly wrenched her head to the side and viciously sank her teeth into his wrist.

He screamed in mingled pain and fury and shook her off, driving the elbow of his gun hand into her back. She lurched forward and spun away from him, ripping free of his grasp before he could react.

ANAYA WAS CLEAR.

Donovan moved lightning fast, grabbing the edge of the table in front of him and flipped it at Nick. Nick grunted and stumbled back with the force of the impact, his face a mask of rage as he raised the pistol at him.

Donovan dove for the bottom of the upturned table, driving it into Nick's legs. Nick cursed and hit the floor, the pistol still in his hand. A shot went off, burying into the ceiling as Anaya screamed.

Donovan shoved up, thigh muscles bunching in anticipation of vaulting over the edge of the table to take Nick down. But out of the corner of his eye he saw Anaya lunge for the stove. He opened his mouth to shout at her to run, but she'd already grabbed the handles of the pot there and hurled the steaming contents at Nick.

Nick's eyes bulged. He went rigid, screaming as the boiling water scalded his neck, chest and back, his whole body contorting in agony for a moment before he wrenched his arm up to aim the pistol at Anaya.

Donovan dove over the edge of the upturned table, hitting

Nick full force in the side. They hit the tile floor with a teeth-rattling thud. A split second later he sucked in a quick breath as the scalding water puddled on the floor burned his skin. He blocked out the pain, his focus narrowed to disarming Nick.

The tackle had knocked the pistol out of his hand and onto the floor when they hit. Donovan shot a hand up to lock around Nick's wrist. Nick twisted beneath him, teeth bared, swinging his free fist in a vicious uppercut, half of his face an angry red.

Donovan's head snapped back with the blow. Pain sliced through his jaw, the impact momentarily stunning him.

Anaya rushed at them, raising the pot as if she was going to bash in Nick's skull with it.

"No, get back!" he shouted. The weapon was still within Nick's reach. Donovan needed her to get out of range.

She darted back just as Nick wrenched to the side and lunged for the weapon. Donovan pounced on him, pinning his arm in place before he could grab it. But the water made him lose his grip.

Nick ripped away from him just long enough to get the weapon.

Donovan seized Nick's gun wrist, wrenching it back with all his might to strip the weapon from him. Another shot went off. Anaya cried out.

He glanced up to see a hole in the wall inches from his head. "Get outside," he growled at her from between clenched teeth. "Go! Call the cops!"

Nick continued to fight him. Donovan dug his fingers into the space between the tendons in Nick's wrist, crushing nerve against bone.

The weapon hit the tile again. Nick bellowed in fury and turned on him.

Donovan took a punch to the face, Nick's fist smashing into his mouth. He tasted blood, managed to hold onto him and then they were rolling on the floor, sliding through the hot water covering the tiles. One of them knocked the pistol, sent it skidding out of reach.

In the background he could hear Anaya's shaky voice while she spoke to someone, the 911 operator based on what she was saying.

Rage and protectiveness blasted through him as he grappled with Nick. This motherfucker had targeted her and Shae. Had almost just put a bullet in her head in front of him out of revenge.

With all his strength, he wrenched Nick to the side, got Nick under him and rolled to his knees, drew back his fist and put all his power behind it. Nick whipped his head aside at the last moment, avoiding the punch. Donovan's knuckles grazed the edge of his cheek instead, then Nick drove the heel of his hand up, going for Donovan's throat.

He blocked it, lost his balance in the puddle of water and slipped, eyes locked on the pistol in Nick's hand as he fell.

A shot rang out.

Nick stiffened, shock flooding his face as he slumped to the floor with a guttural sound of pain, both hands going to his chest. Blood poured from between his fingers.

Donovan whipped around expecting to see Anaya holding the weapon he kept in his nightstand. But his gaze flew past her to the man filling the doorway behind her instead.

TWENTY-TWO

Standing at the junction of the hallway and the kitchen, Anaya staggered back a step, staring at the back doorway where Jean Luc stood aiming a gun at Donovan.

"No, don't!" she cried, automatically rushing over to place herself in front of Donovan.

"Get down," Donovan barked, shoving her back toward the tipped-over table.

Jean Luc didn't move, his gun trained on the other man, his free hand pressed to his belly. The front of his shirt and pants were saturated with blood. More of it dripped onto the tile at his feet, forming a glistening garnet puddle.

His gun arm shook slightly, his face stamped with determination even though he weaved slightly on his feet. "Take her and go," he rasped out to Donovan in his heavy accent, never taking his eyes off the other man. "Go," he barked.

Donovan cautiously rose to his feet, eyeing Jean Luc warily. He moved slowly, keeping his body between her and Jean Luc, and reached back to grasp her hand. "Go out the side door," he ordered in a low voice, moving her backward.

Petrified, not understanding what in the hell was happening, she turned and ran down the hall as fast as her wobbly legs and bad ankle would allow her. At a low, pained groan, she stole a glance over her shoulder.

Jean Luc slumped in the kitchen doorway. His gun hand lowered as if the weight of the weapon was too heavy to hold up a second longer. Then he dropped to his knees, his whole body jerking when he hit the tile, dragging another agonized cry from him.

She stopped automatically, his pain tearing at her. At the edge of the kitchen, Donovan had stilled too.

On the floor in the corner, the man who had attacked her was weakly trying to turn onto his side. His legs were moving, his teeth bared in an animalistic grimace. "You killed me," he accused, eyes filling with tears as he glared at Jean Luc.

"Payback," Jean Luc gasped out, dropping the gun.

Donovan darted forward and kicked it away out of their reach, then looked back at her, features set. "Go outside and call for an ambulance." He immediately moved to the man he'd been fighting, flipping him onto his stomach, ignoring the tortured scream as he used his belt to secure the wounded man's hands behind him.

Anaya staggered to the door at the end of the hall, fumbled to get her phone out and called for an ambulance through chattering teeth. Donovan had flipped the man onto his back now, and it was clear he was dying. His face was ashen, turning slack while blood pooled around him.

Donovan straddled him, stripping off his own shirt and shoving it against the wound. "How long?" he said to her.

"Fifteen minutes," she answered shakily, surprised her voice was working.

A low, strained groan drew her attention back to Jean Luc. He was trying to get up, his eyes locked on her with a desperation that made her heart clench.

She didn't know what to think at this point. She'd thought he had come to kill her tonight. Instead, he had saved her. Then saved Donovan.

She started toward him without realizing she'd moved, grief twisting inside her. "Why?" she demanded, grasping the trembling hand he held out to her.

Anguish twisted his expression. He started babbling in French, his voice barely above a whisper in between gasps. He was cold. Had lost a lot of blood already, and this final act of protection had cost him dearly.

"I'm sorry," he kept saying. "T-tried to…protect you. Please…believe me…"

Her throat closed up and tears stung her eyes. She had a thousand questions. Wanted to shake him and get every answer she was desperate for. But he was dying. Because he had willingly sacrificed his life to protect her.

She gently laid her fingertips over his mouth to silence him. "Shhh. Don't talk right now. Save your energy. You'll have lots of time to explain everything to me later."

Oh, God, his eyes. So tortured, so full of pain that went far beyond his physical suffering as he gazed up at her. "I'm so sorry." Tears glistened in his dark eyes.

She sniffed as her own tears spilled over. "I know. Don't talk. You need to rest now. Save your strength. The ambulance is coming." She sat beside him and curled up her legs, holding his hand tightly in both of hers. Willing him to hold on.

Vehicles roared up out front. No sirens.

She tensed, then heard a familiar voice. "Myers! Anaya!"

"In here," Donovan called out.

Running footsteps came down the hall. Moments later, Callum appeared with a gun in his hand, Walker and Ryder a step behind him, both of them armed as well. They took in the bloody scene with one sweeping glance, then split up, Callum coming to her while Ryder and Walker went to Donovan and the other guy.

"Walker, grab the first-aid gear from my closet," Donovan said, and Walker raced off to get it.

Callum crouched in front of her, his bearing calm and his eyes full of concern. "Are you all right?"

She managed a nod. Physically she was okay. Mostly. Inside…

No. She wasn't okay.

"This is Jean Luc," she forced out, her voice high and tight. Like a wire stretched too taut and about to snap. The way she felt inside. "H-he saved us." The wail of sirens echoed in the background as she finished.

Callum nodded and glanced at Jean Luc. "We need to get the bleeding stopped."

Walker arrived with the first-aid gear and immediately tore into it, passing Callum supplies and tossing Donovan more. Donovan and Callum both got to work.

Jean Luc's grip on her fingers weakened. She glanced at his face. He was still watching her, his eyes only partially open. And the blood.

There was so much blood. She could smell it now. Warm and sticky. A terrible metallic tang to it.

She swallowed, her gorge rising.

A strong arm curled around her. She blinked up at Walker, who pulled her into his side. "Let's get you outside, darlin'," he said gently.

She shook her head. She couldn't leave Jean Luc. "No, I—" She stopped, realized Jean Luc was already unconscious, his hand lax in hers. Slowly she withdrew hers and allowed Walker to help her up, leaning on him while she balanced her weight on her good foot.

He walked her slowly outside. Slipped a coat around her

while he stood with her on the front porch and the rain fell around them, the sound disappearing under the approaching sirens.

Two police cruisers. Walker updated the deputies, who rushed past them into the house. Then an ambulance arrived minutes after that.

Walker moved her over to the end of the porch and sat her down, draping a big arm around her. She frowned, drawing in a familiar scent that didn't match his. Leather and spice.

Glancing down, she realized Walker had wrapped her up in Donovan's leather jacket.

She choked back a sob. Wonderful as Walker was being, she didn't want him here. She wanted Donovan.

She closed her eyes, struggling to keep her emotions contained. How had things gotten so crazy? What was the connection between Donovan and the man who had kidnapped her?

Her eyes flew open when the paramedics emerged from the house pushing a gurney. Jean Luc was on it. Limp and unmoving. "Is he dead?" she blurted, her entire body tense.

"He's alive," one of them answered, rushing past them toward the ambulance waiting with its rear doors open. "But he's critical. We're taking him in now."

They loaded him inside. She refused to look away for even a single moment, not even to blink, in case this was the last time she saw him.

My father.

The rear doors were slammed shut. Then the ambulance was racing down the driveway, lights and sirens on.

It was the sudden silence that did it. An awful, deafening silence as that ambulance disappeared first from view, and then from hearing.

She pressed the back of one hand to her mouth, her shoulders jerking. She was torn between shock and demanding that someone take her to the hospital so she would know what was going on with Jean Luc.

Walker gave her a little squeeze. "Do you want to go back inside now?"

She shook her head, unable to answer. Unable to articulate what she was thinking and feeling. It was all too much, and she needed—

"*Anaya.*"

A sob burst free at the sound of Donovan's voice. She turned, blindly reaching for him as Walker released her. A heartbeat later he was there, dragging her hard against his chest, one arm coming up to lock around her back, his free hand cradling the back of her head to pull her face into the curve of his neck.

She flung her arms around him and let go, sobbing out her fear, confusion and grief over the father she barely knew and was about to lose.

Donovan drew her closer. "Oh, God, baby, I'm so sorry. So sorry. Shit…"

She barely heard him, too lost in the whirlwind of emotions tearing her apart. Absorbing every ounce of comfort Donovan's secure embrace provided.

"Are you hurt?" He eased her head back to look into her face, worry lines creasing his forehead.

She shook her head and buried her face back into his neck, holding on tight.

"I'm so sorry," he whispered again.

She didn't understand. Sorry for what? That he hadn't been able to prevent this? "The m-man in there," she gasped.

"He's dead." Donovan cradled her to him. "But Jean Luc is still alive, and the surgical team will be waiting for him when he gets to the hospital."

Please let him make it, she prayed to the God of her childhood. He'd never answered her prayers before, but maybe He would this time. Just this once.

But even if Jean Luc somehow survived…

He was going to spend the rest of his life behind bars.

TWENTY-THREE

"Hey, man, you wanna come to my place later?" Travis asked him. "Whit, Groz and my dad are coming over for a barbecue."

"Yeah, that sounds good. What time?" Grady took his backpack out of his locker in the staffroom. It had been another long day but a good one. Three healthy babies and mamas on his shift.

"Seven thirty. Don't bring anything, we've got it covered."

"Groz probably has it covered all on his own," he said with a grin. Groz's appetite was legendary, and he somehow still had the metabolism of an eighteen-year-old. It was bullshit.

Travis laughed. "But he's a greedy bastard. Doesn't share his food well." He grabbed his pager from his belt. "Gotta go. See you."

"Later." He palmed his keys and exited the rear doors to the staff parking lot, breathing in the cool, damp air. His truck was parked over to the side. Partway to it, he stopped when he spotted a familiar figure walking through the rain to the back entrance, white-blond hair trailing out beneath her hood. "Everleigh!"

She spun around, seemed to relax when she saw him coming toward her. "Hey."

He jogged up, urging her out of the rain and beneath the shelter of the overhang. The smile she gave him was forced and brittle. She was pale, with dark shadows beneath her pretty slate blue eyes. "What are you doing here?" he said in exasperation. She should be home in bed with someone there waiting on her 24/7.

"Forgot some stuff I need in my locker the other night. I came to pick it up."

Seriously? "Why didn't you call me? I would have brought it to you."

"It's no big deal." She glanced away.

He didn't ask her how she was doing because that was clear. "Do you have anyone at home to help you out?"

She gave a tiny shake of her head. Winced and put a hand to the back of her neck. Whiplash from the accident, on top of everything else. God, if he could get his hands on the motherfucker responsible. "I'll be okay. My parents are coming up tomorrow for a while."

"That's good. But *please*, if you need something, just call." She had his number.

"I will," she said dully.

"Promise?"

At that, her gaze lifted to his. And the raw vulnerability he read there made every muscle in his body bunch with the need to hold her. Comfort and shelter her, even if only for a few moments. He hated to see her so alone and hurting. "Okay."

That was something at least. "Do you need a ride home? I'll drive you."

"I've got a cab waiting outside already. But thanks."

"I'll grab your stuff for you."

She hesitated a moment, then gave him her lock combo on

her locker. He returned a couple minutes later with her bag of things and a paper cup of green tea. "I put two honeys in it," he said.

The ghost of a smile touched the edges of her lips, but it was so sad it damn near broke his heart. "Thank you." She took it, allowed him to carry her bag and walk her over to the waiting taxi. His insides tightened at the stiff, painful way she moved as she got in. "Thanks again," she murmured.

"Anytime." He meant that. Literally anytime. If she needed something, he would do whatever he could to make it happen. "Take care of yourself, and never hesitate to call. Okay?"

"Okay. Good night."

He stood there watching her drive off, wanting to follow her. But that was a total creeper move and she seemed determined to take care of herself.

He turned and strode for his truck, slowing when an ambulance pulled into the lot, no lights and sirens. He recognized Whit in the passenger seat and walked over to meet him. "Hey, how's it going? Hear you're going to Trav's later."

"Gonna be late," Whit said as he climbed out and headed for the back. "Got a shit ton of paperwork to do now."

"Why, what's up?"

He and his partner opened the back and pulled out the gurney loaded with a body bag. "Double shooting over at Donovan Myers's place."

He blinked. "For real?"

Whit nodded and lowered his end of the gurney to the ground, nodding at the body bag. "Word is, just before this guy died, he confessed to hitting Everleigh the other night."

Grady hissed in a breath, his gaze jerking back to the zipped-up bag. *You motherfucker.* "So he did that *and* attacked Myers?"

"Sounds like. I don't know all the details yet, but that's what Callum said."

Grady shook his head. He was glad the asshole was dead. "Myers okay?"

"Yeah, but his girlfriend's shaken up. Apparently, the other victim is her biological father. He's on the table in the OR right now." Whit and the other guy started wheeling the gurney toward the double doors.

Grady rushed past them to hit the automatic button. "I just saw her."

"Who?"

"Everleigh."

"How is she?"

"Not good."

Whit's face hardened. "Well, at least this is some justice for her, I guess." He rolled the gurney past him. "Tell Trav I'll be there ASAP. And make sure Groz leaves me some damn food for when I get there."

"Will do."

Driving home, his mind was still stuck on Everleigh, and what Whit had said. Yeah, the guy at fault dying tonight was at least some form of justice.

But it was a piss-poor consolation compared to the crushing weight of grief she would carry for the rest of her life.

ANAYA LIMPED TO THE NURSES' station in the Emergency Room, where a pretty nurse with light brown skin, dark curls and sea-green eyes looked up at her. "May I help you?" Her nametag read Molly.

"Yes, I'm Anaya Bishop. There was a patient brought in not

long ago. Jean Luc Dumas. He was taken to surgery. Is he out yet? I'm his daughter." It felt so strange to say it.

"I'll check for you." Molly disappeared down the hall and returned several minutes later with a gentle smile. "He's in recovery."

"So he's alive? He made it through the surgery?"

"Yes. He's still critical, but they'll be moving him to the ICU soon."

She sagged, expelling a long, shuddering breath. The past few hours had been nothing short of a nightmare and she was still in shock. "When can I see him?"

"I'll talk to the nurse in charge, but probably when he's moved upstairs. There's a private waiting room in there. Did you want to go sit there in the meantime?"

"Yes, please."

Molly escorted her up to the waiting room and helped her get settled. "Can I get you anything?"

"No, I'm fine, but thank you."

"No, you're not, and I understand," Molly said kindly, squeezing her hand. "Is there someone you can call to come sit with you while you wait?"

"I'm okay for now. Just need some time to ground myself." Nadia had argued with her, wanting to come here. But Anaya only wanted Donovan. And since he couldn't be here with her until they released him from the interviews, she would use this quiet time after the storm to try and recharge her depleted mental energy reserves.

"I get it." Molly released her hand and left the room.

Anaya leaned her head back against the wall, closing her eyes. She was exhausted and numb inside. The police had separated her and Donovan soon after they arrived, and she hadn't seen him since. Then the FBI had gotten involved. She'd done another round of interviews with them, the entire time begging them for information on Jean Luc. Finally, Noah had shown up and offered to bring her here.

The man who had held her at gunpoint was dead, but she didn't know his name. Still didn't know what had happened or about the connection between him and Donovan. All she knew was that someone named Caroline had died, the man had loved her, and he blamed Donovan.

She must have dozed, because the next thing she knew her head jerked upright as the door opened. A middle-aged nurse stood there. "You're Anaya?"

"Yes."

"Your father is in his room now. He's awake, but very weak. You can see him, but only for ten minutes, and only if the visit doesn't cause him stress."

"I understand." She followed the woman down the hall.

Jean Luc was plugged into all kinds of machines, looking heartbreakingly frail in the hospital bed. She sat next to him, reached out to take his hand. His eyes fluttered open, slowly focusing on her. "Anaya," he whispered.

She forced a smile. "Hi. Are you in any pain?"

He grimaced. "*Non. Pas mal.*" He upped the pressure on her fingers, his expression turning desperate. "I'm sorry. You must believe me."

"I do." She swallowed, sifted through all the things she wanted to say. "Why did you follow me here and break into my hotel room?"

Shame flickered over his face. He grimaced and lowered his gaze, as though unable to look at her. "There was a man. He came to my work in Seattle and started asking about you."

"What man?"

Her insides turned cold as he described Riggs to a tee. "What did he do?"

"Threatened to have my immigration status revoked if I didn't do what he wanted."

Her heart began to pound. "Which was?"

He pulled in a shallow breath, grimaced again. "Plant some files from a thumb drive onto your computer."

Oh my God. "What kind of files?"

"I don't know, I didn't see them. But I couldn't do it." He shook his head, torment written into every line of his face. "It was wrong. I didn't want to hurt you. But he is a powerful lawyer with connections. When I got into your room, I panicked. So I took what I could find to get enough money to run."

"I see." It was all starting to make sense now. He hadn't come to hurt or kill her at all, but because he'd felt backed into a corner and had no choice.

"I didn't know what else to do," he choked out, a spasm of pain crossing his face as he laid his free hand on the blanket covering his abdomen.

"Please, don't upset yourself. You need to rest—"

"*Non*, I need to tell you," he insisted, his fingers clenching hers. "He kept threatening me. So I stayed close, thinking of doing what he said. But then I saw that other man following you. I had to protect you. I was never there to protect you when you were little, and by God I was going to protect you now." His voice shook with his sincerity, tears gleaming in his eyes. "But I was too late."

She hitched in a breath, tears blurring her vision. "You sacrificed yourself to try and save me."

"It's the least I could do for you." He sagged against the pillow, looking tired and aged beyond his years. "I'm not a good man. But I wanted to do this one good thing for you." His gaze roamed over her face, the raw emotion there gutting her. "My daughter…"

"I'm sorry," she whispered, wanting to drive her fist into Riggs's handsome, arrogant face. How dare he. How fucking *dare* he. He'd harassed her, embarrassed and threatened her, and now had taken her father away from her.

She would *destroy* him for this.

"*Non, ma chère,*" Jean Luc said. "I'm the one who is sorry. Please forgive me."

Anaya nodded, not trusting her voice. Her feelings toward him were so confusing, but she couldn't shake the sense of loyalty. He was her blood, and he had almost died to protect her. She loved him for that alone.

She wiped the heel of her free hand under her eyes. "Just rest now. You need to sleep."

"Not yet." He turned his head slightly and reached a hand toward the pile of things on the bedside table. "Can you…"

She got up and went to the table.

"In my jeans pocket."

She checked each pocket. Sucked in a breath when her fingers met two objects. One foreign, the other endearingly familiar.

A thumb drive. And her mother's cross pendant. "You didn't sell it," she whispered, overcome. Even as desperate as he was for money to escape Riggs, he'd held onto this, knowing what it meant to her.

"I remember your mother wearing it," he said weakly. He held out his hand. She placed the cross in it and he beckoned for her to come closer.

Anaya came back around the bed and leaned in to let him place it around her neck, helping him with the clasp.

"She was a good woman," Jean Luc said as Anaya straightened, holding the pendant to her skin. "Very beautiful. You remind me so much of her." His weary smile almost broke her heart as he took her hand again. "You are the best of both of us,

Anaya. And while I know I'm not the man you hoped I'd be, always remember that I couldn't be prouder of the woman you've become in spite of where you came from—" He winced, coughed, and his whole face twisted in agony.

Anaya shot to her feet and rushed to the door to call the nurse. The woman hurried toward her, announcing that the visit was over.

Anaya stood outside the room, a tidal wave of grief crashing over her, her mother's cross once again hanging around her neck.

She didn't even remember getting in the elevator.

In the lobby, she stepped out. Looked up. A soft cry ripped from her when she saw Donovan coming through the front entrance.

He spotted her immediately and broke into a run.

She took a stumbling step toward him. He caught her, his warm, strong arms engulfing her just as the world crumbled around her.

TWENTY-FOUR

No punishment could have been worse than knowing he was the cause of Anaya's pain.

Donovan held her close, trying to comfort her while her tears sliced him open inside. "He's stable?" he murmured. He'd been frantic to get to her, but the Feds had kept him for hours going over everything.

She hitched in a breath and shook her head. "I d-dunno. He was so w-weak, and then…" She shuddered.

Resolve hardened inside him, diamond hard. He'd done this. Dropped his fucking guard yet again when her safety was at risk. She'd almost paid the price with her life, and now Jean Luc was upstairs fighting for his.

Sick with guilt and self-loathing, Donovan waited until she'd calmed more before scooping her up in his arms and starting for the entrance. "Let's get you outta here."

A light wind gusted over them when the automatic doors whooshed open, carrying the rain with it. He hurried for his vehicle, hunching over her to shield her. Once she was belted in, he got behind the wheel and pulled out of his parking spot, a dark, toxic mix of emotions churning inside him. "I'm taking you to Nadia and Callum's—"

"No."

At the steel in her tone, he looked over at her in surprise. "You need your family around you right now."

She looked him dead in the eye. "No. I need *you*, Donovan."

He inhaled, hands clenching tight on the wheel. To know that even after everything she had gone through, even though this was all on him, she still wanted him—it shredded him. "I'm the last fucking thing you need," he said bitterly.

"What's that supposed to mean?"

Tell her. Man up and fucking tell *her, you sorry piece of shit.*

She didn't look away. "Who was that guy?"

He stared at the road because he couldn't meet her gaze, and set his jaw. He'd wanted to wait to talk about this until she was more settled and had time to decompress. But she deserved to know, and she would still be leaving in less than twelve hours anyway. The Feds wanted her home until they could wrap up their investigation and ensure there were no other threats to her safety.

Might as well get it all off his chest now.

"I was head of his fiancée's protective detail back when I was a US Marshal. She was the star witness in a high-profile murder case involving a mob hitman in Dallas. On the first day she was supposed to testify, we took her to the courthouse. There was no parking garage, so we had to use the back entrance to the building to get her inside. We'd already swept the courthouse early that morning and had eyes on the surrounding buildings. But it wasn't enough. A hitman used a nearby roof and shot her with an armor-piercing round while she was in the back of our vehicle. She died that night."

When Anaya didn't say anything, he drew a deep breath and kept going. Dreading the moment when she recoiled from and rejected him, yet relieved she would finally know the truth. "I was placed on leave during the investigation. There were no criminal charges brought against me or my team, but the fact remains that Caroline died because I dropped my guard. Nick got in touch with me a few months after I left the Marshals Service. I should have cut contact immediately, but I felt responsible. I met up with him a couple times a year after that. He'd been spiraling lately."

"Is that how he knew you were in Seattle this time?"

He nodded once. "We met on Sunday just before you called asking me to take you to the museum."

"So it was him behind the wheel of that truck?" she said sharply.

"Probably, and then again, the other night on Front Street. The FBI will be looking into all of that."

Anaya was silent for a long, tense minute. "So he's blamed you for her death this entire time, and has been plotting his revenge."

"Not until recently, after the depression and addiction took hold of him. But yes." He swallowed, his heart thudding. "And I'm sorry." It was such a pathetic fucking apology in light of all that had happened.

Anaya turned her head and stared at him. "This wasn't your fault."

"Yes, it fucking *was*," he snapped. "He almost killed you tonight in front of me—" His throat closed up.

She laid a hand on his forearm, her touch gentle but it still made him flinch. "Donovan…"

He shook his head, refusing to look at her. Hating himself more than ever. "It's *all* my fault. Once again, I didn't see the threat in time. I crossed the line with you, then dropped my goddamn guard, and you almost died because of it." Fuck. Fuck, fuck, fuck…

"No, stop," she said in distress, her hand sliding up to grip his shoulder.

He barely kept from throwing her hand off. He didn't deserve comfort, or sympathy, or forgiveness. And he sure as shit didn't deserve *her*. "I fucked up," he croaked. That was his superpower. Fucking up, especially with people he cared about.

"There's no way you could have seen what was happening," she argued. "Not even the sheriff's department or the FBI saw it. So you can't blame yourself for this."

Had she not heard a fucking word he'd said? "He targeted you because of *me*."

"He was angry and crazy and wanted to hurt you as much as he was hurting. And then you risked your life to save me. You're conveniently leaving that part out. You're not superhuman, and you can't see everything."

He shook his head rigidly. It was too soon for her to know what she was feeling. In time she would see the truth. Then she'd hate him. And he would deserve it.

He clamped his jaw shut and sat there stiffly until she finally removed her hand from his shoulder. The rest of the trip to Callum and Nadia's was spent in silence, giving him plenty more time to loathe himself.

The lights in the house were on when he pulled into the driveway. Nadia raced out to embrace her sister. Callum stood in the doorway waiting for them. The women went straight through to the living room. Callum eyed him in concern. "You okay, man?"

He forced a nod, even though he was anything but okay. Then he met Anaya's gaze across the room, and it felt like he was being torn in half. Even after all this chaos and pain, he selfishly still wanted to walk over there and wrap himself around her so tight that she would never leave him. "I should go," he muttered.

Callum glanced to Anaya, then back at him, frowning. "I think you better stay, man," he said in a low voice.

Donovan stood there, unable to tear his eyes off her. He needed to walk away. Right now, for her sake. But his feet refused to move.

I need you, Donovan.

His heart twisted. God, he needed her too. Had never needed anyone this badly. Maybe it was because they were both jacked up on emotion and the adrenaline lash that came with staring death in the face. Maybe it was all heightened by the knowledge that she was leaving tomorrow.

An invisible spike drove deep into his chest, suddenly making it hard to breathe.

"Come sit down," Callum said to him. "You look like you need a drink."

Nadia took Anaya down to the basement suite to shower and change. Callum sat him on the sofa and poured him a scotch. Donovan downed it in two swallows, craving even the tiny bit of numbness it might bring.

"So Jean Luc's gonna make it?" Callum asked after a few minutes.

"Looks like. They'll be taking him into custody as soon as he's released."

"And Riggs?"

"They're going to bring him in for questioning. Not sure if they'll be able to get enough evidence to pin anything on him."

Callum shook his head in disgust. "And you know his rich family's gonna make sure they don't."

"Pretty much."

They sat in silence while the gentle patter of rain on the roof filled the room. Nadia appeared at the top of the stairs to the lower suite. "Anaya's waiting for you. I put out some of Callum's stuff for you to change into, and there's a new toothbrush in the bathroom drawer." She caught Callum's hand on the way by, tugging him to his feet. "See you guys in the morning."

Donovan sat there alone as their bedroom door shut down the hall, listening to the rain as the scotch spread its warmth through his belly. He still felt raw inside. Couldn't let go of the guilt. But now his mind was preoccupied by the woman waiting for him downstairs.

And by what would happen when he went to her.

With purposeful strides, he walked the length of the hall and descended the stairs to the suite. He walked in and shut the door behind him, his heart drumming against his ribs, need and anticipation humming throughout his body.

A soft light came from the bedroom. Anaya sat on the edge of the wide bed, watching him, her dark curls damp and tumbling around her shoulders and the long pink sleep shirt she wore. Her ankle was wrapped in a tensor bandage. There were scrapes on her elbows, and the side of her face was swelling.

The need to take her, claim her, pulsed inside him. He forced it back and knelt in front of her, gently cupped the back of her head while he eased a thumb over the swelling on her cheekbone. He wished he had the power to take away all the hurt. Would never forgive himself for all she'd suffered because of his failures.

"I shouldn't be here," he murmured. "I told myself to walk away, but I can't. I *can't*."

Her hands came up to frame his face, those beautiful dark eyes searching his for a moment before she touched her lips to his.

And he was lost.

. . .

ANAYA COULD FEEL his anguish as she cradled his face and gently brushed her lips over his, feathering kisses across the Steri-Strip on his lower one. His hand bunched in her hair, his jaw rigid. She looked up into his eyes, caught her breath at the raging need she read there.

He curled his hand around the back of her neck and brought his mouth down on hers, heedless of the pain it must have caused him. Desire flashed through her, hot and intense. She wound her arms around his wide shoulders, groaned when he crushed her to him and licked into her mouth, sending sparks of fire racing to her gut.

She could feel his urgency, the pain buried inside him as he rained kisses all over her face before laying her flat on her back and coming down on top of her, wrapping one hand around her calf above her sore ankle to steady it. That show of consideration and protection turned her inside out. His powerful sense of duty and responsibility was one of the things she most admired about him.

But it also anguished him when things went wrong, leaving him blaming himself.

"I want to see you," she whispered, sliding her hands under his shirt over hot, smooth skin. She was desperate to touch him all over.

He came up on his knees to peel it over his head, revealing the muscular, contoured landscape she'd been fantasizing about for weeks. Arousal shot through her, building to a fever pitch as she ran her hands over him while he undid his jeans and shoved the denim down his thighs, along with his underwear.

No more thinking. There was only this moment. Only them.

His erection stood hard against his belly. She curled her fingers around him, heat and power flowing through her at his low groan. Sitting up, she stroked him, feathering her thumb around the crown, her mouth busy kissing and licking his chest.

His hand bunched in her hair once more, then he gathered the material of her nightie across her shoulder blades and tugged it upward. She raised her arms, allowed him to pull it over her head and toss it aside, then went back to exploring his sexy, ripped body with her hands and mouth.

Seconds later he pushed her backward, pinning her shoulders to the bed while he straddled her thighs and raked his searing green gaze over the length of her naked body. Her nipples tightened, sending a rush of heat and wetness between her legs. Donovan's big hands slid up her rib cage, palms curving around her breasts as he leaned down to take a puckered nipple into his mouth.

Pleasure engulfed her. She grabbed hold of him, one hand gripping his hair, her legs curling around his waist. Her sore ankle made it awkward but she no longer cared, could barely feel the pain now, totally focused on the heat of his mouth and the wicked stroke of his tongue across her sensitive flesh.

She turned to liquid, moving under him like a wave as he moved down her body and settled his face between her thighs, melting under the erotic caress of his tongue. She sank deep into it, into this moment and the pleasure he offered, pushing away all the fear and the ugliness. Everything else disappeared until there was only him and the burning need he'd ignited in her.

Already she could feel her body tensing, release gathering deep inside, her breathing growing shallow as he pushed her to the peak. She reached blindly toward the bedside table, grabbed the condom.

"Hurry," she gasped out, tearing it open and handing it to him. She couldn't wait a moment longer. Needed him inside her this instant. Was dying for that most intimate connection with him with every fiber of her being.

Donovan sheathed himself and stretched out on top of her,

bracing his weight on one forearm. She wrapped her limbs around him, lifting her hips while he guided his cock into her. Then, holding her gaze, he braced both hands on either side of her head and thrust forward, burying himself deep.

Her cry was muffled by his mouth, his tongue sliding along hers while he rode her with steady, firm strokes, the intense friction, the sudden fullness awakening millions of hidden nerve endings. She flattened one hand on the small of his back and widened her thighs, allowing her the right angle to rub her tight, swollen clit against his body with each rocking glide of their hips.

Donovan growled into her mouth and slid an arm under her hips, anchoring her to him. Adding to the friction, making the pleasure expand even further. His scent surrounded her, dark and masculine, his body hitting every aching sweet spot with each controlled surge of his hips. He made her feel safe and wanted and adored, his care for her pleasure allowing her to let go completely.

Her muscles tightened around him, ecstasy spiraling up, up until she shattered, crying out her release. He kept her locked to him, prolonged the lovely warm waves of ecstasy by holding his rhythm steady. Only when they began to fade and she melted back against the sheets did he plunge both hands in her hair, fists squeezing tight as he rode her harder. Faster.

He was the most beautiful thing she'd ever seen.

She held him close, nipping and licking at the curve of his shoulder, thighs locked around his hips. She could feel how close he was now, wanted to push him over the edge.

He seemed to grow even harder inside her, his breathing rough and unsteady against her temple before he drove deep one last time and threw his head back. She stared up at him, drinking in every detail. Every muscle within view standing out in sharp relief, his face a mask of sensual agony while he let go, his throttled roar from behind clenched teeth sending a thrill shooting through her.

Gradually his body relaxed. His head dropped forward, coming to rest beside hers on the pillow, warm breaths gusting against her temple. He buried his lips there, pressing a long, slow kiss to her skin, his weight slowly blanketing her once more.

She sighed in blissful contentment, gliding a hand down the length of his bare back, the skin damp over the deep ridges of muscle lining either side of his spine. He was the ultimate weighted blanket. Protecting her. Warming and cocooning her. Sheltering her from the rest of the world, blocking out everything but him.

"So good," she whispered, still coming back to earth. She'd always enjoyed sex, but this had gone way beyond the physical, and Donovan put every other lover she'd had to shame.

She'd never felt this way about anyone else. Had never felt totally free and safe enough to let herself go completely. To surrender her body and soul.

Only with him.

He kissed her temple again, nuzzled her. Shifted to brush his lips over the swelling bruise on her cheek, then skimming down to her mouth. His tongue glided over her lower lip, dipped inside gently to touch hers.

He sucked at her bottom lip, nipped it lightly. Raising his head, he stared down into her eyes for a long moment before bending back down to press a warm, lingering kiss to the center of her forehead. The tenderness and feeling behind it speaking more clearly than any words could have.

Her heart squeezed, a rise of emotion clogging her chest.

His strong arms slid beneath her, and he rolled them onto their sides so that she was facing him. Pulling her close to his chest, he cradled the back of her head in one hand to keep her close and drew the covers over them, reaching back to turn off the lamp.

They lay there in the darkness without speaking while their breathing slowed. Anaya curled into his warmth, absorbing the precious sense of belonging and security she felt in his arms. All too aware of the time slipping away between them, mere hours now before she would be driving to the airport and going back to the other side of the country without him.

A hundred questions crowded her mind, the sudden rise of anxiety corroding the lovely haze she'd been drifting in. What happened now? This couldn't be the end for them. Not after the way he'd just made love to her. Was he willing to at least try a long-distance relationship?

His breathing deepened. The arm around her back grew heavy. Twitched slightly.

He was asleep. She didn't have the heart to wake him. After what he'd been through, he needed the rest.

And besides, she might not like the answers she got.

TWENTY-FIVE

Perched on a stool at the kitchen island with Nadia the next morning, Anaya's heart jumped when someone knocked on the front door. Callum went over to answer it, and her hopes fell when she saw Walker and Shae standing there.

"Morning," Walker said, looking past Callum at her and Nadia.

"Hey, come on in," Callum said.

Shae walked over and gave her a sympathetic smile. "Hey, you." She held out her arms for a hug. "You okay?"

Anaya returned the embrace, glad to see her. "Yes." Battered in heart and soul more than body. Waking up alone had been hard. "You?"

"Yeah, I'm fine." Shae pulled back, her green eyes full of concern. "Is Donovan not here? He didn't answer when I messaged him a little while ago."

"No," she said stiffly. "He left hours ago, before the sun came up." She vaguely remembered him kissing her on the forehead and whispering for her to go back to sleep. There'd been no word from him since and he hadn't responded to her messages.

Beneath the hurt, anger bubbled up. He'd made her feel like she was the center of his universe when he'd made love to her last night, then again when she'd reached for him in the middle of the night. So where was he now? She was leaving in a few hours, and it felt like her heart was in a vise.

Shae winced. "Oh." She looked at Walker, who frowned. "Well, I'm…sure he'll be back soon."

Anaya would bet her mother's necklace that he wouldn't, but she wasn't going to broadcast how devastated and angry she felt. "I'm sure he's got his hands full dealing with everything right now. Anyway, look at you and this outfit! Love the hair too. You use the wand I made you buy?"

"Yes," Shae said with a grin, then sat at the island and chatted to her and Nadia, feeding Ferhana bits of cereal and fruit as she tried to lighten the mood.

Anaya's phone rang on the counter, cutting through her thoughts. She grabbed it, hoping against hope that it was Donovan calling with some logical explanation for leaving her bed in the middle of the night. Like maybe he'd gone home to check on the evidence gathering or cleanup and hadn't wanted to wake her.

But it wasn't Donovan.

Staring at the word Mom on screen, her stomach sank along with her heart. *Not now.* She didn't have the energy.

Walker came over. "Not him?"

"No."

He laid a hand on her shoulder. "Give him time to come around—or pull his head out of his ass, whichever comes first."

She snorted, more anger building. "I don't have time, I'm already down to my last few hours here." Was he seriously going to do this? Make last night their final goodbye and leave without talking things out? The cowardice of it stunned her.

"I know. They're anxious to get you home." He squeezed

her shoulder gently. "Shae, you stay here and visit for a while longer. I'll be back in a bit."

"Where are you going?" Shae asked in surprise.

"Got a few errands to run." He kissed the top of her head, then reached out to ruffle Ferhana's dark curls, earning a giant toothy grin.

Anaya's gaze trailed after him as he stopped and spoke in low tones to Callum, then left. She tried to focus on Shae, Nadia and Ferhana, but her mind was preoccupied and the ache in her heart was unbearable.

She'd been about to hand her heart over to Donovan, and he'd walked away when she needed him most.

DONOVAN'S ARMS TREMBLED, his sweaty face suffused with blood as he strained to complete another rep with the bench press bar. He planned to keep going until his tired, burning muscles gave out. After that…

Shit, he didn't know what came after that. He'd been going over everything in his head for hours now. He knew what he wanted. But he had to think of what was best for Anaya here.

Above the thump of the bass coming through the gym speakers he heard the steel security door clang open and paused to glance over. Then swallowed a groan when he saw Walker stride in.

Walker came over into his line of sight, folded his arms as he leaned against the leg press machine to study him.

"Don't even start," Donovan growled above the music, face set, eyes focused on the ceiling as he shoved the weighted bar upward from his chest.

"Well, this is a damn sight better than finding you at the

bottom of a bottle first thing in the morning, but what the *hell* are you doing here right now?"

"Thinking," he bit out, straining through the next lift. His arms were numb, shoulders and chest screaming, his palms and fingers raw and blistered from the punishing workout. He welcomed the pain. The mindless oblivion the resulting exhaustion would eventually bring.

"How long you been here?" Walker asked, his drawl doing nothing to soften the disapproval in his tone.

"Dunno." He'd come here because he'd known the place would be empty, and because he'd needed an outlet to burn off at least some of what was going on inside him. It was either that or explode.

"Is it helping?"

"Fuck no." The memory of walking into his kitchen and finding Nick holding Anaya at gunpoint haunted him like his own personal demon. That sickening look of terror on her face.

And he was equally haunted by the memory of her face just before he'd left her this morning. Serene in sleep, curled against him so trustingly in spite of all the damage he'd caused, only hours before she would be ripped out of his life. Fuck.

"Yeah, didn't think so." Walker stood there watching him push himself to his limit, until Donovan couldn't lock his elbows at the top of the next press.

His arms shook, threatened to give out and drop the heavy weighted bar across his chest, potentially breaking his ribs.

"Okay, that's enough." Walker stalked over to grab the bar from above.

Donovan glared up at him, panting, his arms trembling as much as his hot, sweaty face.

Walker pulled the bar from his exhausted grip and set it in the top of the rack with a clang.

Donovan sat up, glaring harder. "I wasn't done."

"Yeah, man, you were." He strode over and shut off the music, plunging the room into sudden silence broken only by Donovan's uneven breaths.

"What do you want?" he said, tired all the way to his soul.

"Came to talk to you."

"Fine, so talk," he muttered, dragging a towel over his face. His shirt was soaked through, sticking to his chest and back.

"Okay." Walker leaned back against the wall and regarded him coolly. Scrutinizing him with that superhuman brain of his that never stopped. "You're a fucking idiot."

Walker's deep southern drawl did nothing to blunt the verbal shot, but Donovan was too weary to argue. "Nice. I appreciate that."

Walker cocked his head, watching him with that fucking irritating, assessing way of a guy who'd spent the bulk of his career in the gray realm of intelligence. "Look, I dunno what the hell's going on between you and Anaya, but cutting and running on her after everything that just happened? Jesus, Don, that's a new low, gotta tell ya."

He glanced away, his fists knotting in the towel. Walker was right. It was a new low. "She's better off without me. And she's leaving in a few hours anyway." Going back to her safe, familiar life where she belonged, far away from him and the chaos he seemed to bring everyone he cared about.

Walker rubbed a hand over his jaw and gave a short sigh. "All right, well, this conversation is long fucking overdue, so might as well have this out here and now." He dragged a stool over and parked his ass on it a few feet away, folding his arms to stare hard at him. "What are you doing?"

He so wasn't doing this. Not with Walker. "Leave it alone, man."

"Not this time." Walker's deep blue gaze stayed locked with his, giving Donovan the merest hint of what it must be like to be on the other side of the interrogation room from him. He pitied the poor bastards Walker had dealt with. "You're crazy about her."

Stay the hell out of my personal life, he wanted to snarl. But yeah, he was fucking gone over Anaya. That was the whole problem. "So?"

"So when's the last time that actually happened?"

Donovan lifted a shoulder, refusing to even go there. It didn't matter what he felt for her. That he was fucking dying inside at the thought of losing her. "Dunno."

"Then I'll help you out—never. At least not since I've known you."

"Yeah, and there's a good goddamn reason for that," he snapped back.

"Okay, *now* we're getting somewhere." Walker unfolded his arms and leaned forward, resting his forearms on his knees. "You're selling both of you short by making assumptions that you're not good enough for her—and by making decisions on her behalf without talking to her."

He clenched his jaw, hating every second of this. After a lot of soul-searching, he'd already made the difficult decision to do some therapy and try to work through his shit. That was a big step for him, one he wasn't looking forward to. And he sure as hell wasn't going to tell Walker.

"Think, Don. Think long and hard and carefully about *why* you're doing this and whether it actually makes sense."

He shoved up from the bench, his tired body tensing. Suddenly he was spoiling for a fight. He'd never wanted to hit Walker before, but he was damn close right now. "I don't *want* to think. Don't you get it? I'm fucking well aware of what's going on."

"Good, then explain it to me so I understand."

He clenched his jaw, mind whirling, something wild and

frantic beating at the inside of his chest that made his heart race and his breathing shorten. "Drop it."

"No. You're way too fucking hard on yourself. What happened to Caroline Rothschild wasn't your fault. As for the other? It's been damn near twenty years since you and Jillian were together, and you're still beating yourself up about that on the daily." Walker raised a black eyebrow. "If you walk away from Anaya now because of the toxic bullshit need to punish yourself for the rest of your life, you'll never get over it."

Denial rose swift and hot, the pain twisting inside him until he could barely breathe. But Walker was dead on. "You think I *want* to let her go? I have to, because *I'm* the toxic one. Look what happened with Jillian and Shae, and now the whole fucking nightmare Anaya went through."

"Shae loves you, dickhead. She's not holding a grudge against you. You're the only one doing that."

He shook his head, horrified as a rush of tears flooded his eyes. He choked them back, refusing to lose his shit in front of the guy he secretly worshipped—the guy who was ten times the man he'd ever be. "I can't weigh Anaya down. She deserves better than me."

"That's bullshit, unless you *plan* on letting her down."

He opened his mouth to say something, slammed his jaw shut just before a choked sound could squeeze out of his tight throat. Of course he wouldn't let her down on purpose. But it just kept fucking happening over and over again no matter how hard he tried to make things right.

Walker's hard expression softened slightly. But there was no pity in his gaze, thank fuck. Donovan couldn't have handled that. No, the look in Walker's eyes was closer to hope. More like, *Come on, man, you're almost there. I know you can do this.*

"It's time for you to stop punishing yourself for what

happened," he said quietly, the words hitting Donovan deep inside. That's exactly what he'd been doing. Punishing himself for past mistakes. "You're not that man anymore, and you can't go back and change what happened. Any of it."

He knew that. Hence the decision to finally seek professional help and see if it did anything. He didn't deserve Anaya until he did something about the mental baggage he'd been carrying around.

"What's done is done," Walker continued. "Now you have a chance to have everything you ever wanted but were too afraid to hope for. You deserve to be happy, Don. So choose wisely, man. Otherwise, you're gonna die alone with a shitload of regrets." He stood, clapped Donovan on the shoulder once and walked out of the gym.

Donovan shoved out a heavy sigh, closing his eyes. As far as conversations between them went, that was one hell of a mic drop.

Did he deserve to be happy? He didn't know. But he knew how he felt about Anaya, and that wasn't going to change after she got on that plane this afternoon.

She'd said she needed him. He needed her too. And the thought of causing her any more pain was like a knife driving into his guts.

He stood and strode for the shower, his heart thudding hard against his ribs. God help him, damaged as he was, he couldn't let her go. But for the first time in forever, he felt a faint spark of hope that maybe it wasn't too late for him after all.

If she would forgive him for being a gutless dumbass.

TWENTY-SIX

"Are you sure you don't want us to come to the airport?" Nadia asked, her face anxious.

"Yes. I'm barely keeping it together as it is," Anaya answered, holding Ferhana and giving her a big smile. She was holding her shit together pretty well so far, but if she had to go through an emotional and public goodbye at the airport on top of everything else she was currently coping with, it was going to be waterworks central for sure. She just wanted to be home, where she could process everything in private.

Nadia rubbed her back in sympathy. "Okay. But you'll be back soon. Or we'll come out there. And we're only a phone call away."

She blinked fast, a sheen of tears blurring her eyes. "You're not helping, hon."

"Sorry. Ah, hell." Nadia wrapped her arms around her, engulfing her and Ferhana in a giant hug.

"Oh, shit," Anaya choked, then cringed. "Sorry, Ferhana. Don't say that word. Auntie is bad. *Bad* Auntie."

"Nay," Ferhana crooned, leaning her curly little head on Anaya's shoulder as if trying to comfort her.

That did it.

The floodgates opened. Anaya bit her lip, thrust Ferhana at her sister and then made an awkward run for the upstairs powder room in her walking boot, bypassing a bewildered Callum on the way.

Inside she took a few long, shuddering breaths, ordering herself to get it together. She was entitled to cry. She'd been through a lot of scary, emotional shit the past few days. But that's not why she was crying.

It was Donovan she was crying over, and that just pissed her off. How the hell had she become this hung up on him in such a short time? Especially when he was so shut down emotionally and had never made any promises to her?

A long-term relationship wouldn't work between them. He'd also made it clear he didn't want to be a father again. She desperately wanted to be a mother, so that was an insurmountable hurdle for her.

Logic didn't help the situation, however. She felt how she felt, whether there was a reasonable explanation or not. Even though he'd left her feeling abandoned yet again. For some reason she kept choosing men who did that to her. She needed to figure out why and prevent it from ever happening again.

When the worst had passed, she forced herself to suck it up, splashed cold water on her face and dried off, looking in the mirror. She winced. The bruise on her cheek was swelling and showing purple under her dark skin tone, and the little eye makeup she'd put on after her shower was now pretty much ruined.

Oh well. All in all, she looked not too bad for someone who had been held at gunpoint and nearly killed last night. Jean Luc was stable, at least. The doctor had called to tell her this morning, and the FBI was bringing Riggs in for questioning, since his harassment and intimidation against her had crossed state lines. She had turned in the thumb drive he'd given Jean Luc.

Nadia, Ferhana and Callum were all waiting for her when she came out of the powder room, watching her in concern. "I'm better now," she told them, putting on another smile. "Guess I needed that."

"You ready to get going?" Callum asked.

"Yep." Might as well stop putting off the inevitable and leave now. She hugged her sister, kissed Ferhana's plump little cheek. "See you guys soon, okay? I'll call when I land. Dad's picking me up. He insisted."

Callum went ahead of her, grabbed her bags and carried them out the front door. Nadia followed her with Ferhana. On the front steps, Anaya stopped dead when she saw Donovan's SUV coming down the street.

Her heart swelled, a painful tide of hope rising before she could squash it. The SUV turned into the driveway. Donovan stepped out in his leather jacket, said something to Callum before his gaze cut to her.

She couldn't move, suddenly rooted to the spot. Why was he here? She couldn't take any more hurt or disappointment.

"We were just leaving for the airport. Where've you been?" Callum asked him with an annoyed frown.

Donovan held her gaze. "I'll take her."

Callum glanced back at her, raising his eyebrows in question.

"It's fine," she said, lifting her chin. "I'll go with him." She wanted answers. Closure. It was the only way she was going to be able to get over him—eventually. The two-hour trip to Portland would give them plenty of time to hash things out. And since he was driving, he couldn't avoid her.

Nadia put a hand on her back. "Are you sure?" she murmured.

"Yes." This was happening.

She turned and gave her sister and niece one last hug. "Bye. Love you guys."

"We love you too."

Callum and Donovan loaded her bags into the back of Donovan's vehicle. She paused to hug Callum goodbye, then got in the front seat, on edge and ready to blast him.

"Need anything on the way out of town?" Donovan asked as he steered down the driveway, as if everything was normal.

"No, I'm good." It was unfair how sexy he looked, the scents of leather and spice bringing back so many vivid, erotic images from last night.

His hands holding her in place while he went down on her. Pinning her beneath his weight as he pushed into her, staring into her eyes the whole time. Making her feel on a level she'd never felt with anyone else—and then essentially ditching her.

She waited until the house was out of view before getting down to it. "So where were you?"

He didn't look at her. "Had some things to take care of, and then I had another meeting with the FBI at my place."

What *things*? "I messaged you and called twice."

"I know. I'm sorry."

Oh no. Not nearly good enough. "Sorry for what?" She wanted him to spell it out exactly.

He drew a deep breath, shifting his grip on the wheel. Clearly uncomfortable, but too fucking bad. She'd almost died last night. Had opened her heart to him completely in that bed later. She deserved to know exactly what was going on and where they stood. "I shouldn't have left you like that," he said.

"No," she agreed tautly, hiding her surprise that he wasn't trying to dodge it and glad he was owning it. "So why did you?"

His jaw flexed. "I needed to sort some things out."

Yeah, she'd figured. But she wasn't letting him off the hook he'd hung himself on. "What kind of things?"

"Nick," he answered, staring at the road again. "You. Me. Us. How he never would have targeted you if it weren't for me."

"I already told you, you couldn't have known—"

"Just…wait. Okay? Let me get this out."

She closed her mouth and tamped down her impatience, willing to at least hear him out. Understanding that talking about any of this was hard for him, and that he was trying.

"I kept thinking of all the things I've screwed up in my life. The relationships I've ruined, and that you've been through too much already without me making your life worse." She opened her mouth to argue but he held up a hand and continued. "I don't think I'll ever not blame myself for what happened to you last night. I'm thankful you don't hate my guts."

"Of course I don't hate your guts." She was pissed as hell that he'd taken off earlier.

"Thank you, but I…" He stopped, pulled the vehicle over to the side of the road, put it in park and turned in his seat to face her. Jaw rigid. Green eyes burning. "Don't go."

She blinked, unsure she'd heard him right. "What?"

"I don't want you to go."

She stared at him, stunned into silence. She hadn't expected this. Not even close. "What?" she repeated, feeling like an idiot.

"Stay here. With me. We'll go away together somewhere for a while. Spend more time together doing normal and fun things, get to know each other without all the danger and drama and bullshit."

The hope was back, flooding her chest until she could hardly breathe. He was asking her to allow him time for her to get to know him. The real him. But she was afraid to trust this sudden change of heart. Especially after he'd essentially ghosted her. "Why? What's changed?"

"Everything."

His expression was so earnest it tugged at the softest, most vulnerable part of her heart. *Nope. Don't you dare cave.* "You're going to have to elaborate on that one." She wasn't going to entertain this unless he did an epic goddamn grovel and spilled his guts here and now.

"I've been doing a lot of hard thinking since I left you alone in that bed, and I regret leaving in the first place." He reached out to cup her cheek in his hand, his long fingers sliding into the curls at her temple and shoved out a breath. "I'm sorry. For everything. For putting you in danger, and for making you feel alone this morning. I would never hurt you on purpose. Never."

Dammit, she would *not* cry right now. "Then why did you leave?"

He swallowed. "I'm…damaged," he said, his tortured expression making it clear how much the admission cost him. "But I'm going to try to change that. I've already talked to Mia —Groz's girlfriend—and she's hooked me up with a therapist she thinks will be a good fit for me. I need to do that for myself, but also because I don't want to lose you. I want a future with you."

She caught her breath, the raw emotion in his voice and eyes making her heart clench.

"I care about you more than I've cared about anyone besides Shae. You're sweet and smart and loving. I want you until I can't fucking see straight, let alone think. You make me smile. You make me want things I've never…" He trailed off.

"Never what?" she whispered, heart hammering at her ribs.

"Things I never thought I deserved," he finished quietly.

Oh, Donovan. The pain buried in his words had her fighting

not to throw her arms around him. To hold him and show him he *was* worthy of being loved. "What things?" she said instead.

His thumb moved across her cheek, light as a sigh, his green eyes full of an intensity she'd never seen in him before. "Happiness," he answered. "Someone to share my life with."

Ohhhh... She bit her lower lip, her throat tightening. No, she hadn't expected any of this, or for him to be so open and honest with her. She understood how hard it was for him to say all this aloud to her, knowing she might reject him.

"I don't want to lose you," he repeated.

She shook her head, struggling to take it all in. "Even though my life is back east, and yours is here?"

"Get a transfer."

She laughed, then sobered when she studied his face. "You're serious."

He nodded, holding her stare. "Or I'll move back east."

She shook her head. "You moved here to be close to Shae. I would never ask you to leave her. But I can't stay," she said helplessly. "The FBI want me back home for now until everything is settled with the Riggs situation."

"Then we'll do the long-distance thing until it is. That'll give me time to work on myself more before we take the next step."

She leaned into his hand, excitement and joy beginning to fizz inside her like expensive champagne. "What's the next step?"

"You moving here. Into my place. Your stuff in my closet and you in my bed beside me every night."

A smile spread across her face, her heart fluttering. "That's not moving a bit fast for a guy who up until a few hours ago didn't even want to be in a relationship?"

"No," he said, his tone certain. "I know what I want, and that's you. I also know I'm far from perfect. But I'm going to do better. All I'm asking is for you to give me—us—a chance." His hand tightened on her cheek. "Please. I'll do whatever it takes to make this work. You just tell me what you need."

Anaya took his face in her hands, a sense of certainty overtaking her. Ten minutes ago, she'd been in a dark, lonely place facing the painful aftermath on her own. Now she had a chance at forging something real and lasting with him, and she was taking it. "It's not complicated, Donovan. All I need is you."

He groaned and pulled her to him, holding her tight to his chest. "So that's a yes? We're giving this a shot?"

"Yes," she answered, wrapping her arms around him and closing her eyes.

No matter what happened now, they were going to make this work and find their way back to each other.

TWENTY-SEVEN

Three months later

Anaya folded the ends of the final corner of the wrapping paper and secured it to the box with her last piece of tape. "Operation Christmas complete," she said to herself, hopping up from her kitchen table to place the box in the bottom of her carryon.

The past few days had been a complete whirlwind as she'd raced to get through her to-do list. She'd been so busy, trying to sort out the chaos and put the past to rest.

Jean Luc was in prison awaiting trial for the double murder in Chicago. If his lawyer could get the jury to agree it had been self-defense, his sentence would be far lighter.

As for Anthony Riggs, the FBI had built a case against him using the flash drive he'd given Jean Luc. It contained falsified files that made it look like she had been trying to leak corporate financials and other sensitive documents to a competitor. He'd wanted to frame her, destroy her reputation and career. Now he was the one facing ruin and possible jail time.

Merry Christmas to her.

She was in the bathroom grabbing the last of her toiletries when her phone rang. She glanced at it, sighed when she saw it was her mom returning her call. They'd been playing phone tag all day. Now she was in a rush and didn't feel like talking to her, but... It was her mom, and they weren't going to be spending the holiday together. Which was a relief, to be honest.

"Hi, Mom," she answered.

"Hi. What are you up to?"

"Just packing. Have to leave for the airport shortly, so I can't talk long."

A loaded pause followed, and Anaya braced for the coming confrontation. "Where are you going?"

She wasn't going to lie just to prevent an argument. Not ever again. "Oregon."

"Mmhm," her mother grunted, those two syllables managing to hold a wealth of bitterness and accusation. "So you'll be spending Christmas with Nadia then."

"Yes." She refused to feel guilty about that.

"And your father too, I guess?"

"Yes."

"Well, how nice for you," she said in a clipped voice. "I guess I shouldn't be surprised. You've made it clear you'd rather spend time with him than me."

Anaya dropped her chin to her chest, suppressing a growl of frustration. God, she was so sick of this shit. Of her mother's constant insecurities. Her bitterness, the emotional manipulation, guilt trips and general toxicity.

It was an exhausting broken record. Her mother was mentally unwell and had been her whole life. Those things had all become crystal clear to Anaya now that she had a good therapist and a tight circle of people around her who truly loved her.

"He wanted to spend Ferhana's first Christmas with her."

She didn't know why she even said it. She didn't owe her mother explanations, especially not to justify her father's actions. "Anyway, when does Jason fly in?" she asked to redirect the conversation. Sometimes it worked and staved off more conflict.

At this point, she and Jason were pretty much the only ones who had any kind of relationship with their mother. Between her mother's difficult personality and the unwanted, increasingly radical political and social views she kept spewing at everyone, she'd alienated herself from most of her children, family and friends, and yet seemed bewildered and wounded by everyone "deserting" her.

"Tomorrow night," her mom said, her tone making sure her hurt was loud and clear. "Well, tell Nadia I said hello and give her a big hug. I probably won't even get so much as a text from her on Christmas."

And who's fault is that? She bit the words back, annoyed that she kept allowing her mom to trigger her with her manipulation. Anaya refused to play that game anymore. "I will. Hope you and Jason have a great time together," she said brightly, refusing to be baited. She wasn't responsible for her mother. Was no longer willing to run interference for her.

"Yeah," she said in that same flat, accusatory tone that never failed to grate on her nerves. "Merry Christmas."

Okay, time to end this convo. "Merry Christmas. Thanks for calling, love you."

A sniffle signaled she was on the verge of tears. "Love you too." Her voice cracked on the last word. "You believe that, don't you?"

"Yes." In her own way, her mom loved her. "Bye."

Anaya ended the call and tucked her phone away, letting out a breath and a load of tension with it. It wasn't her fault that her mother was lonely and felt cut off from the rest of the family.

Her mother's behavior was never going to change, so the best she could do was limit her exposure to it. But she didn't have to deal with it anymore for now, and had way happier things to look forward to.

Back in the kitchen, she was just tucking her laptop into her carryon when she heard a vehicle pull up out front of her townhouse. Joy leapt inside her as she hurried to the door and pulled it open. Her father was already inside the gate and coming up the walkway.

His hard features softened with a big smile, a festive red and green scarf wrapped around his neck. "There's my girl. You ready to roll?"

"Ready." When he reached the doorstep, she flung her arms around him, squeezing him hard. "I'm so excited. I don't think I've ever been this excited before in my entire life." She was dying to surprise Donovan. She missed him so damn much she ached inside. It had been almost five weeks since they'd seen each other.

His rough chuckle stirred the hair at her temple. "I'm excited too. Now." He let her go, reached past her for her suitcase. "Let's get to the airport so I can see my granddaughter."

∼

"WHAT DO YOU THINK? Should I go get another set of lights?" Donovan stepped back, hands on hips as he eyed the artificial tree he'd dragged down from the attic an hour ago. "Looks kinda bare to me."

"That's because we haven't put everything else on it yet," Shae answered, busy taking ornaments out of the packaging. They'd already made two trips to the Christmas shop on Front Street to stock up on ornaments and garland. "I think it looks great."

"You were right about the multicolor lights. Definitely the way to go."

"Yep." She moved the white pompom at the end of her red velvet Santa hat to the front of her head and stood, hands full of sparkly silver garland. "Okay, you start winding this end from the top, and I'll follow you around the tree to make sure it doesn't get tangled." She passed him one end of it. "I can't believe this is the first time you've put up a tree since we last spent Christmas together."

Six years ago. "Didn't have anyone to spend it with, so I didn't see the point in putting one up."

"That's just sad," she said in a heartbroken tone.

He shrugged. "Doesn't matter, but I'm glad you're here now." They shared a grin, and he began winding the garland around the tree.

It was the same one he'd bought when she was a little girl. The years he'd been Stateside she would usually spend Christmas Eve at his place, or at least a day somewhere in the Christmas holidays. He'd kept it all these years, dragging it with him every time he moved even though he rarely put it up, because of the memories associated with it. Shae loved this tree.

She was really damn particular about the way the garland went on. He had to stop and fix it a half dozen times before she was satisfied with it, then they started on the ornaments. When it was done, they both stood back to admire their work.

"It's gorgeous. Maybe our best effort ever." She glanced at him. "You feeling any more in the holiday spirit yet?"

"Yeah, super festive," he said with another shrug. Christmas hadn't meant much to him outside of the years he got to spend it with her.

"Good. You're not quite Ebenezer Scrooge level, but you've been pretty miserable lately."

"Have I?"

"Yes."

She wasn't wrong. He missed Anaya like hell, had been looking forward to spending Christmas with her and Shae together, but she'd been called to an emergency work thing in New York until next week. All their phone calls and texts and video chats weren't good enough. He was so desperate to see her, he'd considered showing up there to surprise her, but had decided against it because he didn't want to be a distraction while she was working.

"How's this?" he asked, putting on a giant smile.

Shae eyed him, expression deadpan. "A little terrifying, if I'm gonna be honest." Then she laughed, gave him a playful shove and wandered toward the kitchen. "You want some hot cocoa?"

"Only if it's got booze in it."

"I'll allow it."

He was cleaning up boxes when the doorbell rang.

"Oh!" Shae cried, abandoning the pot on the stove and rushing for the door. "It must be the gift I ordered you. I was worried it wasn't going to get here in time. Don't look," she ordered, pausing with her hand on the knob.

"I won't." He turned his back to the door and kept tidying up as she opened it.

"Yay, it *is* your Christmas present!" she said excitedly.

"I'm not looking."

"Well, that's disappointing," a familiar female voice said.

He whipped around, gaped at Anaya standing inside the door with her arm around Shae.

He dumped what was in his hand and ran over to grab her, hauling her tight to his chest and crushing her to him. He'd better not be fucking dreaming. "Oh my God," he blurted, burying his face in her hair. "Oh my God, you're really here."

"Surprise," she and Shae said at the same time.

Grinning like an idiot, a little choked up, he straightened to take her face in his hands, drinking in the sight of her for a moment before capturing her mouth in an ecstatic kiss.

She laughed against his lips while Shae made a coughing sound. He broke their kiss to look at his daughter. "So this was a setup?"

"Kind of, yeah. We both planned it." She beamed at them.

"Thank you," he said, his damn voice a little rough.

"You're welcome. Love you. Now I've got to, uh, go do some…errands or something." Shae grabbed her car keys—she'd finally gotten her license—winked, then walked out, shutting the front door behind her.

Donovan couldn't wipe the smile from his face as he turned back to Anaya. "I can't believe you're really here. I've missed you so damn much." He kissed her again. And again. And again, walking her backward until she tipped onto the couch with a giggle. He came down on top of her, pouring everything he had into another kiss.

Jesus, what this woman did to him. He'd been insane to think he could ever live without her.

Before he totally lost his head, he paused and braced himself on his forearms to stare down at her. She was so fucking beautiful, those big brown eyes gazing up at him with joy, trust, and…

He swallowed, heart pounding against his ribs. Being apart for most of these past few months had been agonizing. Seeing her only twice over that whole time was torture when she owned his fucking heart.

"I love you," he told her, his chest feeling like it was about to explode. He'd been waiting to tell her in person. This first time had to be in person.

Her eyes widened slightly, then a huge smile broke across her face. "I love you too. Merry Christmas."

Donovan groaned and sank into another kiss. She giggled again, pushing at his shoulder. "I just flew across the country to surprise you. Are we seriously going to make out on your couch like horny teenagers?"

He captured a few curls between his fingers, tugged lightly. "That's exactly what you turn me into." Then he grew serious, possessiveness and determination roaring through him. He didn't want to be separated from her again. "Don't go back after the holidays. Stay here with me. Or I'll move back with you."

She made a little humming noise and raised an eyebrow. "Moving in together, huh?"

"Yes."

"Hmm. I'll think about it." There was a teasing light in her eyes. She'd already told him she loved it here, that she wanted to live close to Nadia and Ferhana, and that her company would allow her to work remotely and commute to Seattle when necessary.

"Need more convincing?"

She stroked his hair, the love in her eyes melting him inside. "No. I'd love to move in with you."

He scooped her up, smothering her laughter with more kisses, almost tripping over his own feet as he headed to the stairs.

They made it to the first landing before he lost his will and pressed her full length against the wall, rubbing his erection against her core, drinking in the soft, erotic little mewl she made. It had been too fucking long since he'd been inside her. Since he'd last thrust into her slick heat and watched her eyes go all hazy, her expression turning desperate while he rode her nice and slow.

"Oh God, we can't," she panted against his lips.

He stilled. Can't? "Why not?"

"Because my—"

The doorbell pealed again. Donovan dropped his forehead against the side of her neck with a defeated groan. "Who the hell's *that*?" he growled.

"My dad."

He lifted his head to stare down at her, incredulous. "Your *dad*?"

Her eyes sparkled with laughter. "Yep. I told him to wait in the car for a few minutes after I went inside. He came to spend Christmas with Nadia and me. And you, hopefully. Shae and Walker too."

He grinned, ridiculously tickled by the idea. "One big weird-ass family."

"Oh, trust me, it's a way less weird family than mine." She looped her arms around him, holding him close. "This is going to be the best Christmas ever. Now go let my father in and say hello."

Donovan disentangled himself from her and went to answer the door. Frank Bishop stood there wearing a hard expression. "Donovan," he said in a tone like granite.

"Sir." He held out a hand. "Good to see you again."

Frank grunted and shook it firmly before lowering his hand. "So, what are your intentions toward my daughter?"

"I'm going to marry her." He wanted it all with Anaya. Wanted everything he'd denied himself before. This was his chance. His shot at redemption and a future, and he was taking it.

Behind him, Anaya gasped. He glanced back at her, saw the stunned look on her face that transformed into a delighted smile. "Is that right?" she asked in a saucy voice.

"That's exactly right," he answered. He'd been thinking about it for weeks now, and his mind was made up.

Therapy was fucking hard, uncomfortable work, but it was helping. He was slowly starting to forgive himself for his past failings, and was even warming to the idea of being a dad again. He and Anaya had talked about it a few times and he knew how important that piece was to her. She would be an incredible mother, and he'd missed out on so much the first time around. When he'd brought the possibility up with Shae, she'd seemed excited and totally on board with potentially being a big sister.

Yeah, he wanted it all with Anaya.

He turned back to Frank, relief sliding through him when the big man's face cracked into a grin. "I was just givin' you a hard time," Frank said. "But that's mighty good to hear, son." He pulled Donovan into a hug, slapped his back a couple times while Anaya watched them with pure adoration in her eyes.

Four hours later they were gathered around Callum and Nadia's living room—including Shae and Walker. Ferhana was like a tiny whirlwind flying around the house, amped up on sugar from all the treats and her new captive audience.

Donovan watched Anaya interact with the others. Her smile and easy, genuine affection. The way she doted on and melted for Ferhana. It was so damn easy to picture her holding a baby of their own, and the image filled him with another surge of love for her.

The sisters exchanged presents. Nadia handed Anaya an envelope with a bow on it, practically dancing with excitement. "Oh my God, open it. I can't stand it a second longer."

Laughing softly, Anaya did. She pulled out the papers inside, frowned. But as she read, her expression shifted to shock, then she darted a look at her sister. "Are you *serious*?"

Nadia covered her mouth with her hands, nodding. "We found your birth mother."

What? Donovan got up and crossed to Anaya, sliding an

arm around her as he read over her shoulder. Holy shit, they *had* found her.

"Who's we?" Anaya asked, a hand pressed to her chest.

"Ivy and me. With a little help from her sister, Amber."

Anaya shook her head in wonder and looked up at him. "She's alive, in Haiti." More tears flooded her eyes. "Will you take me to go see her?"

Her request, her complete trust in him, knitted some jagged parts deep inside him back together again. "Yeah, of course I will." There was nothing he wouldn't do for her.

"Crap, now I'm crying again," she whispered, wiping at her eyes.

He chuckled and pulled her close, rubbing her back while the others all watched them with happy smiles. Ferhana charged over and wrapped her arms around Anaya's legs, saying, "Nay-a."

Anaya laughed and scooped her up, holding her in one arm as she leaned into him, then pulled away and reached for her sister. "Thank you."

Nadia kissed her cheek and hugged her. "Merry Christmas, Nay."

"Best Christmas ever," Anaya murmured.

Donovan agreed. He had never felt so at peace and full of excitement as he did at this moment, watching Anaya while Shae grinned at her like an idiot from the couch.

Everything was finally right in his world. And the future was brighter than he'd ever imagined it could be.

EPILOGUE

Haiti
Three months later

Anaya pressed a hand to her stomach to quell the hot ball of anxiety burning there and reread the message she had composed an hour earlier. She'd rewritten it a dozen times already, wanting to make sure it said *exactly* what she wanted it to.

This was the only way for her to do this.

A phone call was out of the question, and a letter or email explaining her decision was pointless. She didn't need to justify her decision, and her mother would never accept her reasons anyway. No, her mother would rant and rail and accuse Anaya of being cold and ungrateful, cry about how hurt she was, and how she couldn't believe Anaya would ever do this to her.

When in truth her mother had only herself to blame for what was about to happen.

Their last interaction two days ago had been the final straw. Upset that Anaya wanted to reestablish contact with her birth mother, her mom had piled on the guilt about how *she* was Anaya's mother.

How could you do this after all I've done for you? Out of all the children in the orphanage, I chose you. *And this is how you treat me?*

That was something Anaya could never forgive. Her mother had pulled that card out of her back pocket countless times over the years, with Nadia as well.

On top of this latest meltdown, her mother had then spewed hateful words about how violent and dangerous Haitians were —when Anaya was herself Haitian. Using Jean Luc's crimes as evidence, and warning that Anaya's birth mother might have criminal friends try to capture her and ransom her for money when Anaya met up with her.

Anything to try and stop her from going through with this.

It had sickened and infuriated her. She'd sat on it ever since, making sure she thought everything through carefully before doing anything drastic. And had finally decided that she was done. She had forgiven her mother countless times for past transgressions and given her a thousand chances to get help and do better. But her mother refused to change. Almost every time they talked it twisted Anaya into a knot…and *hurt* her.

No more.

Sensing movement behind her, she glanced over her shoulder to find her new husband coming in through the door of the vacation rental they were staying at. They'd eloped eight days ago on the beach at a private resort in the Dominican with just Nadia, Callum, Ferhana, Anaya's dad, Walker and Shae in attendance.

It had been perfect. No fuss. No stress.

Until her mother had found out from one of Anaya's siblings and freaked, resulting in their final confrontation.

Donovan took one look at her and came straight over, frowning in concern. "What's wrong?"

There were too many emotions roiling inside her to answer, but he knew everything that had happened, and the toll it had taken on her. She held up her phone instead.

Donovan scanned it, winced and immediately sat beside her, placing his big hands on her thighs as he searched her eyes. "You sure?" he asked quietly.

She nodded, her throat too tight to speak. Terrible as this decision was, she had no choice now. It had been a long time coming, and she'd allowed this toxic cycle to continue for too long by maintaining a relationship with her mother. It was time to protect herself.

She wanted peace. Needed it desperately. And without taking this drastic step, that would never be possible. She loved her mother. But for her own well-being, Anaya had to let her go.

She read the message again, grateful for Donovan's strong, steady presence and support. Anaya had already blocked her mom on social media and email. As soon as she sent this message, she would block her phone number too.

But holy shit, this was hard. Even though she knew it was what she needed to do.

"Have I thought this through enough?" she asked. The sounds of traffic and people selling their wares on the street below drifted up through the open window, a warm breeze making the gauzy white curtains billow on either side. Palm trees rustled gently.

"Yes," he answered without hesitation. "You did everything possible to make it work and hung in there as long as you could. Probably too long."

"I did," she agreed. It was true. But taking this step had such a terrifying ring of finality to it.

The guilt was crushing.

She cringed at the pain she knew it would cause her mom and dreaded the coming fallout from one of her aunts and several siblings. She wasn't worried about Nadia's reaction, though. Nadia would have her back one hundred percent on this.

A queasy sensation rippled through her stomach as she read the message one final time. It was purposely short and to the point. Clear, concise without being accusatory or giving justification, yet as kind as she could make it.

That was important. She needed to be able to walk away without anger, bitterness or cruelty. Because this was something she was going to have to live with for the rest of her life.

I'm sorry it's come to this, but I have made the decision not to have any further contact with you. Sending love and best wishes, and I hope you can find happiness in your life.

Goodbye, Mom.

Anaya

Donovan slid his palm up and down her bare thigh, lending his silent support. God, this was hard. But she'd made up her mind. On the other side of this, once she'd grieved for the relationship that had never existed, there was the potential for healing and peace.

Do it. Get it over with.

Drawing in a shaky breath, she let it out slowly, then steeled herself and hit send. As soon as it went through, she blocked her mother's number and set the phone aside, then leaned forward to rest her head in her hands.

Guilt tore at her along with a sense of disbelief, but more than anything, there was also a massive wave of relief. That was almost worse than the guilt.

Donovan gathered her close without a word and wrapped his big arms around her. Holding her, holding this space for her while she leaned into his strength, drained. *I'm sorry, Mom. You gave me no choice.*

There were no tears. Maybe there would be later. Right now, there was too much numbness.

She soaked up the comfort Donovan offered, twining her arms around his back and listening to the sound of his heartbeat mixing with the noise of the city outside the apartment. She loved him with every piece of her heart.

Finally, she sat up, twisting to face him fully. The late morning sunlight coming through the window slanted across his face, making his green eyes glow like emeralds. "I did the right thing, right?"

"Yes." He cupped her cheek in one hand, leaned forward to brush a kiss across her mouth.

His quiet certainty helped quell her anxiety a bit. "Okay." Later tonight if she had the energy she would call and tell Nadia. Right now, she had somewhere really important to be. "I guess we should get going."

"You ready for this right now?"

"Yes." She'd been looking forward to this since Nadia had given her the paperwork at Christmas. It was time for new beginnings. She squeezed his hand. "Thank you for being here."

One side of his mouth lifted, his eyes so full of love it almost made her tear up. "I'll always be here for you."

Oh, damn. "I love you."

"Love you back, sweetheart."

She blinked fast against the sudden sting of tears, cleared her throat as she stood and smoothed her hands down the front of her knee-length turquoise dress with little red rosebuds on it. "Let's do this."

The sure grip of his hand around hers filled her with much needed security as he led her through the narrow, crowded streets of the capital. With him beside her, there was no fear, no concern for their safety. Only anticipation and a building excitement that made her heart pound when they got closer to the market.

She could hear it just around the corner out of view, a mix of voices and music, the rich scent of spices filling her with a thousand bittersweet memories from her childhood. They turned right at the end of the narrow, cobbled street and the market square lay ahead of them, a vivid riot of color with all the clothing and produce for sale.

Anaya scanned the various stalls they passed. Her gaze caught on a woman standing with her back to them. She stopped, her breath hitching.

The middle-aged woman's dark hair was pulled back in a thick braid that was liberally streaked with silver. She was scanning the market anxiously, looking for someone, twisting her hands in front of her.

Anaya's heart beat faster, her hand tightening on Donovan's as she angled them toward the woman and finally caught sight of her profile. She swallowed. "*Maman?*"

The woman whipped around. Her eyes widened, a cry wrenching from her. She rushed at Anaya, arms outstretched, face twisting.

Anaya caught her, arms coming around her mother's thin frame as a thousand different emotions swamped her. For so long she had wondered if maybe her mother hadn't really loved her. Wondered whether her mother had missed her.

But her reaction now told Anaya everything she'd ever wanted to know. And the fierce embrace, the way those thin, wiry arms trembled as her mother held her and cried, were the proof.

Her mother let loose with a litany of French as they clung to each other, telling her how glad she was to see her, how much she'd missed her, how she'd fervently prayed that Anaya had been adopted by a kind family and had a better life, and how many times she'd longed for this moment.

Anaya soaked in every sweet word, each one a soothing balm to the unhealed wound she'd carried since the day her mother had taken her to the orphanage.

Her mother eased back slightly and touched the pendant around Anaya's neck with trembling fingers. "You kept it," she whispered, face streaked with tears.

"Yes," she whispered back, her own throat tight.

With a choked sound her mother embraced her again. "My sweet, brave girl…"

Anaya opened swimming eyes to look at Donovan, smiling through her tears. He was grinning from ear to ear as he captured the whole reunion with his phone, his pleasure in her joy clear.

Holding her mother as she looked at her husband, suddenly she knew. All the way to her bones.

She was loved. Had always been loved.

And always would be.

—The End—

*read Grady and Everleigh's story next in *Final Shot*!*

Dear reader,

Thank you for reading ***Protective Impulse***. If you'd like to stay in touch with me and be the first to learn about new releases you can:

• Join my newsletter at: http://kayleacross.com/v2/newsletter/
 • Find me on Facebook: https://www.facebook.com/KayleaCrossAuthor/
 • Follow me on Twitter: https://twitter.com/kayleacross
 • Follow me on Instagram: https://www.instagram.com/kaylea_cross_author/

Also, please consider leaving a review at your favorite online book retailer. It helps other readers discover new books.

Happy reading,
Kaylea

FINAL SHOT
CRIMSON POINT PROTECTORS SERIES

By Kaylea Cross
Copyright © 2023 Kaylea Cross

CHAPTER 1

A cold, damp wind carrying the scent of the sea rushed through the helo's open bay doors, buffeting the Blackhawk as the crew moved in closer to circle the target below. The large freezer trawler that had been caught in a sudden squall, almost capsizing the vessel and damaging the engine. One of the crew had sustained critical injuries while on deck when a rogue wave had hit.

Seated just to the side of the door, Grady reached up and grabbed hold of a strap to steady himself as he scanned the area below, his buddy and fellow PJ Groz crouched behind him, and their team leader Travis poised on the other side of the doorway. The vessel was too far out for the Coast Guard, so their Air National Guard unit had received the call.

A layer of thick, heavy gray cloud stretched overhead, disappearing into the horizon. Down below, the water was a roiling mass of white-capped waves pushing the stricken vessel along. It was mid-June, but the weather sure didn't know it. Last night's storm had dropped the temperature and brought fall-like conditions to the Pacific Northwest.

Two crewmen wearing bright orange overalls were out on

deck, waving their arms. The engineer and rest of the crew were below deck working to restore power to get them underway again.

Grady shifted his weight as the helo's crew chief moved in behind him, speaking over the intercom in their helmets. "Injured crewman's on a spine board in the wheelhouse. He's conscious, breathing on his own, but he's in a lot of pain. Possible spinal injuries in addition to a compound fracture of the lower leg. Likely broken ribs, possible internal injuries. The pilots are going to move into a hover and let you guys rope down."

"Roger that," Travis said. "How are we on fuel?"

"You'll have twenty minutes to get the patient on board."

That was tight. In these conditions, really tight, but Travis nodded. "I'll go down first," he said to them. "Grady, you're with me. Groz, you stay here for now. The patient's a big guy. We're gonna need some extra muscle to get him on board."

"Got it," Groz said, and shifted back out of the way to give them more room while Grady and Trav grabbed their gear. He was a beast, the biggest guy in the unit, with an appetite to match. A bottomless pit when it came to food, and they never passed up an opportunity to give him a hard time about it.

The pilots circled once more and began to descend, moving closer and closer to the deck of the rocking vessel, making sure to keep well clear of the nets and other equipment sticking up from the vessel. When they were in place the crew chief checked the LZ one last time before throwing the nylon fast rope out the helo door and signaling Travis.

Travis got himself in position and slid down to the deck. Just before he touched down, a big wave hit the vessel broadside, tilting it sharply to the side. Travis slipped on the deck but managed to catch himself, then held the end of the rope and signaled for Grady to come down.

Gripping the rope tight with his gloves, Grady slipped out the side of the helo, wound the insteps of his boots around the rope, and let it slide through his gloved hands as he dropped toward the deck. He was six feet from touching down when the boat suddenly dipped into a deep trough.

He squeezed the rope hard to halt his decent and hung there while Travis kept hold of the loose end. Grady glanced up. The rotor wash and wind whipped salt spray into his face, coating his goggles. He looked back down, kept his gaze trained on the deck to time his landing, and as soon as it began to rise, slid down the rest of the way.

An instant before his boots met the deck, another big wave shoved the boat violently upward at an angle.

His left foot slipped sideways on the deck. He gritted his teeth and sucked in a breath as something sharp popped in his knee under the sudden, abrupt force of the rising deck.

Pain shot through it, buckling his leg. He caught himself with his hands just before he crashed to the deck, clenched his jaw and forced himself upright, keeping most of his weight off his left knee that still felt like someone had just driven an icepick through the side of it.

Not good. Not fucking good at all.

He'd had knee injuries before. It was impossible to do this job, do the kind of training and missions they did without incurring wear and tear on your body and joints.

This was different. The pain was sharper and more intense, and his knee was already stiffening up.

He concealed his limp as best he could as he followed Travis through the spray from the waves across the wet, shifting deck to where the crewmembers were ushering them toward the wheelhouse. With every step pain stabbed through his knee, making his leg unstable. Trying to keep his balance on the pitching deck made it even worse.

"Mendoza," Travis said from the wheelhouse doorway, waving him over.

Grady hustled across the slippery, rocking deck, fighting to ignore the pain. It didn't matter if he was injured. The patient waiting inside that room was way worse off. They had to get him stabilized and get him on board that helo ASAP.

That Others May Live. It wasn't just a motto. It was a solemn vow, one that he and every other PJ lived and breathed.

The two crewmen stepped aside to flank the wheelhouse door as Grady entered. The captain and medical officer were kneeling on the steel floor beside the patient. Both men looked up at him and Travis with grim expressions.

"His name's Dave," the captain said, looking at them anxiously.

Travis knelt on one side of Dave while Grady slowly went to his good knee on the man's other side and shrugged out of his med ruck. Their patient was conscious but not alert, obviously in shock. "Hi, Dave. Can you hear me?" Travis said, leaning over him.

Dave's bleary, heavy-lidded eyes focused on them, but he didn't respond, his breathing raspy under the oxygen mask the crew had put on him, his chest and large abdomen exposed by his open shirt. Dave was a big boy all right. Leaving Groz on board to load him had been a good move.

"The rogue wave slammed him into the railing," the captain said. "He started screaming that he'd broken his back, then the boat rolled, and he hit the starboard wall and busted his leg."

Grady completed his visual sweep while the captain spoke. The crew had done a decent job of immobilizing Dave with a spine board and tried to splint his leg to keep it steady. But from the angle of Dave's foot, both tibia and fibula were fractured halfway down. They'd cut away the leg of his waterproof overalls. The fracture was closed, at least.

Travis immediately began doing his own assessment, pulling out a penlight to check Dave's pupils. "How old is he?"

"Thirty-seven."

Travis got on the radio to Groz and the pilots while Grady quickly pulled out a stethoscope and blood pressure cuff to take Dave's BP. "Thirty-seven-year-old male, conscious and somewhat alert. GCS twelve. BP..." Travis glanced at Grady.

"Eighty-five over fifty," he answered, undoing the Velcro cuff from around Dave's upper arm. Low. Definitely a sign of shock, but there could be internal injuries as well.

Travis repeated the info and kept going, palpating Dave's neck, spine, chest and abdomen. Dave grimaced and let out a strangled cry when Travis palpated the region around his left kidney. Could be one of his ribs had fractured and hit it.

"Start a line," Travis said to Grady.

Grady immediately prepped a vein in Dave's forearm and started an IV, his knee pulsing with its own heartbeat the entire time. If there was internal bleeding, they needed to keep Dave's blood volume up on the flight back.

Together he and Travis assessed the lower leg fracture, stabilized the limb better and secured Dave to the spine board along with a cervical collar while Travis stayed in contact with the helo the whole time, alerting the others that they were ready to transport.

Grady administered some ketamine to keep Dave's pain level at a dull roar, packed his gear and grasped the foot of the spine board, mentally bracing for the coming pain.

Travis laid his hand on Dave's shoulder and the man's eyes rolled up to look at him blankly. "We're gonna get you on board the helo now and fly you to a trauma center in Portland. A Coast Guard cutter is on the way to evacuate the rest of your crew. Ready?"

Dave's eyes squeezed shut, his body tensing as if he knew this was gonna hurt.

Travis looked across him at Grady. "On three. One, two, three."

Grady pushed upright. Pain seared through his left knee. He stifled a yell and staggered a step, trying to balance most of his weight on his other foot. Ignoring the look Travis shot him, he clamped his jaw shut as the two of them made their way out of the wheelhouse carrying Dave between them.

Every step was like a knife jabbing into his knee. Waves continued to batter the boat as they crossed the undulating deck. The helo lowered into position above them, the fast rope lashing under the force of the rotor wash. Grady almost groaned in relief when they set Dave down and Travis waved at Groz and the crew chief.

They lowered the basket. Travis caught it, settled it on the deck while the pilots fought to keep a bit of slack in the cable and keep the basket still under the deck's movements.

Balanced on his good knee, Grady helped Travis hoist Dave onto the litter and secure him, then Travis signaled the helo. The basket slowly lifted off the deck, swung back and forth a bit before stabilizing as it rose toward the open helo door.

Groz was waiting there with the crew chief to muscle their patient inside. Once Dave was secure, they lowered the empty cable back down. Travis nodded at Grady to hook on.

He was conscious of the pounding pulse in his knee as the winch hauled him up through the gusting wind. At the doorway he clenched his back teeth together and climbed inside, more pain slicing through his knee every time it hit the deck of the helo.

Groz was already working on Dave toward the back. Grady immediately crawled over while the crew chief sent the cable back down for Travis.

Their team leader came through the doorway a minute later. "Good to go," Travis said as he unhooked from the cable and shut the door behind him.

The pilots banked in a tight turn and then pulled them skyward to begin the flight back to shore. Pushing his physical discomfort aside, Grady focused on his job, working smoothly and easily with his fellow PJs to stabilize and treat the patient, the exact same as he would with his ICU staff.

But his knee was stiffening by the minute. Within fifteen of leaving the boat he couldn't bend or straighten it more than part way. But there was no time to dwell on it. Dave was in rough shape and his core temp was low. Travis got on the radio to the trauma team in Portland, updating them on Dave's condition. They were already prepping the OR in anticipation of his arrival, and a neurosurgeon was standing by.

Once they reached the trauma center to hand Dave off to the team there, Grady's adrenaline had dropped. Without a patient to focus on, his pain level shot up and he found himself wishing he could have a hit of ketamine to take the edge off.

They spent the short flight to base cleaning up the back of the helo. Grady stayed seated as much as possible, didn't utter a word about what was going on. The patient and the mission were paramount. His injury was what it was, and there would be plenty of time to examine it more closely later.

When they climbed out onto the tarmac in front of the hangar with the Pararescue angel painted on the front, however, there was no way to hide he was hurt. His knee was too swollen and unstable to allow him to do more than limp along beside Groz and Travis.

Travis cut him a sharp look. "You good?" Groz stopped and glanced at him too.

"Yeah." Damn, how bad was it? His heart rate kicked up, concern building.

He got his answer after the mission debriefing when he stripped off to shower. His knee was swollen and stiff, and tender to palpation along the medial joint line. Combined with the inability to bear weight, straighten it completely or bend it more than thirty degrees...

He knew what it was. And that he was fucked.

He wiped a hand over his clammy face, telling himself to calm down. Maybe it wasn't as bad as he feared. Maybe it would resolve with some rest, ice and anti-inflammatories. He would wrap it tight, wear a brace if need be to provide extra support. Whatever it took to get back in the game.

Travis walked in and saw him sitting there in his underwear, his gaze immediately zeroing in on Grady's knee. "How bad?"

Medial collateral ligament damage for sure. From the popping sensation he'd felt, probably meniscus as well. Hopefully not the ACL.

Please not the ACL. That would sideline him for at least nine months to a year—after the wait for major reconstructive surgery. He couldn't afford that if he wanted to make SOST this year.

"Dunno." He prayed it wasn't so bad that he would be sidelined for more than a few weeks. Because if he wasn't healed up by early September...

He shook the thought away, refusing to allow it to take root in his mind. He'd worked toward this tryout for five years. Busted his ass putting in extra hours on base and at the hospital, in addition to all the courses he'd taken to earn his certification. Being sidelined by a serious injury now, being unable to go through selection after everything he'd done to prepare would gut him.

Travis met his gaze, blue eyes assessing. "Bill Reinhart isn't working tonight. Want me to call him? I can drive you to see him, get you answers tonight."

Reinhart was former Army and one of the most respected orthopedic surgeons in the region. Grady and Travis both knew him from working at the hospital. "Thanks, but not yet. I want to talk to someone else first." Someone he trusted and hadn't seen in a while. Someone who had the skill and experience to assess the extent of his injury and give him advice on what steps to take next. Someone with white-blond hair and piercing, smoky blue eyes who he'd been thinking about so much for the past nine months.

Most importantly, she had no connection to the military. Because if this turned out to be not as bad as he feared, he didn't want command benching him due to some military official refusing to give him clearance.

Travis nodded, unable to hide the empathy in his eyes. "Okay. Then how about I go find you some crutches."

Grady expelled a breath. Yeah. Walking out of here without assistance wasn't happening, no matter how much he wished it were otherwise. "Thanks, brother."

"No worries. Whatever you need, and any way I can help. That was good work today. We need you back ASAP." He clapped a hand on Grady's back on the way out the door.

Alone in the empty locker room, Grady closed his eyes and started making decisions, the pain in his knee pulsing in time with his heartbeat. First thing tomorrow he was going to be waiting at Everleigh's physio clinic before the doors opened in the morning.

End Excerpt

ABOUT THE AUTHOR

NY Times and USA Today Bestselling author Kaylea Cross writes edge-of-your-seat military romantic suspense. Her work has won many awards, including the Daphne du Maurier Award of Excellence, and has been nominated multiple times for the National Readers' Choice Awards. A Registered Massage Therapist by trade, Kaylea is also an avid gardener, artist, Civil War buff, Special Ops aficionado, belly dance enthusiast and former nationally-carded softball pitcher. She lives in Vancouver, BC with her husband and family.

You can visit Kaylea at www.kayleacross.com. If you would like to be notified of future releases, please join her here:

http://kayleacross.com/v2/newsletter/

COMPLETE BOOKLIST

ROMANTIC SUSPENSE

Crimson Point Protectors Series
Falling Hard
Cornered
Sudden Impact
Unsanctioned
Protective Impulse
Final Shot
Fatal Fallout

Crimson Point Series
Fractured Honor
Buried Lies
Shattered Vows
Rocky Ground
Broken Bonds
Deadly Valor
Dangerous Survivor

Kill Devil Hills Series
Undercurrent
Submerged
Adrift

Rifle Creek Series
Lethal Edge
Lethal Temptation
Lethal Protector

Vengeance Series
Stealing Vengeance
Covert Vengeance
Explosive Vengeance
Toxic Vengeance
Beautiful Vengeance
Taking Vengeance

DEA FAST Series
Falling Fast
Fast Kill
Stand Fast
Strike Fast
Fast Fury
Fast Justice
Fast Vengeance

Colebrook Siblings Trilogy
Brody's Vow
Wyatt's Stand
Easton's Claim

Hostage Rescue Team Series
Marked
Targeted
Hunted
Disavowed
Avenged
Exposed
Seized
Wanted
Betrayed
Reclaimed

Shattered
Guarded

Titanium Security Series
Ignited
Singed
Burned
Extinguished
Rekindled
Blindsided: A Titanium Christmas novella

Bagram Special Ops Series
Deadly Descent
Tactical Strike
Lethal Pursuit
Danger Close
Collateral Damage
Never Surrender (a MacKenzie Family novella)

Suspense Series
Out of Her League
Cover of Darkness
No Turning Back
Relentless
Absolution
Silent Night, Deadly Night

PARANORMAL ROMANCE

Empowered Series
Darkest Caress

HISTORICAL ROMANCE

The Vacant Chair

EROTIC ROMANCE (writing as *Callie Croix*)

Deacon's Touch
Dillon's Claim
No Holds Barred
Touch Me
Let Me In
Covert Seduction